Secret Admirer

Secret Admirer

AMANDA LEES

PAN BOOKS

First published 2002 by Pan Books
an imprint of Pan Macmillan Ltd
Pan Macmillan, 20 New Wharf Road, London N1 9RR
Basingstoke and Oxford
Associated companies throughout the world
www.panmacmillan.com

ISBN 0 330 39236 0

A CIP catalogue record for this book is available from
the British Library.

Phototypeset by Intype London Ltd
Printed and bound in Great Britain by
Mackays of Chatham plc, Chatham, Kent

For Graeme
without whom there would
be no Delilah

Acknowledgements

Ungushing thanks to my stellar agent, Luigi Bonomi, and to everyone at Sheil Land for their unfailing support and enthusiasm. To my editor, Mari Evans, and, in no particular order, to the brilliant team at Pan Macmillan: Clare, Lucy, Nicky, Annika, Jeremy, Naomi, Nadya, Caroline, Elizabeth, every single sales rep and anyone I may have inadvertently forgotten. Enormous gratitude to Tim Jackson and Larry Levy for their help and advice on the dotcom front and to all my mates for their sterling marketing efforts in book stores up and down the country. Keep up the good work.

One

She came that close to throwing it away. A glance in another direction, a less dexterous flick of the wrist and the postcard would have slid into oblivion along with the rest of the junk mail. History. Or, at least, history rewritten. But here it was, safe, sound and resting on the table in front of them now that Jess had finally analysed it to her satisfaction and was preparing to launch into her next favourite pastime. Theorizing. Delilah could hardly wait.

'Well, it . . .'

Delilah leaned forward, anxious not to miss a syllable of the final verdict. A little frown creased Jess's forehead as she tried to frame her words as carefully as possible. Suppressing an urge to snatch it out of her hands and scream aloud in frustration, Delilah confined herself to parting her lips and uttering an encouraging, 'Uh huh?'

Twizzle had no such compunction. Clearly bored with the cautious approach, she took an audible slurp out of her pint glass and boldly declared, 'It stinks.'

They both stared at her in frank astonishment. Frustrating it might be, intriguing certainly, but that seemed to be going a bit far.

'Go on, sniff it. I noticed it right off, in those few seconds before *you* got a hold of it.' Never one to mince her words, Twizzle threw them meaningfully in Jess's direction. It was hard to believe that such polar opposites could be contained within Delilah's life but oddly enough they seemed somehow to rub along together, Jess reining in her more judgemental tendencies whilst Twizz made half-hearted efforts to conform occasionally. Efforts that generally failed in the face of a lustful approach to life, love and the universe at large.

True to type, Jess hesitated a second longer and in a frenzy of exasperation Twizz grabbed the card, thrust it up to Jess's nostrils and urged, 'Smell it, for God's sake.'

A cautious sniff later and a light flicked on in Jess's eyes. 'You're right. There is something kind of perfumy about it . . .'

'You mean . . . it's from a woman?' Now this was a whole new angle on things. Delilah had rather been hoping that some tall, dark stranger lurked behind those flattering words. Or at the very least someone who would not be overshadowed by her highest pair of fuck-me heels. Not that she had anything against a female admirer, of course. Generally speaking. But a tight male bum did it for her every time and, besides, it could prove incredibly awkward, given her clientele. Especially if it were one of them. Her mind began to race off in an altogether alarmist direction, but thankfully she was brought up short by another nugget of wisdom from sniffer dog Jess.

'No, not perfume. Too citrusy . . . rather nice actually. Cologne or aftershave. Givenchy, I would guess. Or Armani perhaps.'

Twizzle had had quite enough. 'You'll be giving us the bloody serial number next.'

Loftily ignoring her, Jess passed the postcard over to an eager Delilah and watched smugly as she inhaled the information for herself. Holding the card carefully by the edges so as not to smudge the thick, black handwriting on the back, Delilah held it up to her own nostrils and then grinned in delight. Jess was right. It was definitely after-shave of some sort. An expensive one at that. Her old headmistress had once suggested that Delilah's greatest talent lay in sniffing out trouble. Be that as it may, it had taken her this far and had been turned to all sorts of things. Now she knew she had found her niche, the perfect reflection of her eclectic taste. Decadence. An oasis to satisfy the most sensual of urges. Lush acres of lace, swathes of satin and silk and the headiness of a dozen delicious fragrances. Creamy white candles, passion red pillows, the light dancing off embroidery and beads. Delilah's shop. Her baby. And it could only be a matter of time before the style press came knocking at her deep purple door. At least, that was what she and Twizzle told each other every day as they tweaked details and rearranged stock. Only a matter of time.

'Although you do have to ask yourself what kind of guy sprays aftershave over a postcard.' Good old Jess. Sharp as a tack and not afraid to sound it. Delilah just wished that once in a while shades of grey might creep in to soften the black and white blow.

'Come on,' Jess continued, 'you have to admit he's probably some sleaze in a neck chain and nylon shirt.' She clearly felt it was time to apply the imagination brakes to Delilah's boundless capacity for optimism.

'With hairy great tufts whopping out of the top. Y'know, Jess, you might have a point there.' For once, even Twizzle was in agreement.

Refusing to be crushed by this joint display of disloyalty, Delilah defiantly declared, 'It could have been the postman's pong for all you know,' placed the card carefully out of harm's way and took a reflective sip of her drink.

'And you two can stop bloody looking at each other like that.' Caught out in a rare conspiratorial glance, both Twizz and Jess leaped up and offered to buy the next round. Twizz shouted loudest and departed for the bar, elbows at the ready although it was hardly necessary in the less than fashionable joint that constituted their local. You could run your fingers over what remained of the faded flock wallpaper at the Doom and Gloom, and it was pushing the boat out to get more than two flavours of crisps, but the old boys kept themselves to themselves and it was blissfully calm. Of course, that wasn't its real name but it suited the atmosphere a whole lot better. And there were plenty of other pubs to champion the good name of Horse and Groom, in spite of an alarming fashion for trendification that seemed to leave no musty corner unfaked.

'If we could just make out the postmark or something . . . might at least tell us where he sent it from.' Jess was worrying away at the problem like a particularly tenacious terrier faced with an enormous bone. Except that this particular bone was not going to crack and yield up its secrets, at least not without the aid of some high-tech equipment and a private detective. They had gleaned what little they could from the card and it was stubbornly refusing to give anything other than the most minimal information away. That is, if you could count a bright pink postcard with 'You Have A Secret Admirer' splashed across the front of it as being in any way minimal. A smudged postmark, Delilah's name and the address of the shop written across the back of it in a thick, bold hand. Written with a fountain pen, no less. Nothing else. No message, no kisses, not even an arch acronym or clichéd question mark to give a clue to the personality of the sender. And a personality he must have if he was willing to make such a gesture, although quite what it might be remained to be seen.

It was definitely a he, Delilah was now sure of that. Something about the formation of the letters and the speed of the writing spoke more of a masculine hand. That, combined with the aftershave, represented the only breakthrough in the half-hour or so they had been subjecting the card to collective scrutiny. Delilah had called an Emergency Summit the minute she had got over the mingled shock and delight of discovering such an item amongst the brochures and bills that generally constituted her business mail. That was their first clue. This was obviously someone who didn't know her too well, or at least not well enough to send it to her home address. So it had to be someone who either came in the shop or knew that she owned it. Someone, perhaps, she had served all too recently. Except that, try as she might, she could not recall a single likely male customer. Plenty of women, certainly. Older ones looking to spice up their lives, younger ones out for a giggle. And some just like her, obviously appreciating the sheer luxury of the fabrics, the hedonistic scents that permeated her small but perfect space.

There had been men, of course, but almost all of them had been of the foot shuffling, dutifully dragged along variety. In the last fortnight she could recall but one lone male and she rather suspected that the lucky recipient of the sandalwood candle and sensuous body rub had been of the hairy-chested variety. There had been a couple of boys prior to that, on the second or third day they had been open, but she couldn't bring herself to credit a pair of sniggering pubescents with such a bold gesture. What's more, the handwriting seemed extremely confident. Far too grown-up for anyone with incipient acne and a tendency to blush at the sight of a French lace bra.

Delilah belatedly realized that she had gone off on one, as Twizz liked to put it. Drifted away from the present and into a world of endless possibility. A world which had spawned the reality of Decadence. Her very own shop. A temple to taste and a home for hedonism. Nothing could have suited Delilah better and everything had been going reasonably smoothly, if a little quietly. Until this. Jerking her focus back to her friends, she noticed that Jess was also gazing off into the middle distance, that little frown once again marring her features. Twizz, meanwhile, was glaring into the bottom of her glass for want of any sort of eye candy on which to fix her attention. There was nothing Twizzle liked more than a long shared stare backed up with body language to match. The local, however, offered nothing more promising than a handful of hoary old subjects on which to practise her pouting, and even that wasn't worth the effort. She doubted, in any case, that they would have either noticed or cared, resigned as most of them were to ending their days happily engaged in completing a cross-word or perhaps examining the bar towels for beer stains.

Delilah ran a ruminative finger over the bevelled edge of the stamp one more time, still careful not to touch the writing for fear of erasing some part of its cryptic contents.

'And you're sure it came this morning, along with all the other post?' As far as girl detectives went, Jess was never going to give Nancy Drew sleepless nights but Delilah patiently answered her one more time.

'I nearly chucked it in the bin until I took a second look and realized there was something handwritten on the back.' Ever since she had signed on the dotted line of the lease, Delilah had been inundated with glossy offers for every-thing from alarm systems to half-built villa schemes in the sun. It was pure and happy chance that had saved the post-card from being consigned to the great waste bin of life. That and the fact that there were only so many ways to rearrange the stock. She had no doubt that the flood of hungry customers would come but until then enforced idle-ness bred ennui and ingenuity in equal measure.

It was in one of her more inventive moments that she had come up with her latest line. Oral Sex. Fat globes of Belgium's finest chocolate, stuffed full of nuts and liqueurs and able to compensate for the deepest emotional deficit, never mind a bad day at the office. Delilah herself could vouch for their efficacy, having spent more than one happy evening tucked up with a paperback and a generous supply. Safe sex at its most sublime and with no nasty side effects. The quiet life had definite advantages and she wasn't about to give it up for anything less than a man with real soul. Or perhaps a bold, black pen.

'Sorry, what did you say?' Suddenly realizing that Jess had been talking, Delilah tuned back to the present and the task at hand.

'I was only saying that it has to be someone you've met in passing, possibly someone you don't even remember.'

'Oh, I think I'd remember the sort of guy who does something like this.'

'How do you know? He's probably some nerdy little computer programmer who got bored with surfing the Web. Or at the very best someone incredibly ordinary.' Sometimes Jess could be too sensible for comfort, although she had an annoying mother-like tendency to be right.

'What if you haven't met him at all?' Twizz had been unnaturally silent for so long that she made them both jump.

Jess snorted derisively. 'Of course she's met him. How else would he know what there is to admire?'

But it took more than common sense to quash Twizz. 'Not necessarily. He might have seen your picture or heard your voice or something and fallen madly in love. It happens.'

'Only in the movies.'

Delilah had to admit that Jess had a point. Pity, really. She rather liked the idea of some man being besotted with her image. It smacked of old-fashioned idealism mixed in with the fabulousness of fate.

Twizz, however, was not so easily deterred. 'So? She answers the phone at the shop all the time. And the local rag printed a photo with that piece on the shop, didn't they?'

It was a thought, but Delilah's optimism was already fading. 'Yeah, right. Grinning like a maniac and with the cheeks of a hamster. I somehow doubt that anyone would fall for that. Unless, of course, he's into fat little rodents.

And the only people who read that paper have nothing better to do in the launderette . . .'

'So he really must be desperate,' Jess finished for her.

'Cow.'

'I love you too.' Only a friendship stretching back beyond the bike shed and that first stolen fag allowed them to insult each other quite so warmly. Having exhausted all possible angles, Jess was getting restless. 'Anyway, I'm sure all will be revealed sooner or later.'

'With any luck,' smirked Twizz, always happy to lower the tone until it hit a real base note.

'Yeah, yeah. And no doubt by then I will have forgotten what to do with it. Now, who's for another? Twizz, bottle of Becks? Jess?' The fascination had grown thin and Delilah knew it was time to change the subject. Carefully secreting the postcard in her bag, she headed off for the bar. By the time she got back with the drinks Jess and Twizz were happily sparring over the issue of self-mutilation in general and Twizz's new piercing in particular. At least she kept it under wraps; the unearthly dullness of the Doom and Gloom would have been shattered forever, dominoes clattering to the floor in astonishment, had Twizz flashed her bits for the world to see. The heated debate lasted them through a couple more rounds and several other issues and ended up with a most satisfying dissection of Twizz's latest date.

Catching herself as she giggled evilly along with her friends, Delilah suddenly realized that she felt at home here, that this was where she belonged. It was such an alien sensation that it took her another moment to realize it was something she liked, very much indeed. It gave her just as much of a rush as receiving the postcard, albeit a gentler, warmer one. Surreptitiously, she slipped a hand inside her bag and scrabbled around until once again she felt the glossy smoothness of the card. Allowing herself just a tiny shiver of elation, Delilah withdrew her hand and turned her attention back to the conversation. Tucked back into its dark recess, the postcard sat silently, not even a tick to betray it as the time bomb poised to explode across her life. Hindsight might well have chucked it into the nearest bin but Delilah lived in the real world and the postcard remained, safe, sound and as dangerous as a slumbering snake.

Two

Dan flicked a couple of crumbs across the table, glanced at his watch and suppressed a sigh. True to form, Matt was running at least an hour late and at this rate last orders would have been called by the time he finally arrived. There was nothing Dan hated more than being made to wait, particularly when he could see everyone around him tucking into their Sunday nosh. The pint of lager he had worked his way through at an inhumanly slow pace had done little to satiate the increasingly obvious demands from his stomach, and he had just about ploughed through every section of the paper, including those bits he never normally read. His own fault, really. He should have known. After all, he'd had the last twenty-odd years to work it out, although even Matt had been forced to bow to the pressure of the playground bell.

Casting around for something, anything, to occupy his attention, he lit upon the only sorry scrap of newsprint he had not yet scrutinized. In the way of prefabricated, fake traditional bars, the artfully scuffed wooden table was spread with every conceivable publication. This one belonged to the genre of local newspaper that relied more heavily on advertisements than on any serious attempt to convey hard news. Although, with front page headlines that screamed 'Car Park to Expand', it didn't seem as if the editorial staff were exactly inundated with ground-breaking reportage. Dan had just about given up on glancing over the inordinate number of DIY advertisements when he turned the page and a fuzzy photograph caught his eye. There was something about the radiant smile of the subject that managed to outshine an accompanying headline that read 'Durber Road Discovers Decadence'. Dan doubted whether the good readers of the *Examiner* even knew the meaning of the word but it intrigued him sufficiently to read on, although to be honest it was the picture rather than the purple prose that had captured his attention.

Scanning rapidly through the leaden paragraphs, he discovered that the owner of the glorious smile rejoiced in the name of Delilah. Oh so '70s – no doubt she had ex-hippy parents and a radical education to match. Her new business sounded wacky enough, conjuring up a vision of sifting through racks of wispy underwear before Dan remembered that there was no space in his life for anything as indulgent as shopping. Every second of his time was squeezed to the max and yet there was always more to do. Even this lunch had been rearranged three or four times until sheer guilt and Matt's heavy sarcasm had forced him to give up a few precious hours of his time. It had come to something when even your closest mate had to lean on the guilt button in order to get to see you.

Thinking of Matt inevitably brought his eyes back to his watch and he had to force himself to suppress his mounting irritation. Great bloke, old Mattie, but his breezy insouciance sometimes went just a little too far, even for Dan. Turning his attention back to the paper spread out in front of him, Dan found his eyes being drawn once more to the photograph. There was no doubt about it, she had a quite extraordinary smile and the sort of lively hair that matched it perfectly. Brown or dark blond, he couldn't tell from the black and white picture but it was springing around her face in a way that practically begged you to run your fingers through it, if only to find out whether they would ever emerge unscathed. As for the face it framed, it became more intriguing the longer he looked at it. Not even the poor quality of the newsprint could obscure a quirkily individual collection of features that added up to an appealing whole. A very appealing whole indeed . . .

'Dan, mate, how's it going?'

His reverie cut rudely short, Dan glanced up at an entirely unrepentant Matt and tried to grin nonchalantly. Matt, however, knew him rather too well to be taken in and immediately offered, 'Bloody car. Must get it seen to. Sorry about that, but you've not been waiting too long, have you? What can I get you? Pint of Stella?' All of this accompanied by a disarming grin and the dumping of a leather jacket and what looked suspiciously like an overnight bag on the chair opposite Dan. Of course. Simple, really. Not so much a car that wouldn't start as a Matt that couldn't stop at the threshold of a bedroom door. If, indeed, he had bothered to walk that far.

Matt soon reappeared with the drinks. That was something he always managed speedily, doubly so if there was a barmaid susceptible to his charms. As he removed the bag from his chair in order to sit down, Dan seized his chance and enquired drily, 'A good night, then?'

'What, this? Just my sports kit, mate.'

'I'll bet.' No workout in the world could produce such a self-satisfied smile. Matt's hair was still damp from the shower, his limbs loose from loving rather than any other kind of limbering. Dan had to admire his stamina, if not his selectivity. It was not so much that Matt went for beauty over brain cells, just that his own form of Darwinism seemed more concerned with the expansion of the mammary than with the growth of the mind.

'So, how's it going?' Matt was all attentiveness, a trick he often employed to divert attention at those times when his behaviour was less than immaculate.

'Oh, not too bad . . . yourself?'

'Yeah, it's good. Going well, really well as it happens.'

'Oh, good. Great.'

A peculiarly male silence descended as they pondered the weight of their exchange.

And then Dan cracked in a most unmale sort of way.

'Fuck it . . . actually, it's terrible. I don't think I've left the office before ten o'clock in the past six weeks or so . . . the bank are being bastards, the landlord's getting edgy, I've got lawyers crawling all over the small print and every day we get a new rash of bugs and glitches. And the bloody coffee machine doesn't work. Apart from that, things are great. And how about you?' For Dan to admit to any of this meant that things must be serious. Matt decided to start with the coffee machine.

'Have you checked the fuse?'

'The fuse?' For a moment, Dan thought Matt had seriously lost the plot. Here he was, painfully baring his innermost fears and frustrations and all Matt could think about was fuses. Looking at the irritatingly helpful expression on Matt's face, he thought he might well blow one of his own.

'In the coffee machine. Used to go every now and then when I had it. Stick a new one in and you'll be fine. I could have a look at it later, if you like.' It never ceased to amaze Matt that a Luddite such as Dan should have ended up running something to do with the Internet. The man didn't even have a telly at home, for Christ's sake.

'Thanks, mate. Sorry to sound off at you . . . it's just been a hell of a week . . .'

'No worries.'

Dan flashed him a grateful grin but continued to run a distracted hand through his hair every now and then, and his thoughts were clearly somewhere else entirely. Matt had never seen him quite this strung out before. Edgy, yes. Dan was not exactly the most laid-back of characters. But things were obviously getting to him far more than usual. They sat in another reasonably empathetic masculine silence for such a long time that Matt began to fear Dan would try to drown himself in his pint, so deeply and morosely was he staring into it.

'What's this you've been reading?'

Dan jumped as if the bank manager himself had barked at him and slapped a guilty hand on to the newspaper. 'Oh, nothing.' Which was, of course, the worst thing he could have said.

'Yeah, right. What is it, anyway? The local rag? Shit, you must have been bored.' Prising the paper out from under Dan's fingers, Matt scanned the page before looking at him in puzzlement. There didn't seem to be anything there, or at least nothing incriminating. A couple of adverts, a bit of copy on some shop or other and a fuzzy photo of a girl . . . His instincts sharp as far as his specialist subject was concerned, Matt took a closer look. Not bad, not bad at all. Quite tasty, in fact, in a sexily unkempt sort of way. Fabulous eyes, from what he could see, a nice little figure . . . and what a name . . .

'Delilah. Hmm, very Old Testament. She's cute. Very cute, in fact.'

A wary look suddenly passed across Dan's face and he shrugged as carelessly as he could. 'I hadn't noticed. I was actually looking at the ads.'

'Need some incontinence pads, then? Christ, mate, I know things are bad but I didn't think you were literally shitting yourself.' Ordinarily that would at the very least have raised a disparaging look, but clearly Dan was not in the mood. Snatching the paper away and tucking it quite deliberately under his arm, he gathered up the glasses and enquired, 'Same again?'

'Dan, let me get these.' As soon as the words were out of his mouth, Matt knew he'd made a mistake. As far as stubborn pride was concerned, Dan could outdo an ox any day. His mouth didn't so much tighten as whiten around its perimeter, but he merely shook his head and turned to fight his way through to the bar. His money might be mostly of the virtual variety but he could still manage to buy a mate a pint. The Sunday drinking crowd was now out in force and it took him a while to get served. No doubt Mattie's magnetism would have shot him straight to the front of the queue, but it took Dan rather longer to catch the barmaid's eye. Nothing to do with a lack of good looks. It just never crossed his mind to strut his stuff in the way that was second nature to Matt.

His fluttered banknote having finally been noticed, he dropped the drinks off at their table and headed to the loo, the beer having taken its inevitable toll. His drink of choice at the moment was whisky, straight up and poured in liberal quantities. It did seem a tad excessive, however, for what was meant to be a quiet drink with a mate. Not that Matt was any old mate – no doubt he wouldn't have raised so much as a well groomed eyebrow if Dan had taken to hitting the hard stuff over a sedate Sunday lunch, but he really didn't think he could bear to be the object of any more understanding, however well intentioned. Although just how good Matt's intentions were remained open to debate, especially as far as women were concerned.

Libidinously blessed, Matt was a great lover of the chase even when his conquests did most of the running. And Dan hadn't liked the look on his face when he caught sight of the photograph in the paper. It wasn't desire exactly, certainly not the sort that had grabbed Dan by the guts and forced him to look at her face again and again. No, Matt's expression had more betrayed the age-old urge that drove grown men to wrestle each other down in the mud as they fought over a ball, or to smash each other to a pulp against the ropes as they staggered around a ring. Fast cars, great flats, top jobs – penis proof par excellence. Dan was buggered if Matt's urge to prove the supremacy of his sperm was going to win out yet again over his finer feelings of friendship. If, indeed, he had any to begin with. When it came to sex, Matt played by a different set of rules. He'd have written the definitive book on the subject if only he'd had a hand free long enough. As it was, his technique was legendary, his reputation unsullied and his partners always gasping for more, probably because staying power was something he reserved purely for the bedroom and his favourite words were 'I'll call'.

Dan supposed that he could take a leaf out of Matt's bulging black book, if only he had the energy for something more than the odd glance at a girl he would never get to meet. Well, OK, 'glance' was putting it lightly. He'd found it progressively hard to tear his eyes away from that picture and harder still to feign coolness in the face of Matt's interest. He wanted to tear her photo out of the paper right now and tuck it possessively away where no one, certainly no one like Matt, could get his grubby hands on it. Or her, for that matter. Dan realized that he had been standing at the urinals for an age as his thoughts had run away with him. And, judging by the expression on the face of the bloke to his right, he had in all likelihood been either pulling some very strange faces or, God forbid, muttering to himself. Both highly likely at the best of times, but doubly so given the stress he was currently under.

Hastily arranging himself and doing up his fly, he sidled out of the toilets, mentally slapping himself for his stupidity. Concentrating on acting normal made him lose his bearings momentarily and Dan somehow found himself heading through the wrong door and into a cramped little corridor occupied by a public telephone and one of those ubiquitous racks of freebie postcards. He was just about to head back the other way when one particularly lurid specimen caught his eye. Standing out from the others by virtue of its bright pink background, the postcard was seemingly devoid of either an image or a product to sell. All it had to offer was a message, splashed boldly across it in a typeface that paid homage to the domestic paintbrush. 'You Have A Secret Admirer.' Very sweet.

Dan plucked it out of the rack and took a closer look, his heart beating faster as an idea began to form in his somewhat strung-out mind. OK, so he might not be charisma central, capable of raising the room temperature with little more than his pulchritudinous presence. He might not even get served at the snap of a sexy smile. But one thing he could do was take the initiative. Proactivity or perish was most definitely his motto. Had to be, with a mate like Matt sending hearts racing faster than Formula One. Dan might not be the dangerous type but he could resort to his weapon of choice – wit. And what better than a provocative postcard to pave the way.

Turning it over in his hand, Dan noticed that the last inch or so of the card was detachable, the serrated edge barely discernible until a thumb was run over it. As he began to pull it away, the purpose of the card became clear. The faint citrusy smell he had barely registered before now intensified, and as he held the separate strip of card up to the light all became clear. In tiny letters across the edge of the strip were the words 'Secret. A new weapon for men.' Talk about the power of advertising – one glance at that and Dan was sold. Never mind that it was about as profound as the average fortune cookie, Dan had been grasping around for a sign, any excuse to go after that girl. And now here it was, slap bang in front of him on an aftershave sample. Even Oprah would be hard pressed to rival that for profundity.

Realizing that the newspaper was still desperately clamped under his arm, he pulled it out and cast a rapid eye over the appropriate page. He knew it was in there somewhere. In the pedestrian way of all local papers it had printed not only the name of the shop but practically the full address as well. And there it was! Ruthlessly ignoring the still, small voice of sanity that popped up to warn him of a huge, impending mistake, he scrabbled around for his fountain pen and wrote out her name and address on the card before good sense could get the better of him. The shop address would have to do; he only hoped that she opened the post herself rather than leaving it for some assistant to giggle over. Or maybe her partner or something, business or romantic – best not even to go there. Although why he should think that a girl like her would be single, never mind open to his attentions. The whole thing was madness. Yet another of those wacky little whims that had all too often led him to the brink of ruin, in more ways than one. He was just about to rip the card into shreds, and his hopes along with it, when a couple fell giggling through the door behind him and practically knocked him flat against the opposite wall.

'Oops . . . sorry . . .'

'Yeah, sorry, mate . . .'

They had the grace to look slightly embarrassed but it was clear as they began snogging with a drunken lack of regard that Dan's presence was surplus to requirements. Looked like another Saturday night that had overflowed into Sunday morning and beyond. That was all he needed. Dan squeezed past them, back to his table and Matt, now happily engrossed in chatting up the blonde at the next table whilst her friend glowered in the corner. Dan knew just how she felt. One pair of young lovers was just about endurable, two was more than enough.

'All right, Danno?' Matt barely glanced up from the task in hand, his eyes busy sending out those not too subtle signals. Dan didn't know why he bothered – judging by the girlish giggles and amount of hair tossing, she was already putty in those practised hands.

Feeling more than slightly superfluous, Dan muttered something about a cashpoint machine and headed out of the front door of the pub and towards the postbox about twenty yards down the road. Digging out his last remaining stamp, he stuck it decisively on the card and threw it into the box without allowing himself a first, let alone second, thought. Striding back to the pub and his pint, he felt as if it was out of his hands and in the far more careless ones of fate. Lady Luck might well have been ignoring him recently, but there was very little chance that Delilah would have any such option. Certainly not when the postcard plopped through her letterbox and lay vividly demanding attention. Who could resist it, lying there in its garish glory and blaring out its irresistibly unequivocal message. If nothing else, it might bring a smile to her face, and beyond that Dan didn't dare think further. God knows what she would think when she picked up the postcard and read, 'You Have A Secret Admirer'. Whatever her thoughts, they wouldn't be of him. Of course they couldn't, they'd never even met and Dan was none too sure that he had the courage, never mind the confidence, to do anything to remedy matters.

Three

Delilah was finding it hard to concentrate. The woman in front of her had an odd look on her face and was speaking loudly and slowly, as if to a foreigner or a total imbecile, although she probably considered them to be one and the same thing.

'I take it you don't have anything slightly less . . . fancy?' she demanded, brandishing a rather hair-raising G-string as she spoke. Delilah's eyes fixed on the flimsy garment as if searching for divine inspiration.

'Fancy? Um . . . I'm not quite sure what you mean . . .'

Where the hell was Twizz when she needed her? She had skipped out twenty minutes earlier in search of a couple of cappuccinos to brighten up an exceedingly dull afternoon and had yet to reappear. Not even Twizz could be taking this long to flirt with the pretty young things who pranced behind the espresso machine. Delilah needed rescuing, and fast. Judging by the set of the woman's chin and the correctness of her clothes, this was going to be no easy ride, particularly not if Delilah's brain continued to refuse to coordinate with her vocal cords. She was clearly losing patience and Delilah could ill afford to lose a customer on a day as slow as this. Or any other day, judging by the snail's pace of her start-up. Flashing an idiotic smile, and merely confirming the woman's worst suspicions in the process, she brightly declared, 'We have far less smarty pants. I mean fancy pants. And much bigger, too. If that's the problem.'

The woman glared at her in stupefied silence before pursing her mouth and uttering a final and rather chilling, 'I see.'

Deciding that she might as well cram her ankle and shin into her mouth while she was at it, Delilah battled on, her cheeks growing hotter as the prospects of making a sale fell to a cold, fat zero. 'Of course, I mean bigger as in wider. So that they cover your, er, bottom and won't, you know, creep up your cr— That is, they won't get caught in your . . . tights or anything.' A lame finish, but anything was better than struggling on such a dangerous tack. With a final snort of disbelief and a look that would ordinarily have withered her to the core, the woman dropped the G-string on the counter as if it were alive and strode out without so much as a frosty goodbye. Laden down with a suspicious variety of carrier bags, Twizz was just in time to catch the swish of her smart A-line skirt as it disappeared into a Jeep Cherokee.

'Strewth – she had fire in her arse. Let me guess . . . she bought six pairs of Thrilling Knickers and a purple thong for Sunday best?' Taking a better look at Delilah's face, Twizz decided that levity was not required. In which case, it would simply have to be hard liquor and a packet of pretzels instead. Delving into her collection of booty, she whipped out a couple of bottles and placed them on the counter before purloining two of the well named CockTail glasses from the shelves and setting to work. Still somewhat dazed and confused, Delilah only realized what she was up to when a brimming glass was thrust into her hand, complete with olive garnish, and Twizz boldly declared cocktail hour open. Taking a tentative sip, she discovered that it was indeed a Martini she was clutching in her shaking hand, and a rather good one at that.

'Stuff the cappuccinos . . . thought we'd go straight to cocktail hour instead. Set you up for tonight. You look like

you could do with it.' Twizz grinned and clinked her glass
against Delilah's. The sound brought her down from whatever cloud she had been inhabiting.

'Yeah, great, cheers . . . God, this is good!' A healthy slug
of cocktail hit the back of her throat and the depths of
Delilah's brain at one and the same moment. Feet firmly
back on the ground, although for how much longer
remained to be seen.

'Still thinking about it, aren't you?' Twizzle wasn't possessed of shrewd Aussie blood for nothing. Delilah didn't
look so much guilty as resigned.

'Wouldn't you?'

'Frankly, no. I'd get on with my life and stop wondering
if every limp-wristed loafer boy I met might just be the one
who wrote it.' Scathing about men in general, Twizz
reserved her most sweeping observations for the denizens
of the local pick-up joints. Although she was right about
the loafers.

'Oh, what the hell. You're right. Let's have another one
and then we might as well close up early. I can't see us
doing any business in the next half-hour or so.'

'But what about Margaret? And all those commuters who
might need to pick up a little something to spice up their
love lives on the way home?' Twizz had a good point;
hardly a day had gone by since they opened without the
redoubtable Margaret popping in to pick up a candle or a
truffle or two, or whatever else she could think of to buy in
order to boost their often meagre takings. In one of her more
disparaging moments, Twizz had suggested that she might
perhaps be stocking a particularly louche sort of bunker but
a sharp look from Delilah had silenced her hyperactive
tonsils.

Margaret had appeared on their grand opening day just
as they were both beginning to wonder whether the entire
street had been nuked and no one had seen fit to inform
them. A most unlikely figure to be visiting an emporium of

subtle erotica, she had carefully inspected each and every item before bestowing a generous smile on them both and handing over a pair of scarlet sequinned mules for purchase. Delilah had struggled to conceal her astonishment at this frowzy woman of indeterminate age and her taste in footwear, but as time went on she began to discover that there was much to Margaret that was surprising and almost nothing that was banal. As she had handed over a parcel wrapped in an orgy of tissue paper and a ribbon which seemed to possess a maverick mind all of its own, the odd customer had murmured her thanks and added, 'That should give that stuffy bastard something to choke on over his cornflakes.'

She'd twinkled naughtily at Delilah's slack-jawed stare and continued in an explanatory fashion, 'My nosy neighbour. Thinks I can't see him twitching his nets and peeking over the garden wall. Adds a whole new meaning to Neighbourhood Watch, I can tell you.'

At this Delilah had been unable to contain herself any longer and burst out into giggles that were fuelled in no small part by the sheer relief of finally having sold something. On hearing those giggles, Twizz had emerged from the stock room with sweet wrappers, fag packet and magazine shamelessly in hand. The ensuing conversation had drifted over life, death and the cruciality of chocolate and, since that day, had ranged much further afield in its capacity for everyday trivia. Now, if for some reason Margaret hadn't appeared an hour or so before closing time, they began to wonder what could be wrong. Except for Thursdays. For some reason, she never appeared on a Thursday, not even to be seen at a distance through the shop window. And that was rather odd, considering she lived two doors away on what was basically a dead-end street. However, no explanation was either solicited or proffered, although Twizz was prone to lurid speculation over a mad sibling locked in a home or even a dodgy lover incarcerated at Her Majesty's displeasure. Delilah suspected there was far more to it than that. Besides which, as she sanctimoniously informed Twizz, everyone was perfectly entitled to a skeleton or two rattling away behind closet doors. At this, Twizz had snorted and muttered meaningfully, 'You wish!' in her uniquely subtle manner.

Knowing that your assistant considered your sex life to be worthy of an obituary was one thing, being forcefully reminded that hers, by contrast, was not only alive but quite literally heaving with health was sometimes a little more than Delilah could stomach. In vain, she would protest her loftier principles and passion for her work, never mind the fact that she had barely enough energy to pull up her sheets at night, let alone get tangled in them. Twizzle knew a convenient excuse when she saw one and was happy to point it out as such on every possible occasion.

The raucous cacophony of the wind chimes above the door cut through a pensive moment, making them both jump. Twizz had assured her that the Chinese considered the wind chime to be a cosmic burglar alarm but Delilah was none too convinced. They hardly added to the sensuous ambience she was aiming for, although she had to admit they were an improvement on those shop door bells that made a sort of 'ping pong' noise. However, until such time as she could muffle the unfortunate wind chimes, or tie them sneakily together whilst Twizz's back was turned, she was stuck with the effect of several dozen dangling cockerels clashing together every time the door opened. In place of the anticipated Margaret stood a woman who looked decidedly the worse for wear, and whose burgundy top clashed unfortunately with the most unlikely head of hair Delilah had seen outside of a hair dye commercial. Which was perspicacious of her because Fran Butler's hair owed very little to nature and an awful lot to the ministrations of the divine Jeremy, a hairdresser without parallel as far as exercising his dubious taste was concerned.

'Shit, what was that?' The clanging cockerels had obviously startled the scarlet woman and once again Delilah resolved that they simply had to go. Either that or be demoted to the cubbyhole that served as stock room, staff canteen and sweet stash whenever Twizz could sneak off to have a surreptitious puff and a munch.

Even before what remained of her nerves had been jangled, Fran had been having a very bad day. A long and lacklustre working lunch had convinced her that there was absolutely nothing for it but to wander home and treat herself to an early hair of the dog, only to get herself hopelessly lost and inevitably caught in a vicious downpour without an umbrella. She had scurried blindly down the nearest side street in the hope that salvation might present itself in the form of a handy pub, or failing that a phone box, her mobile having beeped its way to a noisy death sometime between the coffee and the brain-numbing shock of the bill. No such thing as expenses for a mere freelance; she could only hope that her bank manager would view it as some form of investment scheme.

It was, unfortunately, the sort of street where the doorways were a good ten feet back from the pavement and the railings in between offered precious little in the way of shelter. Squelching miserably over a soggy newspaper, she felt as if she were all out of options. A few minutes earlier and the paper might at least have made a serviceable rain hat, although wet newsprint running down her face would not exactly be a good look. Fran had nothing more effective with her than a notebook in her handbag, and she rather doubted that an interview with a Californian health guru would provide her with any protection from the elements. The woman had been so sanctimoniously radiant that Fran had reacted by ordering a very nice bottle of Saint Emilion and practically draining it all by herself. Childish, she knew, and no doubt she would pay for it, in more ways than the obvious. Probably was already, this rainstorm no doubt being the Californian equivalent of a thunderbolt. Wet, cold and very pissed off, Fran was just about to give up and resign herself to death by downpour when twinkling fairy lights stopped her in her sodden tracks. They were wound through the branches of a tree that she had practically tripped over, snaking down and around and leading back inside the little shop behind. Not caring whether this shop sold tea strainers or toilet paper, Fran had pushed open the door with relief and staggered into a startling scene.

Once the shock of the wind chime had receded she began to take in her extraordinary surroundings. And the more she looked, the more she fell in love with what she saw. The place was a paean to sensuality, every spare inch of wall being covered in a gorgeous array of hangings and fabrics, photographs and prints. The same fairy lights that had served as a lighthouse in the rain ran around the walls and up and over the ceiling, adding sparkle to the crystal and glass arrayed on the shelves and lending an air of enchantment to the whole scenario. In one corner stood an old silvered mirror and above it more lights spelled out what she presumed to be the name of the shop. Decadence. Highly appropriate. On the table in front of her was heaped pile upon pile of lacy little things that just begged you to reach out and touch, which, of course, Fran tentatively did. The most glorious smell filled the air, a mixture of tuberose, vanilla and something spicier to add a huskier note. Even were she stone cold sober, Fran would not have been able to identify it positively but it was definitely intriguing. As, indeed, was this shop.

Peripherally aware that while she had been staring speechlessly around her she had not been unobserved, Fran looked over at the two girls standing in the corner and noted that each held a cocktail glass. And brimming glasses at that. Liking this place more by the minute, she was just about to introduce herself and perhaps join in the party when that damn clanging started all over again, and she heard a voice behind her say, 'My father would have shot the buggers!'

'Margaret! We were just about to give up on you. Come and join the party.' Her cheeks rosy with the effects of undiluted alcohol, Delilah beamed at her most stalwart supporter. Hoping she was also to be included in the invitation, Fran edged closer as unobtrusively as she could. Casting a professional eye over this new arrival, she observed a woman whose appearance could only be described as nondescript. A more searching glance, however, took in the fact that the glint in her eye bore more resemblance to a radar than a twinkle, and that her sensibly shod feet looked entirely capable of delivering a swift kick should the occasion so demand. There was evidently no messing with Margaret and Fran's journalistic instincts were instantly aroused.

Surprisingly, Margaret took one look at the glass Delilah was holding out to her and politely but firmly declined. 'Oh, no, m'dear. Never touch it. Has the most terrible effect on me.'

'I thought that was the whole point,' muttered Twizz into her glass, earning herself a sharp dig in the ribs. Delilah cast around for something else to offer and could only come up with a rather lame, 'Cup of tea, then?' It seemed a shame, however, to waste the cocktail and for a second Delilah was nonplussed. It was then that the walking fruit bowl that was Fran coalesced into something more closely resembling a red flag of opportunity. In best society hostess mode, Delilah smiled at the now gently steaming stranger and sweetly suggested, 'Perhaps I could offer you this instead?'

Fran smiled equally graciously and took the glass, sipping gratefully at what tasted like a particularly lethal mixture. Her bones began to warm, her fingers to unfurl, as liquid fire snaked its way down the back of her throat. Running a relaxed finger up and down the stem of her glass she suddenly realized that there was more to this cocktail than she had at first thought. A good six inches more. Not for nothing was this billed as a CockTail glass, and Fran rather suspected that whoever had blown it was either a screaming narcissist or gay. The thing was tumescently splendid, the stem positively priapic and all the more beautiful for it. Fran gasped and giggled at one and the same time and exclaimed, 'Oh my God, I love it! And I love this place. It's just so naughty without being at all tacky!'

At this, Delilah looked delighted and blurted out, 'Oh, but that's just how I wanted it to be. Naughty and nice all at the same time. Sort of like the *Arabian Nights* meets Madame de Pompadour, if you know what I mean.'

Fran extended her free hand, still smirking like an adolescent caught peeking at a porno mag. 'Yes, I think I do. I'm Fran Butler, by the way.'

'Delilah Honey. This is Twizz, and Margaret here has been my best customer since we opened. Not that we've been open so long. Only a few weeks, really. Takes time, you know, to build and get yourself known but we're getting there. We definitely are.' God, but that cocktail was really working its magic. The words were not so much tripping off Delilah's tongue as falling over each other to get out but, all the same, her enthusiasm touched a chord. Simultaneously charmed and bemused, Fran didn't quite know what to say but fortunately she was spared the effort. Having been safely delivered of her nice cup of tea, Margaret raised it aloft and proposed a toast. 'To Delilah and Decadence and all the success you deserve. And not forgetting Twizzle, of course.'

Twizz came the closest she ever would to looking suitably touched, while Delilah displayed even less restraint. It might have been mostly due to the Martini, but she could definitely feel her eyes prickling with tears. Until that point, her postcard had been the only bright spot in a long and unprofitable week. Now here she was, surrounded by friends old, newish and new, and a glimmer of self-belief was rapidly being reignited. Feeling a rush of sentimental solidarity, she tried to think of something else she could offer them to prolong the party spirit.

'Of course! Oral Sex! And we've just had a whole new delivery.' For a second or two Fran wondered what on earth she was to experience next, but all became clear when Delilah grabbed a handful of positively hedonistic truffles and piled them on to a makeshift plate. She offered them to an awestruck Fran with the immortal words, 'These are absolutely orgasmic. I should know; I've eaten enough of them in bed.'

Along with the majority of the female population, there was very little Fran liked more than to sink her teeth into a yielding lump of chocolate, particularly one as fudgy and succulent as this. She closed her eyes for a moment in homage to its lusciousness and then savoured the velvety aftertaste that always followed on from a major chocolate experience. It was no surprise to her by now to discover that there was a hint of something else, a deeper, longer note that lingered after the first Belgian ecstasy was past. Not coffee, not liqueur . . . something indefinable but infinitely sexy.

'Whoever named these was a genius,' she pronounced, reaching out to repeat the whole divine experience.

'Thank you,' murmured Delilah demurely as she snaffled one for herself. 'Someone else makes them but I make all the suggestions, don't I, Twizz?'

'Mmmm, mmmm,' was the best Twizz could manage in agreement, and for a few more minutes that was the only sound to be heard in the entire shop. Even the cockerels had fallen silent in homage. Finally sated, at least for the moment, Fran waved away the offer of another and declared, 'I feel sick,' hastily adding, 'But a nice sort of sick,' as a hurt look stole across Delilah's face. Taking another sip of her drink and sinking further into a warm feeling that all was now wonderful with the world, she asked conversationally, 'So do you do this every day? Because if you don't, you should.'

'I'd love to but I am rather hoping that it might get too busy for this kind of caper,' responded Delilah, and an idea began to ferment in Fran's busy brain.

'Yes, but it might even work the other way round—' she mused, the thoughts hotting up as they became more concrete.

'I'm not sure I'm following you,' Delilah began but, swept away by her brainwave, Fran interrupted.

'Do this every day. Turn it into a selling point, something that's a signature of the shop. Something decadent at Decadence, a throwback to a time when people had fun and things were more frivolous. Playtime for playgirls, an exclusive little gathering for those in the know. I can just see it now. Your local clientele would love it, and as word got out they'd come from all over the place just to be part of the party.' Fran was away, her tabloid brain visualizing the punchlines even as her glossier side saw magazine potential.

'What a brilliant idea!' Fired up by its instant appeal, Delilah turned to the other two. 'What do you think, Twizz? Margaret? Great, isn't it?' Twizz had to admit begrudgingly that it had potential, despite the fact that she hadn't thought of it. She jealously guarded her joint position as resident creative and fiercely resented anyone apart from Delilah who tried to interfere with their vision. Even she, however, could see that this one had legs. It was just the sort of thing that the style rags would latch on to, smacking as it did of exclusivity at a time when people were begging to belong to something, anything, as long as it marked them out as different. The beauty of it was that it would appeal to precisely the sort of women who had cash to flash and the boredom threshold of the average social butterfly. There was even the hope that a few members of the new demi-monde might wander this far in order to experience life away from the cutting edge, the sort of person Twizz would dearly love to become and whom she avidly admired. Although she would rather be caught shopping by catalogue than admit it.

Margaret was the only one who remained silent, a faraway look in her eyes that made Delilah nervous. Obviously she hated the idea, perhaps resented the fact that their cosy teatimes would become public property. Suddenly, however, she spoke and surprised them all with what she had to say. 'Splendid idea, absolutely splendid. Reminds me of . . . oh, wonderful times. It's all so serious nowadays, but then we had fun. Really knew how to enjoy ourselves. I'm sure you've heard all this before and will think I'm an old bore but I'm afraid it's true. Oh boy, but we had a ball. I'd love to see that again, really I would.'

This was the first time Margaret had made any reference at all to her past and all three of them were intrigued to hear more. Antennae already twitching, Delilah wondered if Margaret had perhaps partied too hard. That would at least explain the thing about drink. Margaret, disappointingly, seemed prepared to leave it at that. Fran, however, could not contain herself and was determined to press the point. Her first instincts had been right, and triumph and tenacity combined to urge her on to dig for the gold she knew was there under that benign exterior.

'So what were they like? These parties?' For a split second she thought she'd succeeded but Margaret merely smiled and said emphatically, 'Fun, they were fun,' and with that Fran had to be contented. At least for the moment. She glanced over at Delilah, who was looking decidedly distracted.

'The thing is . . .' she began, and they all looked at her expectantly. 'Well, it's just that advertising that sort of thing is very expensive. I mean, it *is* the most wonderful idea but I'm not making a lot of profit right now. None really. And I don't think word of mouth is going to do it.'

'It will if we get the ball rolling.' Fran was not to be

fobbed off with practicalities. 'I'm sure I could place a piece somewhere. The monthlies would take too long . . . a style section, that's what we need. One of the Sundays, per-haps . . .'

'A piece? A piece of what?' Delilah was being awfully slow today but she had at least two good excuses, one of which was clutched firmly in her hand while the other lay temporarily forgotten in the depths of her handbag. Fran had no time for minds fogged up with liquid refreshment or literary lust. She barged on, her own mind now occupied with the media minefield ahead. 'A piece! An article or whatever. On Decadence. It would make a great snippet for a Sunday colour section and there are a few people I could call . . .' She was off again, searching wildly for her mobile before remembering that it was out of juice.

'Doesn't matter . . . bit late for this week in any case. Look, I'll knock something together over the weekend and make a few calls Monday morning. See if anyone will bite. I'm not promising anything but I reckon this might just fly. In any case, I'll do my best.' Fran was not sure herself why she was being quite so helpful. Maybe it was the Martini, but more likely it was the immediate sense of kinship she felt with this motley trio and with Delilah in particular. She liked a maverick, recognized a kindred spirit. That, no doubt, was why she was still out there trawling around all and sundry rather than sitting pretty in some corner office at Condé Nast. At least, that was what she liked to tell herself. The real truth, the one she only admitted to herself in uncommonly candid moments, was that she very much doubted Condé Nast would have her and, indeed, whether she would be able to tolerate them in return. Fran preferred to stand on the sidelines, and a state that had been foisted on her by circumstance had grown comfortable with the years. Hence the deliberately outlandish appearance. Might as well celebrate your differences as be ashamed of them.

And whether she knew it or not, that was precisely the quality she had detected in Delilah.

'Well, whatever you can do ... that would be great. But do you really think people would go for it?' Not usually one to hesitate, the last few weeks had evidently taken their toll on Delilah's sense of adventure.

'Oh yeah, most definitely. And we could have theme parties as well ... you know, '30s in Berlin, The Golden Years in Vegas, that sort of thing.' Twizz was away, already glimpsing the possibilities for play-acting ahead. Not for nothing did she style herself a performance artist, even if her best gigs to date tended to take place in the bedroom as opposed to on the boards.

Imagination ignited, Delilah's thoughts began to work in tandem. 'We could dig out some costumes, maybe even style the shop for that week. Like the Vegas theme ... we could rearrange the lights, play the big band sounds, do all that old gangster thing. Sequins everywhere and a shrine to Liberace. Twizz could be Marilyn and I could be ...'

'Rita Hayworth?' suggested Margaret, joining in the spirit of things.

'Rita Hayworth? I don't think I've quite got the figure ...' Delilah ran a nervous hand through her curls, a giveaway gesture if ever there was one.

'Rubbish! You've got curves in all the right places and your hair is exactly the right colour.' There was no arguing with Margaret in this frame of mind, so Delilah did the sensible thing and held on to her tongue. Compliments were not a comfortable area but she knew when she was defeated.

'Yeah, think Gilda, think ...'

Desperate to stem the torrent of ideas, Fran cut frantically across Twizz, 'Hold on a second! Let's just wait and see if anyone goes for it first. With these things you never know.' Almost immediately she wished she'd kept her mouth firmly shut – after all, it was not as if she was treading on Tina Brown's toes when it came to vital telephone numbers.

Fran's contacts were solid but that was part of the problem.
A portfolio bulging with items on DIY makeovers and forty
ways with a lambswool scarf did not amount to a journalistic style challenge. What was meant to be her bread and
butter had unfortunately become the meal in itself and Fran
was rather afraid that she might have missed the boat of
the moment. Perhaps this would edge her towards a different area, open her up to more happening things. She
sincerely hoped so; another thousand words on some pedestrian puff piece and she would have reached the zenith
of her cliché tolerance. That or reduced to a gibbering
mouthpiece only able to squawk out sound bites over and
over again.

'I really must be going, but before I do . . .' Margaret was
casting a practised eye over the shop, searching for some
little item to take.

'Margaret, really, you don't have to buy anything just to
make me feel better!' Much as she appreciated Margaret's
generosity of spirit, it was becoming an embarrassment for
Delilah. Margaret, however, brushed her protests aside with
an uncompromising, 'I don't. I do it to make me feel better,'
and promptly picked out a couple of pure beeswax
candles and a suitable selection of Oral Sex.

'There. All the ingredients I need for a lovely evening.
With the addition of a little Brahms, I think. Maybe
Mozart . . . In any case, I hope you girls have some fun
planned for yourselves . . .'

'Oooh, yes. I think you could say that,' grinned Twizz
with a pointed look at Delilah who looked blank for a
second and then groaned, 'Oh shit, I completely forgot!'

An entire week had passed since the momentous arrival
of the postcard and still it remained a total mystery. Disbelieving her protests that it really didn't matter, and unable
to bear the preoccupied silences, Jess and Twizzle had taken
it upon themselves to hatch a plan and frogmarch her into
a more proactive approach. Hence Project Pick-Up, a

mission that was not so much search and destroy as search for the boy. Jess, ever logical, had reasoned that all they needed to do was retrace their social steps for the last few weeks and the phantom postcard writer was sure to reveal himself in one way or another. Twizz, ever up for it, had enthusiastically agreed. The fact that, other than their local, their recent outings amounted to one sorry night spent lurching through the bars of loafer boy land, dens of iniquity for the public school posse, did not deter them one jot. It was a plan of such cockeyed genius that it was almost bound to work, although Delilah herself remained unconvinced.

Never one to linger once she had made up her mind to be off, Margaret gathered together her little packages and took her leave, cheerily wishing them, 'A damn good time whatever you're doing,' and nodding briskly to Fran as she passed. Not too sure what to make of this, Fran fought back her usual feelings of rank inadequacy, telling herself firmly that the woman was simply an eccentric and perfectly entitled to behave like a crusty old bat. Still, she had set the leaving ball rolling and Fran had a hazy notion that she, too, should be somewhere else. At least it had stopped raining – she didn't think she could face dealing with too harsh a reality after such a surreal experience. For someone who was trying to carve herself a niche as a mover and shaker, Fran really needed to get out more but didn't have the heart for it, never mind the wardrobe. Although she did have the vague feeling that she might at last have spotted a trend before everyone else had consigned it to the great charity shop of life and moved on to the next source of ego-boosting exclusivity.

Fran was not from the Margaret mould of efficiency and it took her a good ten minutes to get it together, but finally she was gone in a flurry of exchanged telephone numbers and promises to be in touch just as soon as she had some news. Left to the sorry sight of party debris, Delilah made an executive decision to leave it till the morning and delegated

Twizz to lock up while she made a frantic effort to tart herself up for the evening ahead. There were an awful lot of things she would much rather do than trawl trendy bars on some misguided mission, but she didn't have the heart, never mind the balls, to call the whole thing off.

As she began to scrabble in her bag for the few sorry items of make-up that might be lurking at the bottom, her fingers inadvertently brushed against the card once again. At least, she tried to convince herself that it was inadvertent, but her conscience and a reasonably perceptive psychologist might have had something to say on that score. Whatever her mental motivation for treating it like a talisman, she kept it very close to her chest.

Finally having located the stubby end of an eye pencil, and noted with no surprise that it was blunt, Delilah made a resolution. Whatever happened, whoever he was, she was not upending her life for some guy just because he made the kind of gesture that would have melted a frozen food factory. She would maintain her equilibrium, once she had rediscovered it. She would be cool, calm and utterly in control. And she would watch forlornly as those pigs flapped past in the sky. OK, so she was hopeless. Better that than heartless. Grabbing a battered lipstick, her contact lenses and the essential concealer stick, she made for the loo and a patch-up paint job. If she had to go out there with the toothsome twosome then she would go out fighting and that meant suitable camouflage. With any luck she might just be able to blend in to the bar decor and leave the other two to be stalked. Either that or be a sitting duck for the mystery man in all his gruesome glory. Cheered on by this bout of positive thinking, she groped around for the light switch and set out her wares in front of the tiny mirror, ready to turn herself into a warrior rather than a wimp or, at the very least, a bird of prey with a perfect pout. It was going to be a long and nauseating night.

Four

The evening did not get off to a flying start. For one thing Jess was late and flustered, and for another Delilah could not see a thing. It was the fault of her thumbnail. She had managed to get one contact lens to stick to a tired and gritty eyeball but the other one had been a bit more troublesome. In her haste to get herself together she had ripped open the packet of the one-day disposables that were a godsend to the lazy or drunk and promptly sliced the lurking lens in half. Not so much bifocal as neatly bisected. There was nothing for it but to remove the one already in her eye and to rely on the others to be her guide girls for the evening.

Now here they were, perched uncomfortably on the minimalist bar stools at Lola's and trying to make themselves heard above the braying sound of a roomful of loafer boys exchanging gossip in their own inimitable style. This seemed to involve an awful lot of hair tossing and eye flicking as the pack tried to outdo each other both in volume and content, continually scanning the room for fresh faces and meat. It bore a close resemblance to the playground at prep school, albeit with the added excitement of the presence of the foxier sex. Delilah was immensely glad that no one had as yet asked her to be in their gang. There were only so many ways you could look entranced at inebriated inanity before boredom and a healthy urge to say something outrageous kicked in. Not that she had always been this cynical. No, it had taken a good three or four similar such excursions before she finally conceded that a Gucci-shod existence was not something she lusted after.

Twizz, of course, was in her element, being too foreign to pin down and too flippant to care what they thought in any case. Not one but three floppy-fringed beauties had already drifted into her sights, and she was happily dispensing sideways glances at the braver boys in the room who stared back as if entranced, before leaning forward to mutter something in a companion's ear. Hearty guffaws and turning heads would then signal that the message had been received and understood and, with the help of another couple of drinks and a mental kicking from his mates, might eventually be acted upon. Until then, she could amuse herself by crossing and uncrossing her legs on the perfectly positioned bar stool and hope that they would not all decide to approach at once.

Jess had joined them at this juncture, full of apologies as she clambered on to the stool they had been reserving with bags, coats and frigid stares at anyone who dared enquire if it were free. Delilah would have been quite happy to sink into their usual routine of giggling, bitching and talking about nothing in particular and everything in general, but Jess had other plans.

'So have you seen anyone likely?' Barely was she settled and she was away, determined that they should not stray from the purpose of the entire evening.

'Ah, well, there is just one problem . . .' Delilah began, but Twizz beat her to it. 'Hah! Only if he's come within a one metre radius.'

'Yeah, well, they shouldn't make those lenses so bloody difficult to see, should they? It's not as if I'm going to recognize him if I see him . . . and he's hardly going to be waving a pen around so I can check out his handwriting.' Really, this whole thing was turning out to be a terrible mistake. She would much rather be at home with a bowl of cornflakes and a good book to drown out the worries that kept whirling around her head. Even a diehard optimist was entitled to an off day and Delilah felt hers was long overdue.

'Oh, for goodness sake, all you have to do is keep an eye out for anyone who might be acting strangely. You know, staring at you a bit too hard, that sort of thing.'

'Thanks. Thanks very much!'

'Oh, come on. You know I didn't mean it like that. Anyway, as you can't see, Twizz and I will have to keep lookout – that is if she can tear herself away from trying to give half the bar a hard-on and concentrate on the matter in hand.'

'I only wish it was . . .' purred Twizz, earning herself a pursed look from Jess and a long-suffering sigh from Delilah, who sometimes wondered if the two of them did it on purpose simply to wind each other up. One head-girlish remark from Jess and Twizz was off, metaphorically chewing gum and blowing bubbles of defiance in the face of authority. Delilah had a theory that they secretly loved it, in fact depended on each other in the way that double acts do.

On this occasion, however, they had a joint mission to accomplish and both realized they had better bond over it. A droopy Delilah left a lot to be desired and they were hoping that whoever so obviously did would rescue them from a lifetime of far-off looks and barely stifled sighs. They wanted the old Delilah back, the one who believed in belittling boys and having her own wicked way with their hearts and minds, wherever they were located. Jess felt that now the shop was up and faltering, the impetus that had driven her through its inception was no longer there. It had been such a long, hard haul, and now that things were staggering along there was not enough to satisfy Delilah's voracious appetite for mental stimulation. As for the physical equivalent, if she'd been a man Twizz would no doubt have suggested that all Delilah needed was a damn good shag. Being her, she said it anyway.

'Don't worry, love. Get it out of your system and you'll be back to your old once-bitten self.'

Unfortunately the prospect of a decent shag was about as likely in Lola's as a sudden onset of social conscience among its regulars, many of whom thought poverty was a communicable disease. As, no doubt, was emotion. Strictly from the roll-on roll-off school of sexual dexterity, they looked back with nostalgia to the days when no conversation was required afterwards and the object of their affection was grateful merely for a place in the first eleven. That, no doubt, was the reason they stuck together like glue, only daring to approach a fancied female if they had a mate firmly clamped to their shoulder for back-up. None of this, of course, could be divined from a cursory glance at the scene. It took time to realize that the charm on display was of the deeply superficial kind and that the perfect smiles bore a close resemblance to the expression of a basking shark.

Delilah hoped fervently that her postcard man was not hiding in the midst of this unpromising throng. Her instincts told her it was unlikely: most of them would be far too cool to make such a gesture and would probably consider it unbearably crass. She didn't think it was crass. Romantic, certainly. Juvenile, maybe. But since when had there been anything wrong with behaving like a fifteen-year-old? And as far as some of these guys were concerned that was probably a generous estimate.

'Don't look now, but that guy over there is definitely staring. It could be *him*, for God's sake. I said don't look! Oh God, now he knows that we know.' Jess gazed fixedly into her glass in a desperate attempt to appear nonchalant, but with companions like hers she never stood a chance.

Turning their heads and taking a long, hard look, they inspected the goods and came to the same conclusion.

Bullseye on Jess and it looked as if he intended to move in for the kill.

'What, you mean the one over there? The one staring at you? The one who's now coming over?' Delilah loved winding her up like this. It got her every single time.

Taking her cue, Twizz enthusiastically joined in. 'Who? Oh, yeah, him . . . yeah, I can see him. Cute.'

Delilah picked up the baton with practised ease. 'Yep. Definitely edging over here. OK, everyone, act normal.'

'Oh, for fuck's sake . . . I really don't know why I let you two do this.' Jess's head was dropping ever lower towards the bar as she tried to make herself as small and inconspicuous as humanly possible.

Mercifully for Jess, the pair of them fell silent as the object of their attentions finally made it as far as the bar, although the sidelong looks and stifled giggles were almost worse than their more blatant efforts. Delilah wondered what he would do next. Perhaps the sideways shuffle until, lo and behold, he stood amazingly close. Or maybe the matey manoeuvre, trying to catch an eye so he could exchange a word or a glance of solidarity at the slowness of the bar staff. That one usually worked a treat, so long as the barman kept up his end of the bargain by being helpfully inefficient. He might even go for broke and buy them a drink, although Delilah had only seen that one done once. In the event, he did none of the above but merely leaned across to Jess with a friendly smile and said, 'Jackson versus Partridge. David Mason.'

For a stunned second they all stared at him before slow realization dawned across Jess's face. 'Oh God, yes. You beat us on that one. Jess—'

'Jessica North. Yes, I remember.' He kept smiling at her in the same friendly fashion while Delilah and Twizz looked on in fascination. On the one hand, Delilah was mentally begging him to stay so she could find out more, while on the other she was shooing him away so they could bombard

Jess with the inevitable onslaught of questions. And questions there would be. No one lingered this meaningfully without there being some history to explain away.

'Well, it's good to see you again.' Jess was twisting the ring on her little finger, a sure sign that she was not as cool as she was attempting to appear, although Delilah had to give her full marks for effort – other than that small gesture, she seemed admirably amenable but distant. David, on the other hand, hovered ever closer the way people do when they are trying to prolong an encounter in order to gain some sort of definite result, such as a phone number, maybe, or even an actual date.

To Delilah's delight, he cracked first. 'Look, here's my card. We must get together and catch up on . . . everything. Call me, OK?' And still he stood there, holding out the card and looking mildly embarrassed with the effort. Just as Delilah was beginning to suspect Jess might coolly refuse, she took the card from him with a careful little smile and said politely, 'That would be nice.'

'OK. Well, lovely to see you too. Um . . .' As he began finally to back away, he nodded to the three of them and turned to walk back to his friends. Only Delilah caught his final glance back at Jess, whose head had somehow burrowed itself into her chest to the great amusement of Twizz. Funny how so much could be conveyed in one loaded little exchange. Now the questions could begin.

'So?' Delilah was in there first, thrilled for someone else to be under the spotlight.

'So what? He's just someone I dealt with on a case, that's all.'

'Must have been a long case.' Delilah was not to be deflected.

'It was, actually. Very complicated. Couldn't believe it when they won. Thought it was too close to call.' It was unlike Jess to become so agitated in such a short space of time. Delilah was intrigued.

'So how come you've never mentioned him before?'

'What's to mention? He's just some guy I worked with. Or rather worked against. That's it, end of story. I don't recall you talking about every Tom, Dick and Harry that walks in the shop.'

'Chance would be a fine thing. Anyway, judging by the way he was looking at you, I'm sure he'd like something more than a working relationship.'

'In his dreams. Now stop looking at me like that. There is nothing more to tell.' Perhaps not, but Delilah had noticed just how carefully Jess had tucked his business card away. Seemed like she wasn't the only one with a hot prospect sizzling away in the bottom of her bag.

'Christ, this place is like a meat market with no steaks. Can't we go somewhere else?' Bored with the ineptitude of Lola's loafer boys, Twizz had drained her drink, stubbed out her cigarette and battened down her eyelashes. There were only so many designer chinos a girl could look at before a desire for rugged set in. Besides, most of them looked as if shaving was something they aspired to rather than resented.

'The Doom and Gloom?' Delilah, too, was keen to get out. The Mont Blanc pens peeping out of top pockets probably saw more action on credit card slips than anything else, and she seriously doubted that any of them would have the imagination to stray from the path of conventional corniness.

'In this outfit? Get real!' Twizz had spent ages layering on her latest look and there was no way she was going to waste it on the local. Jess was similarly intransigent, but for less selfish reasons.

'You must be joking. We're not going home until we've exhausted all the possibilities.'

And so it went on, from one expensive bar stool to another, until Delilah begged for mercy and even Jess had to concede defeat. They seemed to take with them an identikit array of men, all of whom were utterly devoid of talent. Of course, one or two were worth more than a second glance, but they were the ones to whom some gorgeous creature slithered back from the loo only to have a proprietorial arm firmly clamped around her shoulder.

By twelve o'clock Delilah had had more than enough. The thought of work in the morning and the firm hand of Chairman Jess had deprived them of the comfort of total alcoholic oblivion and, as a result, she was beginning to feel like the spare part at a particularly boring party. She was quite prepared to sacrifice her Cinderella moment for the comfort of her own bed and the bliss of her own company. The nearest they had come to a close encounter of the postcard kind had been a beer mat with a number scrawled across it, tossed amongst them as if it were food for starving chicks. A quick cremation in the nearest ashtray sent smoke signals to its diminutive author and provided the three of them with a satisfyingly smug moment. Going out on the prowl was one thing, out on a full scale manhunt quite another. And bloodhound was not a good look, reeking as it did of sheer desperation.

Those boys could certainly drink. Trustafarians to a man, the ability to function the next day had never been an impediment to pleasure. Perhaps on previous occasions Delilah had been too pissed herself to notice, but in the cold light of restricted cocktails she could watch and observe the slow slide from inanity to inarticulacy. It was not a pretty sight. Hair that had been continually swept back through raking fingers began to acquire a sweaty sheen that plastered it to many a damp forehead. Lips that had once pouted began to slacken around suddenly impossible consonants. It was fascinating in its own way but it didn't half make you stop and think. Not only was it uncomfortably like looking in a mirror, it was a salutary lesson in how standards slip when snogging is on your mind and liquid lust is sloshing through your veins. Delilah doubted that she would ever trust her addled instincts again.

Just as they were about to troop out en masse from the latest love lounge, a hand on Delilah's shoulder made her stop with a start. Gritting her teeth and turning her head, she was confronted with a pair of quite nice but very glazed blue eyes that peered hopefully into her own.

'Sabrina?' the owner of the eyes muttered thickly, clearly fighting hard to focus. Prising his fingers off her shoulder, Delilah forced a smile that reached about as far as her upper lip and disabused him with a firm but kind, 'I don't think so.'

'Ah. Shorry.' And he was gone, lurching off in search of whoever had abandoned him. It was the perfect end to an excruciating evening, and the three of them piled out on to the pavement with a sense of relief. Even Twizz seemed happy enough to go home on her own for once. As for Delilah and Jess, it was a silent but companionable cab ride home and then an even more companionable sharing of the vodka bottle until well past the point of coherency, both determined to get as wasted as the evening had so obviously been.

'Could have been one of the barmen, y'know.' Well, they had been the tastiest flesh on display, although Delilah wasn't too chuffed about the idea of a cocktail shaker as a prospective boyfriend. God only knew what he and his wrist action could get up to when she wasn't around.

'Never thought of that. Nah. I'd say posing rather than postcards is more their style. And they're far too busy gazing at themselves in the mirror behind the bar to serve you, never mind suss you out. At least we know one thing . . .' Jess paused tantalizingly, forcing Delilah to kick her sharply. They were curled up at their favourite opposite ends of the sofa, a duvet chucked over the pair of them and copious quantities of vodka warming their pyjama-clad bones. Utter bliss. 'Well, I think we can eliminate the loafer boys from our inquiries. Most of them look as if they'd rather snort something off a postcard than write on it.'

'And if they ever stopped shopping Ralph Lauren would probably go out of business,' added Delilah, secretly relieved that her admirer might have more to him than an expensive habit or homogeneous tastes.

'And it was a mad idea.'

'Insane.'

A few moments passed in comfortable silence as they nursed their glasses and ruminated on what might have been a very close shave. Delilah felt that she was more of a designer stubble girl, having as she did a predilection for black trousers cut tight across the bum and a sexy walk to match. She'd have been better off in a spaghetti house chatting up the staff. This was no good, no good at all. She couldn't afford to be distracted from her shaky career trajectory, and absolutely refused to be shaken from her chosen path by the prospect of a good set of pecs and a nice line in surprise tactics.

'Well, I give up. Whoever he is, he'll just have to make more of an effort or . . . or that's it. We're through. Finished. Kaput. He's history. If you know what I mean.' Delilah thumped the cushion beside her for emphasis, sending an unpleasant spasm through Jess's skull. Looked like the premature hangover from hell was on its way.

'Bollocks. Besides, you haven't even met him yet. How can you be through when it hasn't even started?'

'Don't be so bloody logical,' was all Delilah could manage, and soon after that they both agreed that bed was a better place to be than any other. Tucked up under a mound of goose down, though, Delilah realized that something had started, had done so the second that postcard popped up amongst all her other post. And now the clock was ticking inexorably towards the showup or showdown, her tired brain unable to cope with either concept. Whoever he was and whenever it happened, she could only hope that his shoes were laced up and his shirt collars unbuttoned. And on that gloriously superficial note she drifted off to dream of a hundred polo ponies dancing across top pockets to a background noise of continuous braying, the lullaby of Loafer Boy Land sending her gently to sleep.

Five

Delilah's suffering the next day was intense, made all the worse by Twizz's knowing smile and irritating perkiness. For once in her short career as a shop assistant it was she and not Delilah who was handing out the flat Coke and painkillers, and she was relishing every second of it. Delilah's head was pounding far too hard for her to point out that self-righteousness is not an endearing trait. That would teach her to mix her drinks. Talking of which, there was a message from Fran to say that things looked hopeful but as yet no one had committed. Story of her life, really.

By three o'clock she was ready to throttle Twizz, if only to stop her singing tunelessly to *Abba Gold*. For someone who aspired to be the queen of cool, she was irredeemably addicted to songs that effectively annihilated any pretensions to street cred. Not that she gave a damn. Delilah wished she could acquire some of her attitude – perhaps they handed it out to Australian babies at birth, along with itchy feet and a need to unearth bullshit with the ferocity of a polecat on heat. She was on the verge of rewriting the lyrics and emitting a very loud Dancing Scream when Margaret appeared, bearing gifts of gooey cakes and a few tea bags to replenish stocks. So delighted was Delilah to see her that she clean forgot to mention the topic that had been burning away at the bottom of her bag, until a change of

CD and a blast of 'Postcards from Heaven' sent her scrabbling around for the evidence.

'Here, Margaret, what do you make of this?'

Margaret studied it carefully before glancing up and making an equally searching assessment of Delilah's expression. 'I think it's just what you need,' she stated in her usual unequivocal fashion.

'Don't know about that. It's really doing my head in.'

'And mine,' sang Twizz from somewhere out back, the sound rather muffled by a layer of chocolate eclair.

'Doing your head in? Ah, yes, I see.' Margaret continued to munch philosophically, encouraging Delilah to continue.

'Yeah. Well, it's just so frustrating. I mean, I get this postcard. Obviously from someone who I've met only I can't remember. And all he does is write my name and address, no message, and somehow expects me to guess who he is. Arrogant bastard. Anyway, I don't have time for this. I have a shop to run and things to make and to order and . . . I could do without it. I really could.' She was running a distracted hand through her hair as she spoke and Margaret was not fooled for an instant.

'Hmmmm,' was all she said as she wiped her sticky fingers delicately on a tissue.

'And, you know, it's very important for me to succeed at this. I bloody worked hard enough for it. And for over a week now this has been popping up to distract me. Ridiculous. I shall just put it out of my mind because whoever he is, if he's got any guts at all, he's going to reveal himself eventually. Don't you think?' She flicked an anxious glance at Margaret, who raised an eyebrow in agreement. Taking this as a yes, Delilah rambled on cathartically. 'Anyway, it's just typical of a man. I spend a whole year quite happily on my own – my choice, I'll have you know – and then some bloke decides to upset my nice, sane, happy existence with some little stunt like this. I mean, who does he think he is? Sending out postcards left, right and centre . . . ridiculous. Well, I have better things to think about. So sod him. He'll just have to deal with it. More tea, Margaret?'

Margaret cheerfully held out her cup for a refill and the two of them sat companionably sipping until the dulcet tones of David Bowie signalled the re-emergence of Twizz from musical exile. Soon after that Margaret announced that she had to be off and hauled herself out of the squashy sofa on which much teatime business was conducted.

'Bye, then, Margaret. And thanks for our chat. I feel a lot better about things now.' It was true. She really did feel as if the postcard was bothering her less. A woman back on top, in control and raring to go. At least for the moment.

'Any time, dear. Any time.' Gracious as ever, Margaret twinkled a kindly smile at them both and was gone, the cockerels barely stirring as she shut the door gently behind her. Delilah was just clearing up the cups, Twizz having retired to her turntables, when a much louder jangling signalled what she took to be Margaret's return.

'OK, what did you forget this time?' It was a standing joke, one that underlined Delilah's belief that Margaret's purchases were of the face-saving kind. She must have a hundred and one scented candles by now, not to mention her stockpile of lewd and lacy items. God knows what she did with them but, whatever it was, Delilah was eternally grateful.

But it wasn't Margaret. Slowly, Delilah realized that a puzzled silence hung in the air behind her. Turning around, she came face to amused face with a tall, cute and very cocky stranger. At least, that is what she surmised from the glint in his green eyes and the half-smile playing around a full and entirely kissable mouth.

'Oh, shit, sorry. Thought you were s-s-someone else . . .'

Furious with herself, Delilah realized that she was stuttering. It wasn't exactly the first time she'd clapped eyes on a cute customer. Actually, make that very cute – almost dangerously so.

'Evidently.'

He continued to stand there, giving her a subtle once-over, before grinning sweetly and announcing, 'Hi, I'm Matt.'

'Ha ... right. Well, um, hi. Welcome. Oh, ah, and I'm Delilah. Do ... have a look around. Take your time. In fact ... would you like a cup of tea? Kettle's just boiled.'

'No thanks. I'm fine. But I'd love to take a look around. Great stuff you've got here.'

Quite unabashed, he dived straight into the rack of gorgeous but distinctly provocative little numbers and Delilah could cheerfully have died on the spot. Somehow she had not envisaged an attractive man handling the goods, as it were, and the reality made her go hot and cold all over. Especially an attractive man who was unencumbered by an accompanying blonde of any description. Making his way over to the antique glass cabinet that contained jewellery and other original items, he reached in and fished out a pair of fine, elbow length leather gloves and inspected them carefully. Ravishing though they were, the liberal use of tooled silver studs and fine chains firmly placed them in a category Delilah thought of as bondage-lite. A fashion statement just dangerous enough to raise an eyebrow, and maybe more, in the salons of South Ken. Just when she thought he might ask her to model them or something, Matt threw her a knowing look and cheekily declared, 'Verrrrry nice,' before – thankfully – putting them back and turning his attention elsewhere. Delilah hardly dared move as he took a leisurely trawl among the scents and potions before picking up a CockTail glass and again subjecting it to searching scrutiny. A knowing look lit up his face but he merely smirked before going on to admire the candles, cards and crystals, pausing thoughtfully before picking up one handmade card and demanding, 'Who made this?'

Somewhat taken aback by both the question and his

sudden seriousness of tone, Delilah reddened slightly before answering, 'I did.'

He held it up to the light, admiring the juxtaposition of hand-painted silk, tiny leaves and delicately twisted silver wire before putting it back down carefully in its place with an appreciative, 'Beautiful. And beautifully made.'

He might well have said the same about her. Matt could scarcely believe his luck. Not only was she far sexier than her photo, she was talented too. There was nothing Matt liked more than the killer combination of looks and brains; it made the challenge so much more interesting.

'So do you make all of this?' Now he was standing in front of her, hands on hips and a frankly appreciative look on his face.

'No, I source a lot of it from young designers, import other bits and the rest I have made up. Cottage industry stuff.' Delilah was disconcerted to find that there seemed to be a bottleneck of words in her throat, stuck fast on a lack of saliva. He was still looking at her expectantly and she wondered for a wild moment what he would do if she flung off the cropped cashmere cardie he appeared to find so fascinating and dragged him over to the sofa. Probably respond in kind, such was his aura of complete self-confidence. Of course she did no such thing, merely cast around for something witty to say and thanked heaven above that Twizz was safely tucked away out back and unlikely to re-emerge until closing time. One whiff of this particular pheromonal package and she would have been playing bitch goddess to perfection, something most men seemed to find initially irresistible. Delilah preferred a more soulful approach, and here was one man who was definitely speaking to her inner being. Or more probably her libido.

Suddenly realizing that she had been staring straight at his chest, Delilah raised her eyes with a guilty start and met his, staring straight back at her. That bloody smile would have been infuriating if there hadn't been a matching hint of mischief in his expression, and Delilah was floored for a second. Rapidly pulling herself together, she enquired politely, 'Were you looking for anything in particular?'

Now that was an easy one. Without so much as a flicker, Matt replied sincerely, 'As a matter of fact, I was.' And continued to look at her with high-octane interest.

'Um . . . what, exactly?'

'I'm not too sure, but I thought you might be able to help.'

Shit, maybe he was shopping for a girlfriend or something. Yes, that was probably it. In fact, he most likely flirted with every half-decent woman who came within his orbit. For sport or something.

'Is it a present? For someone in particular?' Studied neutrality was not something that came naturally to Delilah and on this occasion it proved entirely elusive. She glanced distractedly down at her nails and noticed rather belatedly that those were not so much chips in her polish as bloody great cavities. Hastily burying them in the folds of her skirt, she looked up at him brightly and waited.

'Could be. Yeah, in fact it is. A present.'

'Great. Good. Well, what did you have in mind? Um . . . price range? Particular taste . . . ?' Maybe, just maybe, this was for his mother. Or his maiden aunt or something. Although with this bloke around, Delilah had the feeling that any maidens wouldn't stay that way for long. He was positively lethal.

Matt pretended to think for a second before helpfully stating, 'Absolutely no idea. I was hoping you might have some.'

'Ah . . . OK. Maybe you could tell me who it's for . . . or something about . . . them. Hair colour, eyes, age, that sort of thing.' That should just about cover all the possibilities and give her a damn good idea of what she was dealing with. Delilah held her breath and prayed for deliverance.

'Well, kind of similar to you, actually.'

Oh, bugger. Well, at least she was his type. And maybe he had a sister, although if he did she had to be a throwback, there being no way on earth anyone would confuse his studied sexiness with her own more rumpled charms. Pushing one unruly strand of hair away from her face, Delilah brought her mind firmly back to the task in hand.

'Oh, right. Is this a special present, like for a birthday or something?' Or some kind of major seduction number or even, God forbid, a token of his undying lust.

'It's a sort of "hello" present, if you know what I mean.'

Unfortunately, Delilah thought she did. One that said goodbye to her own flickering hopes. She refrained from kicking something very, very hard, and instead drifted over to the rack of frillies he had been so closely inspecting a short time before. At least, she tried to drift in a suitably nonchalant fashion but found it amazingly hard to do so when it involved coming within heart-stopping proximity of what was obviously a very cool customer. It didn't help that the shop was built on such an intimate scale or that he showed no sign of shifting to let her pass. Rather, he seemed to enjoy the fact that she had to squeeze between him and the display cabinet, turning away slightly so that at least it was her shoulder blade that brushed across him rather than anything more disconcerting.

'So, would this be about the right size?' She held up a rather beautiful cream camisole and he took it carefully from her, sizing it up for a second before holding it out at arm's length. 'Looks good to me,' he said, his eyes flicking from her to the camisole as if to measure one against the other. She couldn't swear to it, but Delilah had a distinct feeling she knew what he was getting at.

'Or how about this?' Determined to fight back against the onslaught of suggestiveness, she whipped out a far racier little number and looked him straight in the eye as she held it against her chest.

'Nice. Very nice.' His laughing eyes acknowledged a sort

of professional respect, one flirt to another. 'But perhaps not really you,' he added, throwing her for a second.

'Sorry?' Delilah couldn't help sounding indignant. OK, red and black lace might not be her thing but she was sure she could carry it off. Or make a damn good attempt. She wasn't quite sure what he was implying but she was not certain she liked it either.

'Don't get me wrong, it's lovely. Just a little too... obvious. Predictable. Which, as I'm sure you'll agree, is never a good thing.' His sudden switch to patent sincerity had an alarming effect on her melting point, and she felt herself beginning to simper even as she opened her mouth to speak.

'Oh... er... right. Hmmm.' Catching herself before coyness really took hold, she moved on to the display cabinet, distractedly rummaging through an array of jewels while trying to collect her scrambled thoughts. This guy was brilliant, a past master of effective innuendo. And he managed to do it without sounding the slightest bit corny, a rare quality indeed. A hand appeared over her shoulder and he reached past her to draw out a delicate beaded choker. 'Turn round a second,' he commanded and she obeyed without so much as a murmur. If this was magnetism he had it in spades. He held it lightly against her throat for a moment and frowned as if something were not quite right. Then he reached out and tucked one stray strand of hair gently behind her ear, standing back slightly to admire the effect before pronouncing, 'Perfect. I'll take it.'

'Oh, great,' Delilah squeaked, quite unable to lift her eyes above the level of his shirt collar. Gratefully seizing the opportunity to do something practical and efficient, she took the choker and got busy with her wrapping materials.

'We haven't finished yet.'

Noting an odd emphasis on the word 'we', Delilah smiled a trifle nervously and breezily declared, 'No problem. Whenever you're ready.'

'Well, tonight would be good. Although I expect you already have plans. So how's about tomorrow? Or even the next day? I could pick you up at eight. If that's all right.'

Not quite sure that she had heard correctly, Delilah stopped dead during her tracks and stared stupidly at the little box she had been enshrouding in tissue paper. After a very long pause, in which he remained entirely at ease, she looked up to see if he was joking. Not a flicker of a grin, not even a tiny smirk. Polite and friendly, his expression seemed to indicate that he had asked for nothing more startling than the time or directions to the nearest post office. She licked her lips and thought fast.

'Sorry . . . I, um, don't think I quite got that. Did you just ask . . . ?'

'You out? Yes, I did.'

Deadlock. He was still unnervingly calm about the whole thing, so much so that Delilah began to feel as if it were she who was behaving a bit oddly. Well, perhaps she was. After all, most women would have wet themselves at the chance of a date with a man like Matt. And Delilah was no different.

'Um . . . fine. Yes, OK. Great.' Her answer might have been inarticulate but his face instantly creased into an incandescent smile. He looked as if she had just handed him a large and shiny Christmas present that begged to be unwrapped. An analogy that Delilah would later discover was not a million miles from the truth.

'Fantastic! So . . . tonight, then?'

Retaining a shred of self-possession, Delilah discarded the overeager option. 'Tomorrow would be better,' she demurred. OK, so it wasn't exactly playing hard to get, but then again neither was he.

'Tomorrow it is. So, where shall I pick you up?'

Delilah considered the options before plumping for the one her mother would like best. 'Oh, just pick me up from here. I usually work till late anyway.' Working feverishly on her make-up and hair in the tiny back room, but he didn't have to know that.

'Boss a bit of a slave-driver then?' he teased, and she bridled at the assumption.

'Actually, I am the boss.'

He had known that, of course he had known that. But it didn't hurt to throw in a few red herrings, to make their meeting appear to be pure coincidence. God only knew what Dan would do if he ever found out. Nothing probably. There was precious little he could do, being far too tied up with his company to worry about anything as trivial as real life. Besides, Dan would choose business over bedroom any day of the week. He'd always been the serious foil to Matt's Jack the Lad. And he couldn't be *that* hooked on a girl he'd seen once in a blurry newspaper photo. Probably forgot all about her the moment they left the pub. At least, that was what Matt chose to tell himself. Selective memory was a very useful thing, second only to killer instinct in his book of tricks. And boy, had he made a kill here. He was so close to the spoils he could practically scent flesh. Quashing any faint stirrings of conscience once and for all, Matt brought his focus back to the present and the promise it held for the future. This was going to be fun.

Delilah, of course, knew nothing of the thoughts that were coursing through Matt's mind, principally because he had long ago perfected the art of a charmingly deadpan expression. But her blood was also up, startled into life by his alarming spontaneity, even while a tiny voice at the back of her brain began to nag at her with questions. More to silence those bothersome questions than anything else, she began to busy herself again with his little parcel, wondering more than ever just who the intended recipient might be. This man was more of an enigma than most.

As he waited for her to finish her wrapping, Matt drifted over to the sofa. A small, brightly coloured square caught his eye. Curiosity piqued, he took a closer look. And then another. It took him but a moment to be sure, another to mask the impact of what he had discovered.

'Someone's popular.'

It was an odd sort of statement, but his tone was as light as ever. Delilah glanced up to see him dangling her postcard from forefinger and thumb and realized that she hadn't had a chance to clear up since Margaret's departure. An alarm bell rang somewhere in the back of her brain. He appeared unconcerned, more amused than anything else. Chances were he had alighted on the postcard by accident. It had, after all, been lying there waiting to be found. And yet a small doubt settled into a corner of her mind. Coincidence was all very well but only if you believed that any such thing existed. Long experience and innate cynicism made her an atheist on that score.

'Well, there you go. So many men, so little time.' Although, unfortunately, time enough for cliché-ridden retorts. He didn't even wince as he grinned and handed the postcard over without another word. For some bizarre reason, Delilah felt duty-bound to defend herself.

'Actually, I have no idea who it's from. It's all a bit of a mystery. Probably someone's idea of a joke.'

'Oh, I shouldn't think so.' A loaded response, mischief dancing in his eyes as he spoke. Was that his idea of a hint? She favoured him with a long, hard look but he didn't so much as flicker. Delilah decided that not even an Oscar winner could be that good. There would have been something, a twitch below the eye, a nervous hand to the nose to give the game away. She'd read all that stuff on body language and his sure as hell was communicating something, only it didn't appear to be guilt. Deciding that the jury was still out on that one, she handed him his package with a small smile and took the credit card he was offering in return. Interestingly enough, it was platinum in colour and had the name of a rather posh bank stamped discreetly in the corner, along with his full name. Matthew Stone. Emphatic, strong. Definitely a name to contend with.

The transaction completed, she handed him back his card and tried not to start as his fingers brushed hers. Telling herself sternly to get a grip, that of course it had been unintentional, she nevertheless took a step back and dropped her hand to her side. Delilah didn't think she had ever before met a man who genuinely fulfilled the description of being dangerously attractive. Ludicrously so, certainly. Irresistibly, possibly. But this one had a quality that made her feel as if she had just touched a live wire and couldn't let go.

'See you tomorrow, then. And thank you for all your help.' He inclined his head in a mockery of a little bow, softening the effect by staring at her in a way that suggested everything and nothing at the same time. Delilah mumbled something back and then he was gone, leaving her to heave a huge sigh and yell for Twizz almost in the next intake of breath. This was one story she was not going to believe, although Delilah had a funny feeling it was more of a chapter in what could turn out to be quite a saga. Only time, and the truth, would tell.

Six

The best laid plans often fail to hatch, incubated as they are in a feverish whirl of muddled thinking. And Matt had certainly muddled her thoughts in spectacular fashion. Delilah had had enough time to remind herself that the last thing in the world she was looking for was a relationship, that her business brain superseded her baser instincts, and that her hormones were in happy hibernation and unlikely to emerge for anything so fatuous as a cute smile and a disconcerting manner. Which is why she had spent the last 29 hours shaving her legs and armpits, and gouging several unattractive holes in the process. She'd begged the only available beautician she could find for a last-minute bikini wax that had left her looking like a plucked chicken, and had been fretting over the contents of her wardrobe. Then there was the despair over her hair, the agonizing over her hips and the ultimate dead giveaway – the painting of the toenails. All in all, she was a fabulous advert for the post-Bridget generation and a real flag bearer for female emancipation.

By the fourth phone call Jess was beside herself with boredom. 'Yes, OK, so it could be him. We've established that. And then again, it might not. Why not just give the guy a chance to tell you in his own good time?'

'Oh God, I don't think I can bear the tension. I mean, if it *is* him he might be laughing at me behind his napkin.

And if it's not and I say something, he'll think I'm a total loony.'

Privately, Jess thought that given the way Delilah was behaving this was more than likely to be the case. 'Well then, don't say anything at all about the postcard. Let him do the talking. After all, there's nothing men like better. With any luck you can just sit there and look fascinated until he slips up and lets the cat out of the bag.'

'Cynic!'

'I prefer realist. Now, I really must go. I have a meeting in five minutes.' Delilah could practically hear Jess gathering together her papers as she spoke.

'OK, OK . . . Hey, Jess, just one more thing . . .'

'What?'

'You definitely think the black dress with the boots. And my leather jacket, so it could be either trendy or dressy?'

'Definitely. Now I really must get going. Might catch you later, although I'll probably be back very late tonight myself. And you'd better be tucked up in bed alone, girlie, or I'll have something to say about it!'

'Yeah, right. You can talk.' Jess had suddenly started working alarmingly late, so much so that Delilah was beginning to feel like the spurned one in a love triangle. She could tell that Jess had been there by the occasional appearance of a used mug or a rumpled towel, but for most of the past week they had communicated purely by phone. If Delilah hadn't known better, she would have sworn that Jess was up to no good. But if there had been anyone on the horizon, or even the horizontal, she felt sure that Jess would have told her about it. After all, there was nothing like chucking crumbs to the sex-starved, although tonight might well alter the status quo. Not that she would do anything on a first date. That would be fatal. Well, maybe just a quick snog on the doorstep. Or maybe not, the doorstep then presenting the great coffee dilemma that would inevitably lead to the

even greater danger of the sofa and beyond. Not that
the beyond bit bothered her. Much.

Entirely oblivious to the mental twists and turns taking
place not ten feet away, Twizz kept her eyes firmly fixed on
the magazine she was leafing through, her feet tucked under
her on the sofa and an array of used mugs by her side. She
looked entirely at home for someone who was supposed to
be at work, although Delilah could hardly blame her. They
were still not exactly rushed off their feet, a state of affairs
which should have been commanding her entire attention
rather than being distracted by some hormonal upsurge.
One small ray of hope had been a phone call that morning
from Fran to tell her that she hoped to have something
firmed up by the end of the week. She wasn't the only one.

The thought of free and fabulous publicity had momentarily lifted her business spirits. If only the same could be
said about her sartorial ones. As the hours slipped by and
the day grew dark outside, the evening ahead loomed ever
larger in her fevered imagination. Dark – it had been dark
for quite some time now. One glance at her watch and
Delilah transmogrified into a whirling dervish of activity,
her yelp of alarm alerting Twizz to the seriousness of the
situation.

'Oh, fuck! It's nearly seven o'clock!' Amazing how the
hours could fly past unnoticed when there was absolutely
nothing to do but think.

'Shit, shit, shit . . . make-up bag . . . dress . . . dress . . .'
Casting around frantically, Delilah was on the verge of a
major panic.

'Calm down, will you? They're under here somewhere.'
Twizz coolly extracted a large bag from behind the counter,
in which Delilah had packed three dresses, just in case, the
boots, two pairs of shoes, a sizeable collection of make-up
and the perfume she reserved for special occasions, the one
that practically shrieked seduction.

The definitive dress, the one in which she felt her most

ravishing, resembled nothing so much as a crumpled rag and Delilah's face creased in empathy. 'Oh, no! Just look at it! I completely forgot to hang the bloody thing up and now it's ... it's ...' There was a definite hint of wail in the way that her voice rose. Suppressing an urge to slap her hard, Twizz took the dress and inspected it critically before pronouncing, 'All it needs is a good pressing. Get your face on and I'll have a go at it.'

Throwing effusive thanks over her shoulder and shedding outer layers as she went, Delilah raced for the tiny loo and its even more minuscule mirror. She had stuffed three pairs of disposable contact lenses into her make-up kit to avoid any repeat of that particular disaster but there was still plenty that could go wrong. Shaking hands and subtle make-up are not natural partners, and the last thing she wanted was to resemble a short-sighted drag queen. An entirely natural, devastatingly sexy look was what she was aiming for, something that could only be acquired with trowel loads of slap blended into infinity and a steady wrist when it came to the smoky eyeliner. Which is hard to manage when you're standing shivering with only a pair of old socks, a Muji vest and matching grey knickers to protect you from the elements. Delilah, however, was nothing if not creative. Forty minutes later she was still far from satisfied, but it would have to do. She could hear Twizz making ever louder throat-clearing sounds outside the door, and knew it was only a matter of moments before she lost all patience and dragged Delilah bodily out of the loo. She knew that was imminent when an arm appeared around the door as a particularly unsubtle hint, and an ironed dress was thrust into her sticky hands. Hastily wiping them clean, she slithered into the dress, ran desperate fingers through her hair, applied another layer of lippy just in case, and emerged to a round of sarcastic applause and a critical appraisal.

'Fab. Love the eyes ... verrrry harem girl. How about

with the hair up? Like this?' Twizz scooped a handful of curls up in one hand while reaching behind her with the other for one of the funky hair combs in the cabinet. 'Much better. Now, what about what's underneath?'

'What about it? He's not going to get that far, not on a first date . . . Oh, OK, maybe you're right.'

Admitting defeat in the face of one perfectly arched eyebrow, Delilah grabbed the first pretty set of knickers and bra to hand and a packet of lace-topped hold-ups as an afterthought and disappeared back into the loo. There were some perks to being the proprietor, and purloining the stock in an emergency situation was definitely one of them.

Stockinged-up and suitably underclad, Delilah re-emerged with a strut and a flourish. 'OK, girl, now I'm definitely ready for anything!'

'I'm very glad to hear it.' Matt did indeed look thoroughly delighted as the wiggle died on Delilah's hips. Behind him stood Twizz, making innocent gestures with her upturned palms and rolling her eyes in self-absolution.

'H–ha . . . hi!' Slinking to a halt right in front of him, Delilah was grateful for the firm hand that reached out and held her shoulders as he kissed her lightly on both cheeks. Air kissing was not really her thing, but he did it with such grace that she felt she could forgive him, just this once. Well, maybe twice if her flesh kept tingling under his hands in that disconcerting way.

'So, shall we go?' Clearly he was a man of action, already holding the door open for her as she scrambled for her bag and the carefully chosen leather jacket.

'Sure you're going to be warm enough like that?' His concern was touching, charming even, but Delilah was well past the little woman stage.

'Course I am. Twizz, you don't mind locking up do you?' Too bad if she did, rotten guard dog that she was.

In response, Twizz favoured her with a most demure expression and a sweet little, 'Of course not. Now you go

and have a good time and I'll see you in the morning . . .'
When you can tell me all about it being the implicit message,
right down to the nitty-gritty of whether or not he got to
admire those expensive underpinnings.

Once safely outside, Matt strode purposefully towards
the cars parked alongside the pavement, and Delilah
wondered which one would respond to his finger on the
magic button knowing that boys just adore their toys and
the remote control key was definitely designed with them
in mind. Lights flashed and beeping noises went off at his
first attempt, almost as impressive as a taxi screeching to a
halt the second a man raises a nonchalant hand. And in the
impressiveness stakes there was definitely more to come,
the car in question being a sporty little BMW in a tasteful
silver. Delilah slid into her seat without comment, although
she was busily adding this latest piece to the Matt jigsaw
puzzle.

He flicked on the CD player and an unknown symphony
poured into the car. Classical music was not Delilah's area
of expertise but she could certainly appreciate it. She supposed it was because her brain worked in such a visual
way. Show her a gallery and she could unerringly pick out
the finest pieces, hum her an aria and she was stumped.
Still, it was lovely just to let the music wash over her as they
sped smoothly along, Delilah keeping one observational eye
on Matt's approach to the open road. You could tell a lot
from the way a man drove – more than from the way he
danced or behaved with waiters, but perhaps not as much
as from the way he kissed. The very thought sent an involuntary shiver up her spine and she stole a sideways glance
to see if he had noticed. Matt slid his eyes sideways at
exactly the same moment, the corners crinkling attractively
as he smiled.

'You're a bit quiet. You OK? Long day?'

Realizing she had been silent for a fraction too long,
Delilah hastily perked up and began to babble, 'Oh, I'm fine

thanks. Bit tired . . . well, no I'm not really. No, waking up now, as it happens. You know what it's like, people coming in and out of the shop all day, never a moment to think. Talking to them all of the time. Keeping the customer happy. You sort of run out of things to say . . .' Which, of course, was a blatant lie, but there was no way in hell she was going to tell him that her vocal chords had frozen over through lack of use. She and Twizz had refined the meaning of 'companionable silence' to the point where shared grunts over endless cups of coffee represented the high point of their intellectual exchange. Not great for keeping up one's social skills, but as sign language went it was very efficient.

His smile widened. 'Somehow I doubt that.'

'Doubt what?' Maybe it was the daily overdose of caffeine, but Delilah rose very swiftly to the bait.

'That you would ever run out of anything interesting to say.' Oh, very good. She had to give him full marks for that. In fact, the whole set-up so far was fairly faultless, bar an alarming tendency to put his foot down rather hard on the accelerator and a subsequent heavy reliance on the brakes. That didn't bode too well for his bedroom technique, never mind his tyre tread. And the fact that it was a BMW said something in itself . . . Delilah whipped her mind away from what was becoming dangerous ground. Just this once she would reserve judgement, suppress those instincts that threatened to do her a disservice.

In this sanguine spirit of open-mindedness, she kept her mouth firmly shut when he cut up a black cab, fair game that they were, and exhaled very quietly when they finally parked right outside the restaurant. She looked up at it with only a slightly sinking heart. It was very big, very flash and very fashionable, and Delilah's hopes of a romantic tête-à-tête faded the minute she registered the decibel level. Things began to look up, however, when they were led upstairs to a much more restful room and installed at a discreet corner table beside the window. Good sign: either he was known here or he had called ahead.

They studied the unwieldy menus for a moment until a waiter appeared at their side and enquired, 'Something to drink?'

'Champagne to start with, I think. If that's all right with you?' It was more than all right, it was positively one of her most favourite things in the entire world. She didn't say that, of course, merely smiled sweetly and said, 'That would be lovely.'

'Bottle of Veuve Clicquot, then. Oh, and an ashtray, please. Doesn't bother you, does it?' He asked as an after-thought, the cigarette packet already out on the table in front of him. As a matter of fact it did – there was nothing in the world worse than kissing a walking ashtray. But as they hadn't got that far, and as she was sitting in a very nice restaurant having been driven there in a very nice car by one of the cutest men with whom she had ever locked eyeballs, she did nothing but smile sweetly all over again. Not that she was superficial or anything; it had just been a long time since any of this had happened to Delilah. 'No, not at all. Fire away, so to speak. Ha ha.' He didn't seem to get that one, but the awkward moment was smoothed over by the ceremonial arrival of the champagne bucket and the uncorking of the bottle.

Matt raised his glass. 'To us. And a very good evening.' She liked the way he said that, with just enough humour to take the edge off the cheesiness. Delilah slowly began to relax.

Matt was happy to take up the conversational baton, a rare quality in a man. Delilah was beginning to like him more and more, not least because his charm was so easy even if his physical presence wasn't. Such tangible testos-terone was terrifying, far too scary to contemplate when your recent pucker practice has consisted of snuggling up to a battered teddy, and the warmest thing you've had in your bed is a hot water bottle that has gone cold by morning. Bit like a man, really. No, that was unfair. Here she was with a member of the species who not only oozed sex appeal but was surprisingly in possession of all the normal faculties. And what faculties they were . . . Delilah could spend forever watching that mouth as he spoke. Just the right mixture of fullness and form – promising rather than pretty.

'I love your shop. How long have you been open? I don't remember seeing it there before.' That might have had something to do with the fact that ordinarily Matt would not have been seen dead in such a glaringly unfashionable part of town. Up and coming was all very well, but he preferred to wait until somewhere had truly arrived.

'Actually, we've only been open a few weeks. Four and a half, to be exact. Could even tell you the hours if you like – there've been plenty of them.' Now she sounded like the sort of sad cow who marks off the minutes of her day in some sort of mental calendar. Trying to be more upbeat, she added, 'What with all the work setting it up and so on. Making stuff, sourcing it. It's hard work, I can tell you.'

'I didn't realize it was such a recent thing. I'm sure you're going to do very well.' Was that a hint of respect in his eyes? Delilah sincerely hoped so. She liked a man secure enough to applaud success. Even if that success was a bit slow in coming.

'I hope so. It's taking a while to get off the ground.' She hadn't meant to be so honest, but Matt seemed to bring it out in her. Maybe it was the way those green eyes looked so directly at her, inviting confidences.

'All it needs is for word to get around and they'll be fighting to get in the door. Trust me, it took a good three months before anyone really came near my gallery and now things are going great.'

Now this was a revelation. Delilah had assumed he was something suity. 'You own a gallery?'

'Yup. Well, I have a couple of backers on side. We deal

mostly in commercial contemporary works, with a few emerging artists thrown in to keep things exciting. I always think that those who are already established should help the up-and-coming. And you never know, I might find the next big thing.' Not even the cigarette he was carefully aiming away from her could detract from his increased lustre in Delilah's eyes. A man who made his living from art but still fought to be ethical. This was almost too good to be true.

'Wow, that's fantastic. What sort of art? Paintings? Sculpture?'

'Mainly paintings, yes, although I do have some more conceptual stuff. Americans especially go for it. In fact, there's a great installation at the moment you might be interested in seeing – part of my new show.'

'I'd love to.' Her words were a lot cooler than her thoughts. Delilah forced herself to stay cool. An invitation to his gallery meant nothing. A friendly gesture, that was all. No reason to start going off at the romantic deep end. Even if plunging headlong into those waters was becoming a more attractive prospect by the minute.

'Are you ready to order?' Saved by the service. With that alarming ability to pop up out of nowhere, a waiter had appeared, notebook poised and pencil at the ready.

Frantically scanning the list of starters, Delilah went for the easy option. 'Oh ... ah ... um ... what are you having?'

'The Thai-style salad is good, so is the seafood linguine. But I think I'm going to go for the risotto to start with and then perhaps the monkfish. I've had quite enough red meat for one week.'

She only wished she could say the same.

'Sounds great. I'll go for that too.'

Neither original nor sophisticated but Delilah didn't care. She had far bigger things to worry about than what she was going to eat, one of them being Matt's cool hand

lightly holding her wrist as he inspected the ring on
her index finger. Tactile was obviously his preferred
approach.

'Lovely. Is it one of yours?'

'It's from one of my discoveries. She comes up with
some great pieces – really delicate but different at the same
time.'

'So I see. Suits you.' Mercifully, he relinquished his touch
just as her heart rate was about to soar beyond the recom-
mended safety level.

'We kind of do a similar thing, don't we? Find unknown
artists, get their work seen. Of course, yours is in a totally
different league . . .' Was it her imagination or was she
taking off the babble brakes again?

'Oh, I wouldn't say that.' Again that warm and confident
smile. But not too confident. She liked that. 'There's no such
thing as a different league – just different media. Mine might
be more expensive than yours but that doesn't make your
pieces any less valid. Or beautiful.'

This last was definitely loaded in her direction, and her
pulse obligingly started to go beyond a gentle jog again. He
must have known the effect he was having, probably did
this number all the time. Not that she was objecting. Just
being cautious. Quite why, she wasn't sure.

'You're right, of course. But at the moment my artists are
definitely in the "undiscovered" category. Although not for
much longer, not if I have anything to do with it.' Never
squashed for long, Delilah's fighting spirit rose to the
surface and her eyes gleamed with determination. The effect
was not lost on Matt. He loved a woman who crackled with
that kind of energy.

'I'd put money on it. And I'm very good at sounding out
what will sell. Something I picked up in a former incar-
nation. It's come in very handy, I can tell you.'

'Oh yes? How so?'

'I used to be an advertising exec. Very corporate. I

know, I know . . .' He threw his hands up at her involuntary look of disgust. 'All I can say in my defence is that I got out as soon as I could. Well, as soon as I could afford to.'

'Is that how you financed your gallery?' Her initial reaction had hardly been fair, and he did seem well on the way to rehabilitation.

'Partly through that, yes. I took my final bonus and ran. But you can't knock it entirely. Some of the clients I used to deal with are amongst my best customers. Surprising what the most conservative of people will buy. I would have thought that you of all people would know that.' Touché. And she had to give him brownie points for patience and humour in the face of knee-jerk prejudice.

'Right again. Happy now?'

'You bet I am. You're here, for one thing.' There it was again, that ability to deliver a line that by rights should stink of Stilton. Only the way he said it, it made perfect and highly seductive sense.

'Hmmmm,' was all she managed as a safe response, swiftly followed by an even bigger 'Mmmmmm' as her main course was placed in front of her and her wine glass filled. A bottle of well chosen Chablis had appeared by some mysterious sleight of the sommelier and it slid down remarkably quickly. Unsurprising when her glass was not only huge but in a permanent state of refill. He was either eager to impress or desperately keen to get her into the sack. No, that was unfair. For one thing he was driving and for another he was only trying to make sure she had a good time. She was the one who kept throwing the spanner of suspicion into the works. Ballsy was one thing, bitter quite another. God forbid that she should slide over the fine line between the two.

Whatever his nefarious intentions, the conversation flowed as easily as the wine. So easily that when he threw her a curve ball of a question it threw her for a second.

'So what were you doing before you opened the shop?'

He was looking at her expectantly and for a moment Delilah hesitated, hovering between the edited and the unexpurgated versions of the truth.

'I . . . worked in retail.' That should about cover things, more or less. Matt, however, was not the sort to be so easily fobbed off.

'What sort of retail? Department store, large chain, boutique? Were you a buyer, in marketing . . . ?'

'Actually, it was a market stall and I ran the whole show. Bought the raw materials, made most of the stock, sold it and froze my arse off often enough in the process.'

So there. Only he didn't seem at all fazed by her admission, simply looked even more intrigued than before and politely asked, 'And where was your stall? In a street market, I take it.'

'Mainly, yes. I did Camden at the weekends, Covent Garden in the week and then I branched out and had another stall at Greenwich as well. I had to keep plugging away until finally I earned my permanent pitches, but it was worth it in the end. Although you've no idea how much work is involved keeping up three separate sites.'

Matt raised an eyebrow. 'My God, positively an empire!' His teasing, however, was more admirational than provocative.

Encouraged by his attitude, Delilah grinned back. 'Hardly. But I learned a hell of a lot, enough so that when this place came up I knew I could make a go of it.' Quite unconsciously, she dug her nails into her palm as she spoke. She wasn't quite at the hair-tearing stage yet, but the strain was beginning to show in the forced brightness of her smile.

'And you will. It's a fabulous idea, I'm telling you. People need a bit of fun and glamour in their lives, and you're flogging it to them with just the right attitude. Cheeky without being sleazy and pretty classy as well. You've obviously got a good eye for things.' Oh, but she certainly had. And from where she was sitting things looked very good indeed.

'Your assistant's quite something else, isn't she?' Matt continued.

For a split second Delilah felt a pang of what she sincerely hoped was nothing more than insecurity rearing its insidious head. 'That is one way of putting it. No, Twizz is great. In fact it was she who ran the other stall for me in Greenwich whilst I did Camden. That's how we met – she wandered up one day and asked if I needed anyone to help out, and next thing I know she's helping me empire build, as you call it.'

'Weird name, that.'

This was a little too interested for her liking. She had to work not to make her response too dismissive. 'She was christened Theresa but her baby brother couldn't manage that so Twizzle, or Twizz, she became. Suits her better anyway, and it's good for professional purposes. She's a performance artist, you know.'

'I didn't, but it wouldn't surprise me at all. She has that look about her.'

Hating herself for it, Delilah watched him carefully as he spoke. Twizz, after all, did tend to trip over the tongues hanging out in her wake. Odd because she wasn't classically pretty or drop dead sexy. Sure, she was tall and bleached blonde but you could hardly call her the baby doll type. She just had something. Something Delilah often wished she could bottle and sell at a ferocious rate.

'And what look is that?'

'Oh, you know. A lot of fun but mad as a brush. Far too much like hard work, if you ask me.'

The rush of relief that roared through Delilah would have flattened a juggernaut in its wake. Fantastic. Twizz wasn't his type. Of course, that was no guarantee that she was either, but things were looking hopeful. Especially when he added, 'I like my women to be sorted, know what they want. Like you, for instance. You've got a passion and you're going for it. And good for you.'

Several things passed through Delilah's mind simultaneously as he said this. The first was how incredibly sexy he was when he went all serious like that. The second was an irresistible urge to hug him. And the third was an insane desire to burst into tears and demand, 'Does that mean I'm your woman?' in a way that would have shamed Nashville's finest. Naturally, she did none of the above, simply looked a little flustered but flattered and murmured, 'Do you think so? Um, well, yes, I suppose I am, really.'

Getting a grip was becoming harder and harder. Lack of practice may have made her rusty in the flirtation stakes but she was having trouble even speaking coherently. Not the best state to be in when you consider your brains to be your greatest asset and your self-sufficiency a given. Being reduced to a heap of romantic rubble in so short a space of time was downright humiliating, although her mind had admittedly been less lucid of late. Primed up by a corny postcard, rendered incapable by a piece of pink cardboard and five short words. Little wonder she was having so much trouble formulating a sentence. Although now that the card had once again impinged on her consciousness . . .

'You have a secret admirer.' The words fell of their own accord out of her mouth before she had a chance to catch herself. That's what came of living some of the time in your own little world and the rest of the time in everybody else's. Matt took a beat before reacting, but she could have sworn that something flickered in his eyes. She hoped it was interest, although it seemed more akin to alarm.

'I beg your pardon?' He made great play of filling her glass and she wondered if it was to cover his own confusion or hers.

'God, I am sorry. That just sort of popped out. It was on that postcard . . .'

'Postcard?'

An awkward pause as she waited him out, watching his face for the slightest sign. Nothing, not a single clue beyond that initial response. He was either the greatest poker player in the world or he really didn't know what she was on about.

'You know. The one you picked up when you came to the shop . . . it's got that written on the front . . .' Still fishing and still he was not taking the bait.

'Really? Can't say that I remember. Probably too busy sussing out the sexy knickers to notice.'

There it was again, that irresistible glint and a half-smile that held plenty of promise. There was nothing more Delilah could do to push the point, and besides, she was getting distracted all over again. It really was like getting back on a bicycle; a long look here, a shy smile there and you were away, en route to loved-up land and the bedroom beyond. Pushing back her chair, Delilah stood up and announced, 'Back in a minute,' before weaving hazily towards the loo and a lipstick moment. She'd held off for as long as she possibly could, but there comes a moment in every date when the table ricochet has to be risked. At least she had her contacts in. Many was the time she'd headed hopefully in the direction of a likely looking door, only to find it led to the kitchens, or worse. She was on nodding terms with half the kitchen workers in town. There had to be a job for her in immigration if all else failed.

A pause for thought on the throne, a quick fluff of the hair and she was ready to return to the fray, or at least the dessert menu that was sitting in wait.

'Oh, nothing for me, thanks.' She smiled at the hovering waiter.

'A coffee then, madam?'

'Do you have decaf? I don't really drink coffee late at night . . .' she offered apologetically.

'Bang goes one excuse for inviting you back, then.' Matt was straight in there and Delilah didn't know whether to blush or smack him one. Hard to tell if he was teasing or not when his mouth was saying one thing and his eyes quite another. God but he was gobsmackingly gorgeous.

'You're confident.'

'Hopeful, I think is the word.'

'Oh, yes?' Ouch. That was arch.

'Yes.' And that was so soft and sincere that she melted faster than butter on a hot plate. Bastard. He knew exactly the effect he was having. Thank goodness for the lack of caffeine – her hands were shaking quite enough already. It was hard even to put the cup back on its saucer without a telltale rattle of china. She took refuge in stirring with great intent.

'Do you know, there's this artist I represent who lives entirely on black coffee and baked beans. Figures they act as the perfect creative fuel.'

'Gives him a kind of explosive energy, does it?' Delilah was delighted that she could still dredge up the odd funny when the occasion demanded.

'Oh ha ha, very good.'

They grinned at each other in juvenile empathy. He looked searchingly at her and his smile subsided into seriousness. Reaching across, he brushed her hand lightly and quietly asked, 'Shall we go?'

This was always the tough bit. After dinner, where next? Nerves twanging like a badly tuned guitar string, she nodded mutely and began to scrabble for her purse. There was nothing she hated more than to feel bought off by a date, but Matt was way ahead of her on this one. While her fingers were still reaching around in her bag, he had summoned a waiter and slipped him his credit card in one ultra-slick action. Delilah knew when she was beaten. In the

smoothness stakes Matt was in a league all of his own. And
he managed it without being slimy. Miraculous, really. He
even held her jacket out for her in such a way as to avoid
her normal inelegant wriggle into the armholes, and passed
over her handbag without a murmur of offended masculinity. Heaven only knew what planet this man came from,
but wherever it was, they were shit hot on the halo effect.

Once in the car he made a great play of fiddling with
buttons and dials, turning to ask with unfeigned consideration, 'Are you warm enough?'

With an internal body temperature nearing meltdown,
there was little Delilah could do but murmur a platitudi-
nous, 'Oh, yes,' before settling down to enjoy the ride. And
what a ride it turned out to be. Matt headed the car towards
the river, swooping along with a careless grace until they
reached the bridges, all aflame with fairy lights. Delilah
loved the river, particularly at night. She had even been
known to beg cabbies to take her on a wide detour home,
cost fading as a consideration beside the lure of the lights
on the water. She turned to tell him as much, her eyes
shining almost as brightly as any of the megawatt bulbs
suspended high above them.

'This is wonderful . . .'

Mistaking her enthusiasm as being entirely for him, Matt
smirked in response and reached across to squeeze the
closest available bit of her thigh. Delilah froze, uncertain
whether this was a definite come-on or merely his way of
empathizing. She soon got her answer when, with a flick
of an indicator and unparalleled audacity, he pulled the car
over and her into his arms in one unbroken action. Shock
delayed Delilah's reactions, tripping a time lapse between
her brain and her mouth. Thanking God for autopilot, she
dimly began to realize that it was indeed her tongue that
was twining with his, her jaw that was beginning to ache
under an extremely enthusiastic onslaught. Finally able to
pull back and draw breath, she resisted the urge to lick her

lips and settled for a coy look up under the lashes, just as he was gazing down at her with the sort of expression cats usually reserve for their more interesting prey. Playful but deadly at one and the same time.

'That was nice.' He made it sound as if he had nibbled at a particularly luscious chocolate and found himself wanting more. Which, Matt being Matt, he took without any hesitation, this time adding a thorough exploration of her upper torso to his endeavours.

Boy, but he was a fast mover. Feeling a bit like a born-again virgin, Delilah squirmed decorously away from his more daring forays up and down and around her front. Not that it didn't feel fabulously good, but there were limits and hers were not about to be breached on the strength of dinner and a satisfying snog. To give him his due, his hands did take no for an answer, even if they simply regrouped and tried again elsewhere. She had to admire his intransigence. Finally, even he had to concede defeat. Drawing back, he cradled her face in his hands in a sweetly affectionate gesture, kissed the tip of her nose and remarked, 'You can't blame me for trying.'

Delilah didn't know what to say to that, so wisely said nothing at all, just peered up at him and marvelled at the length of the lashes about eight inches from her own. He was running his thumb gently up and down her temples, stroking the back of her head with his fingertips. The sensation was immensely soothing but Delilah couldn't let go. This was definitely one dangerous player and she wasn't going to drop her guard, not for an instant. Which is why he totally disarmed her by giving her one final kiss on the forehead and murmuring, 'Well, I suppose I had better take you home.'

Disappointment surged treacherously in her throat as she nodded dumbly in reply. It was one thing to decorously fight off his advances, quite another to have her supply suddenly cut off. Delilah kept her eyes fixed to the road for the remainder of the journey, directing him as crisply as she could even as her mind worked overtime.

Matt, meanwhile, was enjoying himself hugely Everything was working to plan. The first lunge to catch her off guard, an enjoyable if frustrating fumble to follow. Keep her on tenterhooks until he was good and ready. By the time he'd finished she'd practically be begging for it.

As they drew up outside her place, Delilah wrestled mentally with the coffee question for a good twenty seconds before turning to him and suggesting, 'Coffee?' in a take-it-or-leave-it tone of voice.

Unbelievably, he glanced at his watch before responding. 'Sure. But just a quick one – I've got training in the morning.'

For what? Teasing a woman mercilessly? Torturing her with the hot and cold treatment? He certainly seemed a master of the art. As she let them in, Delilah hoped that Auntie Jess would not be there in her slippers and ratty old dressing gown to greet them. The flat, however, was silent and obviously unoccupied. Judging by the uncollected pile of post, Jess hadn't even been home. Probably slumming it with a bunch of her fellow solicitors in some chichi joint, happily putting the world to rights for a liquid fraction of their usual hourly rate. That didn't mean, however, that they wouldn't be disturbed at any second, although judging by the way Matt was behaving, it looked like there wasn't going to be much of a party to break up. It would appear that he was one of the few men with a heartbeat who took an invitation to have coffee literally. Stung by his apparent indifference, Delilah held up a jar and inquired sweetly, 'Instant OK?'

'Yeah, great. Milk, no sugar.' And he turned away to inspect her bookshelves.

Gritting the teeth she wanted to grind in frustration, Delilah busied herself and handed him a steaming mug before perching on the edge of the sofa with her camomile tea, wondering if he would join her or if he was just going to wander around all night casing the joint. Happily for him, Matt got the subliminal message, sprawling across the cushions and reaching out an arm to drag her down beside him.

'This is nice.' To make it absolutely clear that he wasn't necessarily referring to the coffee, in the next breath he added, 'Being here, I mean. With you.'

Delilah's spirits instantaneously lifted and the tight feeling in her throat dissipated. It was going to be all right after all. In fact, more than all right. Things got interesting again when he took her mug and put it aside before moving in for more full-on Matt. This time his rambles across her form yielded results as Delilah entwined her arms around his neck and arched against him in a far more abandoned fashion. They both emerged ruffled and red faced. Delilah thought she had never seen anything so adorable. His breathing was definitely faster than before and he took time to compose himself before dropping his forehead to touch hers and muttering, 'I'd better go.'

It took a superhuman effort not to beg him to stay. Begging, however, was not a good move and Delilah had no intention of buggering things up this early. Taking a deep breath of her own, she sighed in what she hoped was a wistful rather than a thwarted fashion and murmured, 'I suppose you had.' Excellently played, if she said so herself. If he'd been hoping for resistance there was to be none forthcoming. And perhaps he had, because he hesitated for a moment longer before slowly drawing back, grinning at her and running a hand through his tousled locks. How anyone could look so bashfully beautiful and yet so irresistibly naughty was a total mystery. She had to keep a tight hold to prevent herself changing her mind and ripping at his buttons there and then. Delaying gratification had never been so hard.

'Well, thank you for a lovely evening.' The subtext was all in her brightest smile. Oh, please, please ask me out again. Please just tell me you'll call and actually mean it. Take my home phone number, take my address, take me for that matter . . .

'Thank you for coming. I had a great time and . . . I'll give you a call, shall I?' He was slipping his jacket back on, heading towards the door.

'That would be lovely.' When? How? Would you like me to write the number down for you? And still she stood there, looking studiedly nonchalant about the whole damn thing.

He was dangerously close to crossing the threshold, possibly never to be seen again, when Delilah threw dignity to the wind and blurted out, 'But you haven't got my number!' Matt stopped dead in his tracks, slowly turned and paused for a very long moment. Delilah's stomach lurched in anticipation. Surely he wasn't just going to wave goodnight and walk out the door? Although recent experience had taught her that was entirely poss— Thoughts silenced by the best snog yet, Delilah knew what people meant when they talked about legs turning to jelly. Hers were so wobbly she was surprised to find herself still standing when he finally let her go.

'I found you once, didn't I? Trust me, I will find you again,' were his parting words before he disappeared into the night.

Delilah heard the front door bang behind him but she was too caught up to care about the neighbours and their fussy little signs. The way she felt right now she'd happily bang a hundred doors out of sheer euphoria, and a hundred headboards after that. If only she'd known how close they'd come to doing just that.

It took Matt a full minute of breathing deeply outside the front door before he could saunter in a rather stiff-legged way to his car. His departures from the scene were not normally this precipitous, but she had really got to him. Her walk, her smile, that crazy hair . . . he put the mental brakes on hard. If there was one thing Matthew did not do, it was fall in love. Lust he could do, passion was not a problem. But as for emotion – he was allergic to the very idea. For that reason alone a hasty exit had been the smartest move. That and the fact he always liked to leave them panting for more. There was no doubt about it, she was ripe and ready. Next time she'd be desperate. The very thought brought a wolfish grin to his chops and a swagger to his step. Sanity regained, Matt gunned up the engine and headed for home, the return of his careless confidence only too evident in the way he drove.

Back inside, Delilah heard the engine start up and wondered what had taken him so long. And once she had started wondering about one thing her thoughts led her inevitably to another. Like his parting words. Strange way of putting things . . . as far as she was concerned they had met quite by chance. So why did he use the word 'found'? Was it just a figure of speech? Maybe it was more than that. Maybe the search had started even before he came in the shop. A week or two before. A week or two before when he had found out her address and sent her the postcard. No. Ridiculous. She was certain she had never seen him before in her life, and she wasn't likely to forget a man like Matt. But what about that thing Twizz said . . . meeting him without her knowing it. The postcard man. Could it be him? Would it be him? Was it in his nature? Delilah had absolutely no idea.

Punch-drunk with thinking and dizzy with desire, Delilah swayed off to bed and her raggle-taggle teddy. Once safely tucked up, she kept the events of the evening running around in her head on a continuous loop until sheer exhaustion ground them to a halt. A couple of thoughts nibbled away at her even as her eyelids fluttered and her breath grew heavy and slow. The first was the possibility that she had found the phantom postcard sender. The second was a sneaking suspicion that, wherever Jess was, it was not where she was supposed to be. And whatever the whys and wherefores, she fully intended to get to the bottom of both.

Seven

'I can't believe you didn't check it out. Not even his signature ... couldn't you have tried to cop a look at the credit card slip?' Twizz was practically slapping her forehead in incredulity.

'I could hardly hang over his hand and watch him fill in the total, now, could I?' Delilah was becoming irritated – one of the side effects of lack of sex.

'OK, OK. No need to chuck your dummy. Well, did he have the right sort of pen on him? Does he seem like the kind of guy who'd pull a stunt like the postcard? Can he talk in joined-up sentences, for Christ's sake?' Clearly impatient with Delilah's dull-witted responses, Twizz was indulging in an accurate impression of a drill sergeant. A dull ache began to throb right in the middle of Delilah's forehead.

'I ... don't ... know. And I don't care either. Isn't it enough that he's incredibly attractive and that he's not an axe murderer?' Or an axe grinder, come to that. Delilah had lost count of the number and variety of neuroses she had come across in her encounters of the masculine kind. They all fitted so neatly into their Freudian boxes: the mummy's boy, the mixed-up boy, the one who wanted to be everybody's boy ...

'If you say so.' A clearly disgruntled Twizz obviously did not agree, but she had decided that delving into a packet of M&Ms was infinitely more rewarding. Feeling unaccountably like a failure, Delilah decided that a peace offering was in order, if only to wipe that expression off her assistant's face.

'Coffee?' she suggested diffidently.

'Latte?' Now Twizz was really pushing it. A latte meant a trip down to the end of the road. Away from the telephone. Not that she was hovering by it or anything so obvious. Just twitching over its reluctance to trill, and picking it up every so often in case the line was dead. There was, however, no getting out of this one. Gritting her teeth and grabbing her purse, she conceded defeat and completed the swiftest coffee run on record.

'Nothing worse than a lukewarm latte,' she pronounced to a sceptical Twizz, before giving the game away by oh so casually enquiring, 'Any calls?' as she involuntarily glanced over at the phone.

'Not in the last six minutes, no.' That knowing smirk was back, playing around Twizz's mouth like a magnet for a swift left hook.

'Oh, right.' Not that she would expect him to call quite so soon. Bit too quick, not to mention keen. No, he'd probably leave it the requisite three days, four at a push. Five would really be going too far, although better that than nothing at all. He'd call. Of course he'd call. He'd been interested. She'd held back. He'd been left wanting more. Not that she believed in all that crap . . . although it did seem to work. Unfortunately. Treat 'em mean, keep 'em keen. But was there such a thing as too mean? And surely she had as much right to call as he did? Female initiative, making the first move. Men were supposed to love that kind of thing. Only they didn't, not really. Delilah could vouch for that, having once or twice let her fingers do the dialling thing only to have them royally burned. The poor loves couldn't handle it and the ones who paid lip service to new manhood were the worst of the lot. Old wimphood, more like. Which brought her back to Matt and the age-old question.

'So, do you reckon he'll call?' Twizz couldn't resist teasing, although she rather suspected he'd take his time, being just a little too pleased with himself not to play games.

Delilah winced. Twizzle was either reading her thoughts or, more probably, they were plastered across her face for the world to see and read.

'Dunno. Might do. You know how these things are.'

Brilliantly executed, but she was wasting her time. The darting glances over at the silent instrument of torture and the air of utter indifference gave the game away more easily than a prize fighter paid to take a dive. Busy. She really had to get busy. And her shop along with herself. She wondered vaguely what Fran was up to – nothing, in all likelihood. It was par for the journalistic course to wax and wane between outrageous enthusiasm and total apathy. The response to her shop opening press release had been remarkable only for its almost total non-existence, the honourable exception being the local paper, although stories on school fêtes and planning protests did not exactly constitute stiff opposition. A new game had evolved out of some of their more desperate Wednesday afternoons, where she and Twizz would take it in turns to come up with ever more fanciful takes on tabloid exclusives. 'Elvis Spotted in Saucy Knicker Store' had been a front runner until Delilah had come up with the clear winner: 'Suburbia Mad for Oral Sex'. Geographically that might be stretching a point, but this was one urban myth that was definitely based on fact. And she had the sales receipts to prove it. At least her chocolates were a winner.

As if to prove a point, the door opened, the cockerels clanged and a small group of Japanese tourists wandered into the shop looking about them as if they had stumbled across a particularly eye-popping exhibit. Twittering excitedly, they came complete with designer togs and a keen eye for a photo opportunity. By the time Delilah and a reluctantly roped-in Twizz had finished posing for shots, they felt as if smile rictus was about to set in. To give the oriental posse their due, they purchased a gratifyingly large number of items, unable to resist the lure of the kinkily kitsch. There was much giggling behind hands and long discussion before seven pairs of frilly knickers, four sets of bejewelled cuffs, a couple of outré candles and almost the entire stock of CockTail glasses were handed over to be wrapped. These were the source of much amusement as dawning realization produced a collective chorus of 'Waaah!' followed by an explosion of mirth. Delilah could only assume that phallic objects were not big in Japan.

Once their visitors had taken their excessively polite leave, it seemed quieter than ever. So quiet that when the phone did ring, both Delilah and Twizz jumped out of their skins and ended up clutching each other in a white-knuckled kind of way.

'Well, go on then. Answer it,' ordered Twizz.

'No, you,' came the pathetic response. They both stared at the phone for a second before another insistent trill broke down Delilah's defences.

'Good afternoon, Decadence. Can I help you?' Uncomfortably aware that she sounded like a hotel receptionist, Delilah held the receiver as if it were a live and potentially dangerous reptile.

'Delilah? Is that you?'

The sudden release of tension sent the air swooshing out of Delilah's lungs. Whoever this was, it wasn't *him*. Not unless someone had kicked him hard in the cojones.

'It's me. Fran,' the voice rushed on, sounding as if its owner were standing right in the middle of a three lane motorway. 'Just come from a meeting with Jan Howard . . . Sunday style section . . . wants an excl— Hello? Hello? Are you there? Oh, bugger this thing! Hello?!'

'Fran? I can't hear you. Fran?'

'Delilah? Hellooo?! Hang on a sec, I'm just shifting into this doorway—' And then the line went completely dead. Delilah looked at the receiver stupidly before replacing it and shrugging at Twizz. The second she did so, the phone rang again and she snatched it up before the communication gods could once again cut the connection.

'Fran? Can you hear me?' She yelled down the receiver and a momentarily deafened Fran responded with an only slightly sarcastic, 'Loud and clear.'

'Great . . . so, what were you saying? Jan somebody or other—'

'Jan Howard. Editor of the style section in the *Sunday Herald*. She wants me to do an exclusive on the shop. Y'know, all that stuff we talked about. She loved it, loved the concept. Thinks her readers will go for it in a big way. It took some talking, I can tell you, but I gave her the big sell. Promised her an exclusive, went on about the cocktail thing. Told her they'll be coming from all over town once word gets out. She totally agrees. Seems pretty keen to come along herself in fact . . .'

Paralytic with delight, Delilah let the words flow over her while she tried to absorb their impact. Beside her, Twizz hopped from one foot to another impatiently, anxious to be let in on the big secret. Clearly something wonderful was afoot. She could tell that merely by looking at Delilah's face and its expression of pure, unadulterated amazement.

'I don't believe it! That's just . . . just . . .'

Fran cut short Delilah's spluttering with a modest, 'Incredible. I know. I'm over the moon myself. I mean, the *Sunday Herald*. Do you know what their circulation is? Phenomenal, absolutely phenomenal. And their readership . . . I tell you, Delilah, you could not ask for a better target audience . . .' Far be it from her to preen, but in her doorway Fran was practically purring with well deserved delight.

'Fran, I can't thank you enough. Look, why don't you

come over and we'll celebrate. You can tell us all about it over a glass of something. I'm sure we can dig out a bottle from somewhere.' This with frantic hand signals to Twizz who, arms firmly folded, had no intention of going anywhere until a few questions were answered.

Fran sighed regretfully down the phone. 'Shit, I'd love to but I've got to get this piece finished for first thing tomorrow. How's about tomorrow night instead? I could come along just before closing and we could get going on some ideas. Pick out the things you particularly want to feature, get some bio on you, that sort of thing.'

'Fab, great, whenever you want,' Delilah's eyes were darting around the shop as she spoke, trying to pick out newsworthy items while in fact not focusing on anything at all. 'There's so many things I'd love you to mention. I just don't know where to start . . .'

Fran's answering chuckle was just a little constrained. 'Yeah, well, don't get too excited. We've only got about 750 words in which to do this. But it's a start. Definitely a start.' Still huddled in her doorway, she tapped her foot involuntarily and gripped her mobile a bit tighter. Hell, why should she feel defensive? It was still a coup, albeit one limited by the demands of the copy editor and the need to prove herself. Well, she'd show them with this one. No more scrabbling around the lower reaches of glossy land. This was the big one, a broadsheet no less. Quality stuff, and Fran was determined to turn in the goods, whatever it took. And if that meant orchestrating events and massaging a few facts then she was the girl for the task.

On the other end of the phone Delilah was still beaming into the receiver. Even after they had said their goodbyes and Fran had disappeared into the ether of the airwaves, she continued to hold on to it for a few moments more, afraid to let go in case her news proved similarly ephemeral. Twizzle was beginning to think she might have to snatch the receiver out of her hands when Delilah snapped back to reality, slammed down the phone and grabbed her with a great whoop of joy.

'We've done it! We've done it! We've bloody well done it!' They were both feeling slightly queasy by the time they'd finished jiggling around but, Delilah's excitement being highly infectious, they were also grinning like loons. Exhausted with emotion, Delilah flung herself back into the depths of the sofa, her arms wide and her face shining. Even her hair was more electrified than ever, spreading out with similar abandon across the top of the comfy old cushions. Her happiness was all-encompassing, the aura of benevolence extending to where Twizz stood bemused and again beginning to wonder what on earth it was all about.

'Care to share?' she demanded, still none the wiser.

'We're rich, we're famous. We're only in the *Sunday bloody Herald*!' Judging by the hyperbole, Delilah was already halfway into tabloid land. Too bad she hadn't done a deal with one of the red-tops. No, not too bad at all. Broadsheet was where she wanted to be, slap bang amongst the sleek and shiny with purses and wallets to match. As far as breaks went it was akin to the chorus girl stepping into the lead, an analogy Twizz of all people should understand.

'Bloody hell!' was, in fact, her intelligent response once Delilah had finished filling in the details, followed by the inevitable, 'This calls for a drink.'

'You bet it does. Let me see if I can get hold of Jess. It'd be great if she could join us.'

'Yeah, fantastic.' A deadpan response which was wasted on Delilah, already reaching for the phone and dying to let the whole world in on her news. Or at least the whole of her own particular universe. Even as she was dialling, it flashed across her mind to tell Matt. Oh, no – she'd got that urge to share. A sure sign she was on that slippery slope to slushiness.

'Hi, is Jess there, please?' Delilah didn't recognize the voice on the end of the phone. She could only assume it

was the latest in a long line of temps, most of whom lasted
only as long as it took to save up the money for the nice
long holiday they needed after working the hours that commercial law demanded. No wonder Jess was hardly ever
home, welded to her desk by sheer weight of work and
expectation from on high.

Sure enough, Delilah got the standard response. 'She's in
a meeting at the moment. Can I take a message?'

'Can you just tell her that Delilah rang and it's urgent.'
Probably not as urgent as some multimillion-pound
company going belly up over a dodgy deal, but Delilah
didn't care. As far as she was concerned her news beat some
suity negotiations any day of the week.

'Delilah? Is that D-E-L . . . oh, just a moment. She's just
this second come out of her meeting.'

Funny, that. Still, Delilah was feeling generous enough
to overlook the small matter of call screening. That was the
trouble with the temp turnover. Just as she had one trained
to recognize her voice another one came along and she was
back on that bottom rung of the ladder labelled 'fob-offable'.

'Delilah, what is it?' Hardly the welcome she'd been
looking for. Jess sounded both hurried and harried, her
voice guarded in a way that signified she was not alone.

'Nice to speak to you, too! Do I take it there's someone
with you?' Delilah's cheery tones contrasted sharply with
the formally hushed manner in which Jess was speaking.

'Look, can I get back to you? I'm right in the middle of
something here.' She was sounding strained now, even for
Jess. Almost strangled, in fact. Disappointed though she was
not to be able to gush forth her news, Delilah felt a pang of
alarm. Something was cooking at Jess's end and it didn't
sound as if it was anything digestible.

'Uh, sure. Course you can. Speak to you later.' Whenever
that would be. Delilah had never understood those TV programmes where flatmates coexisted on a claustrophobic
basis, but this was going to the other extreme. She hadn't

even had a chance to dissect her date with Jess, never mind spill the beans on the latest bit of excitement. And she couldn't help but feel miffed, even as the warning bell clanged somewhere in the back of her brain. Mystified but determined not to show it, she proposed a frothy hot chocolate as a stopgap celebration.

Twizz had been hoping for something with a few more bubbles but graciously conceded it was her turn to fetch the goods. She was ready for a little male interaction and perhaps even a welcoming kiss from Flavio. A girl had to brighten up her day any way she could, although by the sound of things such time-filling measures might well become a thing of the past. Soon they would be far too busy coping with the fashionable hordes to pause for anything as pedestrian as a coffee run. At this rate she might even get her own assistant to dash around and do the dirty work.

While Twizz tripped off happily, thoughts of her most camera-ready outfits already whirling through her head, Delilah took a moment to savour events all over again. It just proved the old truism – lucky breaks happen when you least expect them. Maybe if she forgot hard enough about Matt there would be a similar cosmic effect. Not that he was at the forefront of her thoughts or anything, merely lurking in the wings until the spotlight swung back in his favour. No doubt he was used to it, even metaphorically speaking. Men like Matt were just meant to be centre stage, and all without apparent effort. The princeling effect – she'd met more than a few who were afflicted by it. But maybe not Matt. So far he'd exhibited few, if any, of the tendencies. No overuse of the I pronoun, no overbearing arrogance, no sodding phone call . . .

Delilah had had enough. Against all her better instincts she reached out a hand and picked up the Yellow Pages. She flipped the book open near the beginning, scanning rapidly for the section entitled 'Art Galleries and Dealers'. Justifying her actions was all too easy. Who said the guy always had to make the call? She could phone up and thank him for a lovely time, find an unbearably arty question she burned to have answered. Or how about suggesting a visit to some exhibition or other? A play, a film, some other vaguely cultural event? Then again, she could always just tattoo 'Welcome' on her stomach and lie across his front doorway doing her best impression of a hairy doormat.

There was no denying it, make that call and she would lose in the balance of power stakes faster than Twizz could say, 'I told you so.' Third millennium it might be, but when it came to the dating game there were certain men you had to play by the book, even while every fibre in your feminist body screamed otherwise. Fair it most certainly wasn't, but it was futile to complain. The thrill of the chase did not extend to getting the golden boy, so she would just have to stash away her hunting instincts and keep them in reserve for matters of a material kind.

'Got you a large one, seeing as we're celebrating. With extra choc on top.' Saved by the bell, or in this case by the birds bashing together above the door. Twizz made a timely reappearance, rattling on as she parked her packages on the counter, dumped her jacket in the back and produced some wicked biscotti to dunk. Pausing for breath did not come high in her list of priorities and she was halfway through some story about one of the pretty coffee boys before she had even begun to prise the lid off her cup.

'So Flavio says, why you never want to come see the cinema with me, and I say to him, not on your life mate. I know what you Italian guys are all about, I've lived in . . . Delilah, what are you doing?' Uncanny. In full flow, off on her favourite subject and it all comes to a dead halt when she smells something is up. Delilah had to hand it to her, her senses were sharper than those of a hound on heat.

'Doing? Nothing. I'm not doing anything.' A shade too defensive and Twizz was on to her, an emotional Exocet missile homing in on its target.

'So what are you looking up in the phone book? Or should I say who?'

'Nothing. No one. I was just—'

'About to blow your chances? Delilah, I am ashamed of you. Now, go on, be a good girl and close it. That's the way. And put it back where it belongs. Excellent. Now come over here and sit down beside me. And don't even *think* of phoning him while my back is turned. Got that?' Blonde crop aquiver, Twizzle could really come on like the head prefect she never was. Possibly a case of unfulfilled potential, or even wishful thinking. Whatever it was, there was no arguing with her, especially not when it came to her specialist subject: man taming in ten tortuous steps.

Feeling absurdly guilty, Delilah took a slurp of her chocolate and tried not to feel cheated. Even Twizz's self-righteous, 'You'll thank me for this one day,' only fuelled a childish attack of belligerence. And her fingers still itched to dial those digits, no matter what her self-appointed love minder thought. Perhaps a spot of displacement activity would do the trick. Jess might be too busy to talk, Matt a forbidden fruit, but she could call somebody else. It was always like this when she had something to crow about. An overriding desire to tell the world and his wife, or at least ten people who gave a damn. Conversely, when things went wrong it was her battered old teddy who got the ear bashing and who generally came up with the sage advice that got her through. That, at least, was how she liked to see it.

Unable to settle now until she had burbled away to at least one other person, Delilah mentally ran through her address book. There were certain people you rang for certain things. Some were great twice a year to meet up for a drink and a giggle, others were brilliant stalwarts who were there whenever.

'I know. Kate!' Brilliant. Kate was the sort of mate who was always happy to play and still there when time and life got in the way and your friendship was reduced to telephone tag and email jokes. They went back to college days, when a shared sense of the absurd had got them through some chaotic times. Kate had loyally shown up on the first Saturday they'd been open, clutching a large bunch of lilies and going away with the most frighteningly expensive items she could find. Delilah's protests had been cut through with a cheery, 'Well, if I don't wear it I can always use it at the next brainstorming meeting,' bringing to mind the delicious picture of a roomful of marketing types applying their lateral thinking skills to a feathered bustier and a crystal-encrusted riding crop.

'Kate, hi, it's Delilah.' Oh, for the joy of direct lines. Delilah had an aversion to switchboards and an even bigger one to secretaries with the instincts of guard geese.

'Delilah!' A gratifying shriek of joy in response. 'How are you, girl? How's the gorgeous shop? Simply heaving with people, I'll bet!' Ever since she'd risen to the rank of account director, Kate had begun speaking in superlatives. A hazard of the job and Delilah forgave her for it.

'Not quite heaving but things are going nicely. Well, they will do now. That's why I rang . . .' She was off and running, babbling along on one breath as the excitement began to build again.

'That sounds fan— Sorry, what did you say? Delilah, sorry love, can you hang on a sec . . .' The sound of muffled talking as Kate placed a hand over the receiver and engaged in some urgent confab. At least she hadn't used the hold button, that being another telephonic pet hate. A few moments later Kate came back on the line.

'Sorry about that. Look, can I call you back? Something's come up and I have to deal with it now. Two minutes and I'll get back to you, OK?' What could Delilah do but agree, even as she had to choke back her story for the second time. Feeling thoroughly thwarted, she slumped over the counter and gave up on ever being able to share the good news. Almost immediately the phone rang again, and she tried not to sound too grumpy as she answered.

'That was quick, crisis over then?'

'I didn't know I was having one,' came the laconic reply, and Delilah's hand flew up to her mouth in horror.

'Matt . . . hi. How are you?' Without looking she could feel Twizz shaking her head in despair. Bit of a giveaway to recognize his voice straightaway, and totally against the Twizz method of making them work for it. Oh well, failed at the first fence. Again.

'Pretty good. Rushed off my feet but you know how it goes.'

Not really, but Delilah's heart soared despite herself. Of course he was incredibly busy. Things to do, people to meet, paintings to flog. No wonder he'd taken a full fifteen hours to call her.

'Oh, I know. It's been really hectic here, too.' Comparatively speaking, but he wasn't to know that.

'Well, I won't keep you . . .' Oh, do, please do, she wanted to shout but of course restrained herself. 'I'd just like to invite you to a private view we're having. Nothing huge, but I thought you might find it interesting. I meant to mention it last night but it clean slipped my mind.'

Yessss! He wanted to see her again and on his own turf. Cool be damned. Delilah felt herself brim over with happiness.

'Sounds great. When is it?' She hoped Twizz would be proud of her controlled tone of voice. She was certainly proud of herself.

'Um . . . that's the thing. It's tomorrow night. I know it's short notice but—'

'No, no, that's fine. I'm free as it happens.' She tried to make it sound as if that were a rare and startling occurrence.

Matt was obviously the sort of person who was so inundated with invitations that social spontaneity occurred a good week or so in advance.

Hence, no doubt, the initial hesitation and then the surprised but delighted, 'You are? Fantastic!'

A flurry of pen finding and address taking ensued before he rang off with an affectionate, 'See you tomorrow then. I'm looking forward to it.'

Not half as much as Delilah was. Had a customer not walked into the shop at that very moment she would have punched the air with excitement. Instead, she contented herself with beaming benevolently at the woman, even when she handed over one solitary truffle to be wrapped. Poor love was obviously suffering from a lack of endorphins. Delilah treated her with all the sympathy of the soon to be satisfied to the sex-starved, conveniently forgetting that all too recently she had been numbering herself amongst them. Well, not any more – fingers crossed. She knew all about not counting her chickens and so on but a little flutter of anticipation was allowed. Actually, too much anticipation made her nervous. Best not to dwell on that until the moment presented itself. It was just like riding a bicycle, except that bikes didn't demand quite such a high level of interaction.

Anyway, there were far more important things to think about than the prospect of a night of passion with Matt. Like what on earth she was going to wear to what sounded like an event out of *Pretension Monthly*. There would probably be aspiring artists and screaming queen critics all over the place, simply dripping with effortless style and edgy appeal. Black, she supposed, would be the order of the day. Never one to follow a fad, Delilah had always preferred to carve her own sartorial path. It might be idiosyncratic at times, but at least it was always a reflection of her. For once, however, she felt that might not be enough. Or perhaps not enough for Matt. A definite case of wardrobe crisis and who better to advise than the resident expert on all things arty and street.

'Twizz, he's asked me to some arty-farty show. I've got absolutely nothing to wear.'

'Haven't we been here before?' came the response, bringing Delilah up short in the realization that she was in severe danger of losing her post-feminist credentials. Flapping around over a first date was just about allowable but any subsequent panic was going a superficial step too far. Although she had a sneaky suspicion that it was not so much the beauty of her soul that was captivating him as the rest of the packaging. Everyone knew that men were visual creatures – she only had to look around her own shop for proof.

'OK, point taken,' she muttered, her mind working furiously through her wardrobe.

Twizz sighed. Delilah was a hopeless case but she couldn't in all conscience let her cock this one up. 'Well, by the sound of things I don't think you should break out your best frock and pearls. Go minimal but funky – you know, blend in with the art. That is his kind of thing, right?'

'People don't really dress up for these things, do they? Yeah, you're right. Think Damian Hirst . . .'

'Or maybe not. Cow is so last season.'

They looked at each other and burst into fits of giggles. Delilah was still laughing when the phone rang for the umpteenth time and Kate's bemused voice asked, 'Delilah? You all right?'

'Fine . . . yep, I'm fine. You'd have to have been here . . .'

'I wish I was. Sounds like you're having a riot.'

She was, she most definitely was. And the fun was only just starting. As she settled down to one hell of a catch-up chat, Delilah felt that frisson of expectation. It was all happening at the same time, her life coming together on every front. And if the thrill that rippled across the pit of her stomach was due more to terror than anything else, then Delilah chose to remain in blissful ignorance. An entirely human, if ostrich-like, response.

Eight

For an arty party it was surprisingly short on excess. The buzz of chatter would not have disgraced a solicitor's drinks party, while the crowd had hardly raided the outer reaches of fashion for their outfits. Delilah supposed that she ought to be relieved although in truth she was somewhat disappointed. At the very least she had been hoping for a dreadful dowager and a couple of wannabe Quentin Crisps. Instead, the only crisps on offer were of the hand-cooked root vegetable variety, and the nearest she could find to eccentricity was the dishevelled creature holding court in a distant corner. His dress sense was compellingly awful, compounded by a haircut that would not have disgraced a flea-ridden marsupial. He simply had to be one of the artists.

'Hello, gorgeous. Glad you could make it.' Matt swooped down from behind and kissed her just above her right ear. Delilah jumped and the glass of warmish white wine she had procured splashed over her hand and down her front. Matt looked appreciatively at the damage.

'Can't wait for the wet T-shirt contest,' he quipped, admiring the effect, and her mortification turned instantaneously to mirth.

That was one thing to be said for basic black – great when it came to concealing a wet patch. All would have been well had she not felt compelled to dab at it with a crumpled tissue, leaving behind a liberal dusting of tiny white shreds in the process.

'Don't worry about it. Come and meet some people.'

Matt took her by the hand that had been flicking ineffectually at the dandruffy mess and led her off into the throng, skirting a Perspex podium piled high with oranges as they traversed the room. Beneath the podium a rubber snake was coiled and above it a large plastic daisy dangled. As they edged carefully past, Delilah caught sight of the card attached. 'Temptation', it read. But of course.

So many people were packed into the rest of the gallery that they had to proceed in single file but never once did he let go, despite having to twist his shoulder at an impossible angle just to keep a hold of her hand. Pressed up close behind him, Delilah inhaled his musky scent and felt her loins liquefy. A fabulous mixture of laundered shirt, warm flesh and a spicy trace of something scented; she could have buried her face in his back forever. It was probably fortuitous then that Matt stopped in front of a small group who had carved out their own spot to one side and were engaged in animated conversation.

'Jane, Tom, Doug, I want you to meet Delilah.' His tongue rolled over her name, highlighting its exoticism in contrast to the good old-fashioned efforts. Monosyllables were so much more user-friendly, and far easier to hide behind.

Jane, a woman of a certain age and dress sense, was first to react. 'What a lovely name! Is your father a radical vicar or something?' Funnily enough, Delilah had heard that one before, but politeness compelled her to smile and trot out her standard response. 'No, but it could have been worse. Jezebel was the other hot favourite.'

'And, of course, entirely inappropriate.' Matt's arm was warm against her shoulder, his words light whilst his hand conveyed a more contradictory message. Jane let out a tinkly little laugh.

'So, how do you two know each other?' she enquired

pleasantly, if not originally. 'Matt been up to his old tricks again?'

Delilah had often wondered what people meant when they talked about someone's face darkening. Observing a shadow flit momentarily across Matt's features, she suddenly knew exactly what they were talking about. An abrupt change of subject was obviously called for and the rather dapper Tom thankfully filled the breach.

'I must say you've got a good turnout. This new find of yours is definitely flavour of the month. Where did you stumble across him?' Behind the bespoke suit and magenta silk hankie in the top pocket Delilah could discern a pair of shrewd but kind eyes. The sort of eyes that strip you down to your fundamentals without making a snap judgement of any kind. She warmed to him, grateful for his intervention in what had been an unaccountably sticky moment. Matt, too, seized happily upon the diversionary tactic.

'Ivan? Destined for the big time, no doubt about it. We came across him at art school, snapped him up on the spot. Of course, it was Lizzie who spotted him first. I can only claim credit for persuading him to accept our deal rather than that of one of the bigger boys . . .' He was looking straight at the woman who had joined them, slipping up so quietly that only Matt noticed her presence at first.

'Lizzie, my love, how *are* you . . .?' Nice Tom engulfed her in a fond embrace and Jane extended a cool little smile. Delilah noticed Doug slip a proprietorial arm around her and wondered how she fitted into the relationship picture that was forming in front of her.

'Lizzie, this is Delilah. Delilah, Lizzie – my active partner in the gallery. Her husband Doug here is the silent one.'

'As you can probably tell,' said Lizzie with an affectionate glance in Doug's direction. 'Delilah, how lovely to meet you. Matt has been talking about you a lot.'

A remark which clearly hit home, although in a different way to Jane's earlier effort. Delilah wouldn't swear to it, but

Matt's cheeks did seem to have acquired a ruddier aspect. He recovered himself enough to grin ruefully and exclaim, 'Oh, thanks, thanks very much. What are friends for but to drop you in it!'

Delilah was beginning to relax and enjoy herself more and more. His discomfiture was endearing, the fact that he had been talking about her heartening. And his friends, although somewhat older than either of them, seemed perfectly nice. With the possible exception of Jane – Delilah had her marked out as a woman to watch.

'So, Delilah, what do you do?' Lizzie looked her straight in the eye as she spoke and Delilah got the distinct impression that she was being subtly but soundly scrutinized. Smiling back at her despite the sudden tightening around her jaw, she responded, 'I run a shop called Decadence.'

'Really? Sounds absolutely fascinating. And what do you sell?' Lizzie's eyebrows had shot up in amusement but she appeared to be genuinely enthralled.

'Lingerie, oils, candles and so on. We've not been open too long. It's meant to be sensuous and fun rather than outright sexy. Kind of hedonistic but with humour, if you know what I mean.' Delilah hadn't meant to sound quite so defiant but Jane's sarcastic smirk was beginning to get on her nerves. Approbation came, however, from a quite unexpected source.

'Grand idea! You've obviously got a good eye for a niche market. How are sales?'

The broadness of Doug's northern accent startled her almost as much as his actually speaking. His quiet demeanour and nondescript appearance hadn't signalled anything much but now that he was animated, Delilah could feel the force of his personality. Probably not a man to be trifled with, at least not when it came to business. He obviously saved his pussycat side for his domestic arrangements. And now that he had spoken, his relationship with

Lizzie began to make more sense. Delilah had been wondering what such an elegant and self-possessed woman was doing with a man who appeared to have no conversation. It would seem that he preferred to ration his words as the occasion and his interest demanded.

'Not too brilliant,' she reluctantly admitted in answer to his question, 'but they're bound to get better. In fact, I've just had a bit of good news on the publicity front, so fingers crossed . . .'

'You won't be needing that, not once your word of mouth builds up.' Doug smiled at her kindly and Lizzie butted in with an explanatory, 'Doug's first company was a ladies' underwear outfit. What was it called, darling?'

'Fantasy Fashions. Very popular with the lower end of the market. Not the sort of thing you're selling – that's what they all want now. Bit of quality, class. If I was still in it, that's the way I'd go myself.' There was a definite hint of nostalgia in his voice. Clearly, Fantasy Fashions had meant a lot to him, despite its dubious name. To her amusement, Delilah could detect a pained quality to Lizzie's indulgent smile. She would bet that when Doug had moved on to bigger and better things, it had not been without a gentle guiding hand made of socially motivated steel. Not that Lizzie was a snob – on limited acquaintance she appeared genuine enough – but she was obviously a woman who preferred refinement to a bit of rough and had worked hard to polish her diamond of a spouse.

'Will you excuse me a moment? I see that our artist is stuck with that God-awful little man from Art International . . .' A knowing murmur went around the group and Lizzie was off to the rescue. Delilah followed her with her eyes, intrigued to see what the fuss was about. Disappointingly, it wasn't to the darkly interesting character in the corner that Lizzie headed but towards a short, well muscled guy clad in his take on a suit. Being of a creative persuasion, he had eschewed a shirt and tie in favour of an

orange T-shirt so tight fitting that it was practically transparent, but other than that his appearance was almost
mundane. Close-cropped hair, an angelically sweet face and
a liking for eccentric tailoring. It was probably safe to
assume he was not a man who spent a lot of time painting
female nudes.

As if party to her thoughts, Tom turned to Delilah and
asked, 'Have you managed to see any of the work yet?'

She smiled at him in guilty amusement. 'No, I haven't.
It's rather hard to get a proper look with all these people
around.'

'Oh, I know. I always think private view is a bit of a
misnomer. It really ought to be called a public scrum or
something.' Tom twinkled conspiratorially at her while
beside him Jane was busy scanning the room, her eyes
flicking as she assessed and discarded each person according to social worth or potential. Delilah felt like giving her a
good, hard kick in her stringy shins.

'Well, these things are really just one big PR exercise. The
buying and selling comes later when things have calmed
down and the good clients come in to take a proper look.'
Matt spoke equably enough but he was clearly anxious to
move on and work the room. She couldn't blame him for
that – it was his job, after all. 'Can I get anyone another
drink . . . Jane, Delilah . . . ?' A classic manoeuvre which they
all recognized.

'Not for me, thanks. In fact, isn't that Tristan Tyler over
there? Must go and say hello . . .'

'Ooh, yes. I'll come too . . .' cooed Jane in response to
Tom's graceful get-out and they were off, squeezing through
the throng until they reached the side of a tallish man in an
improbably white suit. Matt was already dragging Delilah
by the hand in the other direction, and for a moment she
felt a slight pang of guilt at leaving Doug standing there on
his own. The next time she turned her head, however, it
was to see that he had wandered off to join his Lizzie and

her coterie of art critics and clients. Clearly he was happy to let his wife shine in her own element. A rare enough occurrence, particularly so from a man of his generation. Delilah liked him all the more for it.

'Fraid this is as good as it gets.' Matt was apologetically holding out another glass of tepid white, which she took from him with an understanding grimace. 'Got caseloads of it free from Lizzie's renegade brother – his latest little scheme,' he offered by way of explanation, before placing a hand on the small of her back and guiding her across to yet another chattering knot of people. The pressure of his hand on her coccyx sent a power surge through parts which had yet to be breached. By the time they got there, Delilah was about ready to explode. Never mind the free booze, they could have powered the entire show on the electricity crackling between them.

More hellos were said and opinions solicited. Matt listened intently to each and every person, giving weight to what they had to say and simultaneously keeping the party mood going. You had to hand it to him, he was very good at his job. Whatever that was. Delilah was still trying to make sense of the business arrangement. Her guess was that Lizzie had the contacts and Matt the charisma, whilst Doug kept an eye on the books and bank balance. An interesting triumvirate, and Delilah intended to quiz him about it when they had a moment to themselves.

Whenever that was, because it certainly wasn't going to be tonight. As they flitted from group to group and person to person, the names and faces began to blur into one amorphous mass of nodding heads and a burble of art speak. Never before had Delilah heard the word 'concept' bandied about with such fervour and intensity and, as far as she could tell, with such differing opinions. Apart from his fruity effort, Ivan's work was variously attributed to a rebellion against the march of monochrome, a comment on society's more primal urges, and his own childlike dance with life. And those were some of the less florid efforts. From the limited glimpses that she had snatched, Delilah judged his work to be perfectly inoffensive in a colourful, splashy, basic sort of way. Not quite Picasso but not *Playschool* either.

Even though the crowd had thinned considerably, there were still a number of late arrivals. Just when she thought there couldn't possibly be any more people to meet, she heard Matt cry out, 'Dan, mate, glad you could make it!'

Might as well go for the brazen approach, even though inside Matt experienced an unfamiliar flicker of uncertainty. All was fair when it came to love and more, but he and Dan went back a long way. And he could read the expression on Dan's face where others might have seen nothing untoward. Danno was good but Matt knew him better. To back down was suicide, so might as well push ahead and savour his victory.

Not party to the significance of this silent exchange, Delilah turned round to take a good look at the new arrival and found herself being assessed in equal measure. Evidently not shy, Matt's friend was eyeing her up even as he extended a hand in response to Matt's introductions. Had she but known that Dan was more stunned than anything else, she might have taken a less defensive stance. As it was, her instant reaction was to bridle at his unflinching appraisal.

'Delilah, my best mate, Dan. Dan and I were at school together, so if you want any dirt there's your man.' Dan couldn't have put it better himself.

'Hi, Dan. Nice to meet you.' She withdrew her fingers after the barest of contact.

Dan smiled weakly in return and then dropped his eyes, unable to look at Matt for fear that he might hit him hard in the solar plexus. The bastard had done it. Sneaked in there, while his back was turned, snatched her from under his nose. He must have realized, there was no way he'd missed that thing with the newspaper. But he couldn't resist it, couldn't stop himself from proving that when it came to women, Matt won every time. He should have known. After all, it wasn't the first time. Torn between banging his head against the nearest wall or using Matt's as a battering ram instead, he took several deep breaths and finally felt sufficiently in control to speak.

'Looks like it's gone well . . .' He couldn't help loading his words as he lifted his head and stared straight into Matt's baby blues. Now he knew how Banquo felt. There was barely a flicker in those pools of innocence. Always one of Mattie's greatest assets. Dan, however, knew him of old. Right behind the shine of friendship lay the unmistakable glitter of triumph. Yes, Danny boy, I've done it all over again. And what are you going to do about it? Dan knew it was futile to put up any sort of fight, and in any case, he wouldn't give him the satisfaction. His guts felt hollow and his mouth was dry. He took a long gulp of the rancid wine. Its very acidity felt entirely appropriate. This time Matt had gone too far.

Delilah was saying something to him and the only way he could manage to answer halfway intelligently was to stare somewhere over her left shoulder. He was sure that if he looked at her, something would definitely crumble inside. In the flesh, she was so much more appealing than in the photograph, intensely vibrant and alive. And God knows the photo had had a strong enough effect.

'I'm sorry, what did you say?'

Delilah couldn't work out why this guy was so unfriendly. If there was one thing she absolutely hated, it was someone who wouldn't look her in the eye. He was either shifty or a social climber in the mould of Jane, and both were equally abhorrent.

'I asked you what you do for a living.' Hardly plumbing the shallows of small talk, but if he was going to behave like this she couldn't really be bothered with anything more imaginative.

'I, um, the Internet. You know – e-commerce.' He cleared his throat nervously and continued to look about him as if fascinated by the art on display.

She might have known. A geek. No social skills to speak of and probably slept with his mouse under his pillow. Sweeping stereotypes came easily when faced with someone who clearly had no interest in human interaction. No doubt he preferred interfacing on the Internet to contact of the more personal kind.

'Yeah, how's it going, mate?'

Matt was all concern but Dan didn't fall for it. One look at his face should tell Matt all he needed to know. The fine lines, the bloodshot eyes and the dark circles complementing his greyish complexion all pointed towards too many hours spent out of the sunlight and in e-commerce hell. Although if anyone had asked Dan, he would have had to confess to actually enjoying the ride, stomach-lurching moments and all. It beat a roller coaster for thrills any day. It had been a major sacrifice to tear himself away and make it over here in time. Now this. Greeted by a fait accompli, the modern equivalent of a thrown-down glove. Well, from what he could remember, duellists were always given the right to choose their own weapons. Matt might have the obvious ones to hand, but staying power was Dan's strong point. He had learned to be a patient man, not to mention a persistent one. And the war wasn't won yet, not by a long chalk. He could tell that much by the way Matt was still dancing attendance, darting those appraising looks at Delilah whenever he thought she was looking elsewhere. A sure sign that they had not yet dived under the duvet together, although for how much longer that would be the status quo, Dan could only painfully surmise.

Thank goodness for the well toned arm and flurry of blonde bob that interrupted his uncomfortable thoughts.

'Matt, darling, must be off. Big kiss.' The arm reached up to pull him closer for a kiss that was more than social in its intent. Looking on, Delilah noted that not an ounce of her lipgloss had shifted in the encounter. Bitch. As if reading her thoughts, the blonde flicked a dismissive glance at Delilah before lingering rather longer on Dan, standing alongside. Clearly she liked what she saw. A consummate man's woman, if ever there was one. Delilah's antipathy was instant.

Matt, meanwhile, was suppressing a groan. This was all he needed. First the cuckold and now the cock-tease. The evening was growing more complicated by the minute. Plastering on a passably pleased expression, he dropped a dutiful peck on her cheek, successfully avoiding the most rapacious red lips in town while making a mental note to phone her as soon as he possibly could. There was one more place left on the trip and she might be the perfect person to fill it, unbeknown to Delilah, of course.

'Serena, sweetheart, it's been lovely to see you. Give me a call when you've settled into your new offices.' He was handling it well, holding himself at a respectable distance even while he came over all roguish. You could always tell from the placement of the pelvis what was really going on, and his was definitely tilted away. Small comfort to Delilah, as she observed that the kittenish Serena had no such scruples. There was nothing she hated more than a woman who actually batted her eyelashes.

'Darling, let me give you my new number . . .' Serena began a fruitless hunt in her dinky bag, a no doubt horrendously expensive item that could not have contained more than a lipstick, a credit card and the teeniest of mobiles. But no cards. Fluffy and fragile to the last, she looked helplessly at Matt and wailed, 'I don't believe I came out without my cards!'

'Not to worry. I'll just scribble it down on this,' suggested

Matt, pillaging the drinks table for a paper napkin. 'Um . . .
Dan, you don't happen to have a pen handy, do you?'

Reaching into his jacket pocket, Dan passed him his
favourite pen. His precious, thick-nibbed, postcard-writing
pen. As he did so, Delilah remembered Twizz's words.
Craning forward, she kept a close eye as Matt leaned over
the table to write on the napkin. His first attempt was not
too successful, the nib tearing the napkin as he attacked it
ineptly.

'Shit but these things are a bugger to write with . . .' he
muttered as he made a second stab at it, obviously more at
home with a biro than a fountain pen. At that very second, a
happy shriek emanated from Serena and she cooed, 'Found
them! I *completely* forgot I've got this little pocket for them
in my mobile case. Look, isn't it clever? Aren't I silly?'

Forbearing from agreeing with her out loud, Delilah
gritted her teeth as Matt handed back the pen and tucked
the card safely away. Thwarted again. Dammit. As Serena
finally flounced out of the door, Matt rolled his eyes and
offered, 'PR girl. And, amazingly enough, very good at her
job. Wouldn't trust her as far as I could throw her.'

The irony of the moment was not lost on Dan. Having
had quite enough of Matt-inflicted masochism for one night,
he put down his drink and offered his apologies. 'I should
be making tracks. I only wanted to drop in and see how
things were going.' Very well, by the look of things. On all
fronts.

'But you've only just got here!' Was it his imagination or
did Matt seem genuinely put out? Tough. A taste of his own
medicine would do him the power of good. And it was
better to leave before he did something they all would
regret. What, after all, could he say to Delilah? I saw you
first? She'd only wonder from which playground he'd
emerged.

'Sorry, but you know how it is . . . I'll give you a call
when things are a little less hectic.' And when I don't feel

quite so much like giving you a good hammering to match my heartbeats. Masking his truer feelings beneath a swift clap to Matt's shoulder, Dan forced himself to look straight at Delilah.

'Delilah, it was lovely to meet you.' No need for prevarication on that one, although the effort it cost him was considerable. But if that was all he would get to hold, then her gaze would have to do. Hard though it was to get his head around that one.

Delilah inclined her head in an oddly formal gesture and uttered a polite, 'Likewise.' She couldn't fathom him out. One minute he was acting like the light switches held more interest than her efforts at conversation, the next smiling at her in a way that would have softened up the toughest toffee bar. So much sexier when he loosened up, although apparently unaware of the fact. An enigma, probably even to himself.

Whether by accident or design, Matt came out with a parting shot. 'How about that game of squash? It's been a while since I showed you what winners are made of.'

'I wouldn't be too sure about that.' Dan's delivery was deadpan, his countenance unsmiling.

'I'll call you then. Set up a game.' Or duel, more like. Matt was driven by some demon to persist, even when it was clear to them both that it was game, set and match.

Dignified to the last, Dan departed, head up and step swinging, although to the very core of his soul he felt profoundly cheated. They both watched him as he went, Matt's expression unreadable, Delilah's ditto but for very different reasons. She wasn't given much time to ponder, however, as Matt's arm snaked around her waist and drew her close to him.

'Enjoying yourself?' he asked the top of her head.

'I've had a brilliant time,' she lied, tilting her head up to look at him. 'So many interesting people.' With so little to say. If vacuity were an art form, this lot would have hoovered up first prize.

She thought she'd ironed out any edge in her voice but Matt obviously detected a bum note. 'The really interesting ones are the collectors. The majority of the people here tonight turn up to all of these things. Freeloaders most of them but they have their uses. There are, of course, exceptions. Tom, for instance.'

Fearing that she'd been a touch churlish, Delilah was quick to agree. 'I liked him. And Doug – intriguing bloke. Not what you'd expect.'

'How do you mean?' Only the well schooled would have clocked the sudden hint of wariness.

'Oh, you know. He's very quiet and unassuming but I bet he's a tiger when it comes to the boardroom.'

Matt's grin was positively feral as he flashed his riposte. 'If not the bedroom, although you never heard that from me.'

Taken aback by the vehemence in his voice, Delilah stuttered, 'Oh, right . . . well, whatever,' and then fell silent. Not only could she think of nothing else to say, she felt as if Doug's betrayal would be compounded by any further discussion. She had instinctively liked the man, warmed to his unassuming manner. Matt's enjoyment at this unwelcome titbit was unexpected and seemed entirely out of character. Perhaps sensing that he had overstepped the mark, Matt wrapped his arms tighter around her and whispered, 'Ready to leave?'

Delilah's insides swirled so vertiginously that she swayed perceptibly. Wedging herself against him, she muttered into the depths of his chest, 'But don't you have to clear up?'

Matt looked at her in some amusement. 'The cleaners will do it in the morning.'

'What about Lizzie? And Doug?' she muttered hastily, an inexplicable sense of panic beginning to rise.

'What about them? The party's pretty much done.'

It was true. Even Ivan the artist was making tracks and only the diehards loitered, overloud voices betraying the amount of booze they had consumed. All out of ideas, Delilah thought fast. He was evidently no slouch when it came to detecting a delaying tactic. This called for a short, swift inner tussle over her dating game plan. As it turned out, it was not too much of a struggle to toss the rule book aside and any cautionary thoughts along with it. It had been far too long and he was far too horny to act on anything other than her basest instincts. Backing momentarily away from those heat-building hands, Delilah smiled gamely and announced, 'I'll just get my coat.' The look on his face said it all. It was amazing, really, how much inane grinning went on between two people who were falling in lust.

Delilah didn't remember much of the journey to his place. They had headed there by tacit consent, and on the way one thought kept running round her head like a mantra: What am I doing? Oh God, what on earth am I doing? Such was her preoccupation that she didn't at first react when he flung open the front door to his flat and ushered her straight into what appeared to be his living room and kitchen combined. Compact would be the kindest way of describing the apartment, although the location was to die for. Right on the fashionable fringes of Soho, with every desirable coffee shop and boutique bang on his doorstep. Must have been hell to find parking, although Matt had managed it with ease, squeezing his precious car into a space that was tailor-made if a bit of a tight fit. It would have made a Milanese proud.

Despite being just one storey up from the street, very little noise filtered through the large windows at the far end of the room. Perhaps the piles of clothes everywhere acted as some sort of buffer – there certainly weren't any curtains to speak of. Instead, a pair of black paper blinds hung halfway down, and through the bottom halves of the windows Delilah could see straight into the building

opposite. Interesting how a well lit window always draws
the eye; she couldn't help but stare at the bloke prancing
around in a tiny thong and very little else. At an educated
guess, he was warming up his moves for the night ahead,
and doing so entirely oblivious to the possibility of being
seen. Either that or he was possessed of the most extraordi-
narily exhibitionistic tendencies. This was Soho after all.

Busy clearing space on the futon/sofa, Matt missed her
absorption in his neighbour's antics. It was only when he
looked up and commanded, 'Come and sit down,' that
he noticed he did not have her complete attention. 'See
you've met Sparkly, then.'

'Sorry?' She swung her head round, catching sight as she
did so of some of the less savoury elements of the room.
Matt was obviously not one for washing up.

'The bloke opposite. We call him that on account of his
dress sense. Now come and sit here – I'll get you a drink.
Vodka OK? Sorry about the mess, by the way, but the
cleaning lady's been off with the flu or something. Here you
go. Cheers.'

Matt snuggled in next to her on the crowded sofa and
she wordlessly accepted a glass of the Stolly he'd retrieved
from the iced-up freezer compartment. She took a couple of
gulps as she groped around for something to say. Thankfully, Matt seemed to be more interested in action than
words. Deciding that she had had quite enough refreshment,
he removed the glass from her grasp and kissed her very
thoroughly indeed. His mouth was cool from the vodka, his
tongue all too clearly spelling out his intentions. They were
heading scarily close to that invisible line and Delilah began
to feel very nervous indeed. Suddenly, he stopped, lifted
his head and murmured, 'Tell me if I'm going too fast. It's
just that I find you totally irresistible.'

Her sentiments exactly. Succumbing again to kisses that
grew hungrier by the minute, Delilah didn't raise so much
as a whimper of protest when his hands slipped under her

clingy little top and began to ease it over her head. Whoever invented Lycra, it was clearly not Casanova. After much wriggling and squirming, she emerged tousled and flushed and feeling rather exposed. Always a hard one, having less clothes on than your partner. Especially when you've decided to do without a bra on the grounds that it would spoil the line. Naturally enough, Matt was thrilled by the ease of access and gave his new-found friends a comprehensive kneading until Delilah decided that it was time to even up the score. If there was one thing she hated, it was someone twiddling her nipples – a tough thing to convey to someone who's never met your chest before. Re-education was obviously to be the order of things – a not unfamiliar state of affairs.

The only thing to do was to distract his attention with something even bigger and better than her boobs. Her whole body, for instance. But first a little equality was called for. She reached across and, in one impressively swift move, unbuttoned Matt's trousers. He had already hauled his shirt over his head, revealing a very respectable musculature and a nice, sparse sprinkling of hair. Thank God – there was nothing that turned her off more than a chest that looked as if it had been carpeted in shag-pile. Nothing, that is, except a back that fitted the same description. Kneeling up so that she could slither more easily out of the rest of her clothes, Delilah took the opportunity to brush against the smooth expanse in front of her, fixing her lips on his as she did so. The effect was electrifying. With barely a flick of elastic Matt had removed the scrap of lace that constituted the last, flimsy barrier and was busily exploring the elasticity of her buttocks. She had to hand it to him, he'd have made a terrific baker.

It wasn't quite so easy to free Matt from the confines of his chinos. Removing a man's clothing in a suitably seductive manner is difficult enough, but she was severely hampered by his efforts to pull her on top of him as his hands roamed across every available crevice. A change of position was definitely called for.

'Matt . . .'

'Mmmmmm.'

'How about we go into the bedroom?'

'Hmmmmmmmm.'

Realizing that it was going to be well nigh impossible to drag his nose out of her cleavage, except by brute force, Delilah put each hand on either side of his chest and levered herself upright. Matt looked as if his favourite toy had been snatched away. Ignoring the trembling lower lip, Delilah tried again. 'Matt . . . the bedroom . . .'

Her words had a Pavlovian effect on him. Years of rewarding reinforcement had obviously done wonders for this particular word association. Bedroom. Bonking. Yessss. With an impressive display of speed in spite of their tangled limbs, Matt somehow heaved them both up and into the next room. Head dangling over his shoulder, Delilah took stock. If the living room had been cosy, this was positively bijou. A large bed practically filled the space, and what was left of it was adorned with yet more heaps of discarded clothing, the odd magazine and what looked suspiciously like an empty champagne bottle under the bed. The deep red walls, iron bedstead and gilt-framed picture of a nubile nude above the bed meant it was sexy in an obvious way, if a touch gothic for Delilah's taste. Surprising – she had been expecting acres of space adorned with the odd mini-malistic touch.

Still, the duvet was soft and the mattress springy beneath her back. She had landed on it rather quickly, levered there by Matt's insistent grasp and kept there by the weight of his body. And what a body it was. Her surroundings faded into insignificance as her hands roamed across his muscled back, reaching down and around the base of his spine and beyond. As bottoms went Matt's was practically perfect, combining as it did the right percentages of tautness and pertness. And not an ounce of fluff. Marvellous.

Her wandering fingers were just beginning to tantalize the top of his thighs when, without warning, he rolled over and pulled her on top of him. Obviously a man who was more visual than most. Delilah tried not to feel self-conscious as he openly admired the lushness of the flesh at his disposal, but she rather wished he had turned on the bedside lamp instead of the overhead light. So much more flattering. He was pulling her against him now, rubbing her hard up and down the length of his thigh. His breathing spoke volumes about the height of his desire, as did the impressive protuberance of his penis, alert for action and so purple it was almost bruised. She hadn't paid too much attention to it, either visually or manually. It didn't seem to need a great deal in the way of encouragement and it felt rather rude to stare. Matt, in the way that men are, was inordinately proud of his little pal. So proud that he clearly wanted her to take a closer look. Delilah knew what it meant when his hands started pressing down on her head, and she wasn't that sure she wanted to comply. An eyeful was one thing, a mouthful something else. Always a sticky subject – to blow or not to blow on a first encounter.

She knew what was coming next and sure enough it did. Matt wriggled up, his hands bore her further down and she was on nodding terms with his prize possession. There was nothing for it but to act as any self-respecting twenty-first century woman would. Ignoring the delights of what was on offer, Delilah took matters in hand and maintained her grip as she trailed a tactful line of kisses back up his torso until they were once again in ocular contact.

'Mmmmmatt . . .' she murmured into his overworked lips.

'Uurgh?' Oh, good. The hand distraction ploy was working.

'Do you have a condom?' A pause as her words

penetrated his befuddled brain. Then the implications sank
in and he was reaching across to the bedside table, his hand
scrabbling around under a pile of papers and tissues for the
entry requirement to the main event. A tearing sound, much
fiddling about and he was ready for action. Only Delilah
wasn't. Her suggestion had been more of a pre-emptive
kind than an out and out invitation to get it on and she felt
decidedly hard done by. Perhaps sensing this, Matt was
busily making up for matters, although judging by his hand
action, he was impatient to get started. This was not quite
what she had imagined. Consoling herself that it was the
first time, they were both nervous and things were bound
to get better, Delilah relaxed slightly and began to respond to
his efforts at arousal. Taking this as a green light, Matt
made his move and before she had time to think about it,
Delilah found herself impaled on top of him, her initial
shock replaced almost instantaneously by awe. It hadn't
looked that big before, although admittedly seeing it from
above and in close-up was not an accurate gauge.

Now that she had far bigger things to worry about than
the overhead light, Delilah adjusted well to the moment.
She wasn't given time to become complacent, however, as
Matt was obviously eager to get things rocking. With one
firm hand on each hip, she had no choice but to indulge in
a series of movements which would have done a belly
dancer proud. Clearly he liked to vary his strokes in one
way or another. Her thighs were soon beginning to scream
but there was no let-up. In any case, there was no way he
would have noticed her desperate expression, his eyes being
shut tight in grim concentration. She leaned further forward
over him and a few beads of sweat from her brow dripped
attractively on to his face. Result! He opened his eyes and
stared blankly at her before declaring, 'God, you are the
most fantastic shag!'

A romantic to the last. In the heat of the moment, she
didn't have too much time to think about that one. With a

few more thrusts and grinds, he was there. His legs stiffened, his head went back and a guttural groan signalled
that it was all over bar the post-coital chat. Delilah didn't
know whether to laugh or cry but she had enough savvy to
realize that neither was appropriate. Instead, she clambered
gracelessly off and flopped resignedly at his side. Great.
Her celibacy duck broken by that.

After a few moments of deep breathing and contem-
plating his inner sex god, Matt reached a lazy arm over,
drew her close and sleepily whispered, 'That was amazing!'
as his hands fumbled for his cigarette packet.

Would that she could say the same. Finding it hard not
to feel utterly choked, Delilah said nothing. Her silence must
have got through to him on some subliminal level because
after a short while, he rolled over so that he was half on
top of her, began to stroke her belly placatingly and had the
grace to admit, 'Got a bit carried away there. Sorry.'

Even with his eyes shut he managed to look unbearably
contrite. Delilah fought down an urge to clutch him to her
bosom and smooth his hair until everything was better. He
played that little boy number to perfection and even while
she realized it, it nevertheless struck a protective chord.
Damn him. Still, she felt that some sort of soothing response
was required. And he was stroking her stomach in the most
delicious manner.

'It's OK. Really it is,' she murmured and with that he
seemed content. So content that within half a minute he was
fast asleep, unlit fag in mouth and snoring gently into her
cleavage. Of course, there was no way that Delilah could
follow suit. She extracted the cigarette with finger and
thumb and lay back against the thin pillows to contemplate.
For hour upon hour she lay there, reluctant to shift his dead
weight and suffering from that curiously maternal malaise
that inflicts a surprising number of women after sex, good
or otherwise. Finally, a numb leg and total desperation
forced her to heave him off, a feat that required a consider-

able amount of brute force and persistence. And still he slumbered, oblivious to her presence and sleeping the sleep of the totally satisfied. Delilah curled on her side and, as the pins and needles subsided, managed to drop off into a far more fractious state of unconsciousness, where her dreams were invaded by great tidal waves that threatened to engulf her in Jungian messages straight from her soul. She was awoken from this restless state by the tentacles of a sea creature like no other, although as she swam back up towards lucidity she realized that this was not so much a marine encounter as one of a much earthier persuasion.

Rested from his earlier exertions, Matt decided that pre-dawn was as good a time as any to go for a second shot. Well pleased with the way their first erotic encounter had gone, he momentarily paused to admire Delilah in repose, her chest gently rising and falling as she breathed. Poor thing – he'd clearly exhausted her with his ministrations. Trouble was, he preferred them awake, if only to see that look of amazement on their faces. Not too much of a problem. Once he got started she'd be alert soon enough, aroused in the best possible way. 'OK, babe, time for action,' he muttered as he reached reluctantly for the condom packet, making a mental note to dispense with the horrible little hoods just as soon as she could be persuaded otherwise.

It was the rustle of the wrapper that cut through her dreams, dragging her almost to wakefulness, and she thought for a sleepy moment he might be about to clamber straight aboard. This time, however, he was taking things nice and slowly and his free hand was repeating the rhythm right where it counted. Half asleep and her limbs still heavy, Delilah was more than happy to lie there and let him do all the work. She could feel the heat of him all along her back, the arms reaching round her holding her steady as he sank deep into her from behind. Lovely. All she had to do was lie there and enjoy, and this time Matt made sure she did. He held her even tighter as she cried out in delight and then minutes later he was there himself, his own moans of pleasure more muted than before but still gratifyingly prolonged. Dreamlike encounter over, Delilah dozed off and sank straight back into the real thing. This time, however, the waters were still and she slept calmly in his arms.

Nine

'Well, you've certainly got a glow about you,' observed Margaret, sipping away at the tea she insisted on drinking despite the fact that they had decamped to the coffee house on the corner.

'Beard rash, more like,' growled Twizz into her extra tall, extra fatty latte, working away at the bottom of the glass with a long spoon to try and stir things up as much as she could.

'Charming.' It was true, though. She had the lot – the goofy grin, the sparkling eyes, the air of supreme self-satisfaction. Oh, and the exfoliated chin and sandpapered cheeks to complete the picture. A bit of fashionable growth was all very well, but it didn't half make a mess of your face.

'I take it the postcard man has presented himself?' Margaret chose her words delicately, but there was a definite hint of amusement lurking around the corners of her eyes. At this Twizz extracted her spoon with a final flourish, gave it a good lick and said disgustedly, 'She doesn't bloody know, does she!'

In response to Margaret's interrogatory eyebrows, Delilah shrugged and declared happily, 'It's true, I don't. I have absolutely no idea if it was Matt who sent the postcard and quite frankly I don't care.' Selective memory syndrome already at work, she had wiped their first fumbling encounter from her mind. The second attempt had more than made up for it, as had the croissant and cappuccino he had insisted on buying her before he dropped her off in the morning. There had been no hope of anything edible at his place, but this was something she intended to work on just as soon as the cleaning lady recovered and there was somewhere safe to store food. He might not be the kind of guy to whip up supper à deux, but Delilah was fond of her creature comforts. At the very least, she could bring round some decent coffee, orange juice with bits in, a few things to assuage the midnight munchies . . .

'Are you telling me you couldn't see a single thing that he'd written on? No lists, no letters, nothing?'

Post-coital planning rudely cut short by pugnacity, Delilah sighed out an answering, 'Nope,' and refused to recoil under Twizz's withering stare. Not for the first time she reflected that her assistant was a sad loss to the Australian branch of the secret service, if indeed they had one. Probably too up-front a country for such a subversive notion, if Twizz's outspokenness was anything to go by.

'What do you want me to do? Fingerprint the guy?' Reluctant to let practicality marr the romantic aftermath, Delilah was beginning to lose her patience.

'It's a thought.' At this they all had to laugh, including an unusually lacklustre Margaret. Even in her hormonally heightened state Delilah had noticed that she seemed rather pale and quiet. She was reluctant, however, to intrude on private property. Easy though it was to share confidences with Margaret, it was very much a one-way trade.

'Do you think the lights are back on yet?' Clearly regarding Delilah as a lost cause, Twizz had her nose up against the window in a futile bid to look right around the corner and back down their street.

'Dunno. The electricity people said it would be about an hour or so.' Anxious as she was to get back to her beloved shop, it was going to be hard to leave the light and warmth of the coffee shop and brave the dismal November weather. Mercifully, they had been unaffected by the power cut that had plunged the other end of the street into an entirely unromantic gloom. It had always been a mystery to Delilah why baby booms resulted from electrical failure. People were obviously total telly addicts or desperately lacking in imagination. At least vibrators ran on batteries.

'Shall we risk it?' Margaret was up and ready, coat on over the thick layers of cardigan and jumper. There seemed to be rather more padding than usual. Probably coming down with one of the millions of bugs flying around – that would explain the pallor and dip in energy level. Safe in the knowledge that her internal Ready Brek radiator pro vided total immunity, Delilah gave her an affectionate squeeze. Margaret appeared slightly stunned at this breach of British restraint but refrained from commenting.

'You all right, Margaret?' What the hell, thought Delilah, might as well break down another barrier while she was at it.

'Of course I am. Just got some silly sniffle or something.' As if to prove her point, Margaret dabbed at her nose with her hankie and Delilah had to concede it did look rather red.

'It's going round. Half my housemates are down with something. Bloody British weather,' remarked Twizz cheerfully, conveniently forgetting that the vast and shifting population of her shared abode represented more germ potential than a nippy November day ever would. 'My shout,' she added with true Antipodean generosity and tripped off to pay.

'Are you sure? Very sweet of you,' murmured Margaret, for once not up to insisting on paying. Sweet my ass, thought Delilah, all too wise to Twizz's tricks. With a fawning Flavio and at least one other pretty Italian boy to play with, it was worth the price of two coffees, a pot of tea and a plate of biscotti.

They parted from Margaret outside the shop. The lights were indeed back on and she was anxious to get home, leaving the two of them to wrestle with the shop door. The lock was being its usual impenetrable self although they had just about perfected the necessary manoeuvres. Stick the key in, then pull it out slightly, jiggle ever so gently, give the door a shove and bingo! The phone was ringing as they burst over the entrance and Delilah made a dash for it. When she heard who it was, she wished she hadn't bothered. One of her suppliers, frostily suggesting that payment was now well overdue. They realized, of course, that this had never happened before and that naturally it would never happen again. As for the post, they had had no problems at their end and could only suggest she pop another cheque in it forthwith. That very day, in fact.

By the time she came off the phone Delilah was steaming harder than Flavio's cappuccino machine. 'Bastards! They know perfectly well I paid on the nail when I had the stall. It's not as if they're the only candle makers in the universe.'

'Yeah, but they *are* the best ones.' Twizz had a point.

'I know, I know. It's just . . . it all gets a bit much, y'know? Three red bills this morning, another one yesterday, then the phone call . . .' Even Delilah's hair seemed to share her distress, its natural bounce as flat as her spirits. Or maybe that was the weather.

'Don't worry, love, it'll be all right. Honest.' Twizz's softer side was seldom seen but when it was she was almost marshmallowy in her concern. The effect on Delilah was bracing and instantaneous. Things had to look bad for Twizz to behave like that. She had to boost morale, and fast.

'Yep. You're right. It will. Of course it will. Now, let's get going with the window. Shift it around like you suggested. Entice them in even if we have to put the Diet Coke bloke in the window and dress him in a G-string.'

'It'd work for me.' Twizz's grin was part reaction and part relief. In the same 'sod it' frame of mind, they dived on the window display and began carefully but systematically to tear it apart. Scissors flashed, fingers draped and tweaked and a good two hours later they were done. It was way past closing time when, flushed, triumphant and in total disarray, they surveyed the results of their efforts. And what results they were. In pride of place lounged the mannequin who had previously lurked beside the lingerie rail. She had been twisted, painted and pulled until she did a creditable imitation of a supine starlet, limbs provocatively outstretched and her weight resting on one arm, while the other hand was raised to her newly scarlet lips. The lipstick had been a master stroke, bringing colour to an otherwise lifeless countenance and providing her with the perfect pout that clashed marvellously with the hot pink backdrop. A CockTail glass rested in her hand, its ingredients authentic down to the olive on the stick. This was clearly a mannequin on a mission to enjoy.

'Least we can do if she's got to freeze her tits off in the window,' declared Twizz, and Delilah had heartily agreed. The fact that they had also imbibed in a spirit of solidarity had pepped them up, adding a whole new spirit to their work. Rock bottom had never been such an inspirational place. To complement the cocktail mood, they had draped the mannequin in a black satin robe, her leopard print underwear just peeking through to hint at the animal within. Propped at an angle against a pile of fake fur cushions, realistic bunches of grapes and an empty bottle at her side, Ms Mannequin was definitely in the party mood. To help her along, a mirrorball twirled on its string above her head and fairy lights flashed in syncopation at her painted toenails. For sheer kitsch value, the window display was a masterpiece and a couple of happy bunnies headed for home and a hot bath.

Across town, Matt was celebrating the sale of an altogether more traditional work of art. Or as traditional as Ivan's evocations of *Playschool* primal would ever be. Lizzie was still dealing with the paperwork but it was a done deal and the buyer, a portly gentleman of Middle American extraction, looked very pleased with his purchases. No doubt they would be adorning the walls of his Wichita oil company offices just as soon as he could ship them back home. Art with a capital A, something to which every self-respecting man on the make aspired sooner or later.

As soon as the final signatures were in place, Matt shook him warmly by the hand and convincingly declared, 'A fine choice you've made there, sir, if I may say so.'

'You certainly may, young man. Pleasure doing business with you.' His hand caught in an enthusiastic handclasp, Matt kept up the shiny countenance until Mr Marinkowski had exited into the night, his precious pictures safely stashed away until they could be transported to their new home-stead. Carefully tucking the papers into the appropriate file, Lizzie smiled benevolently at him.

'Well done you. Time for a drink?'

Matt knew it was more of a command than a request. Mentally dropping any plans he might have made for later, he made the sensible career move and graciously acqui-esced. They both knew where the bucks were buried. In any case, this could be a good time to have a little chat, pave the way for some of Matt's more ambitious new ideas. For one thing, there was the New York trip and the possibility that this time he might get a chance to tag along and learn the ropes. His purchasing eye had sharpened immeasurably under Lizzie's expert tuition, but the art market in the Big Apple was a whole different ball game. One that required the dazzling dexterity of a Michael Jordan or the fancy footwork of a Ronaldo if he was to keep up to speed.

'That would be great. Where do you want to go?' He prayed it was somewhere local, although the choice was limited to a few uptight pubs or one desperate wine bar.

'How about the American Bar? We can call it a small

celebration,' Lizzie suggested, an airy arm indicating the red 'sold' stickers on the three paintings behind them.

Shit. The American Bar meant at least a bottle of champagne, more if some of Lizzie's chums were in attendance. It wiped out any chance of an evening on his own terms.

'Fabulous. Your car or mine?' An expressive pause followed this, Lizzie's sarcastic half-smile indicating exactly what was on her mind. OK, so technically speaking his car was of the 'company' variety. She didn't have to act as if that made it hers by right. Thankfully, she chose not to labour the point. This time.

'Don't be silly, darling. Let's just leap in a cab. Parking's hell round there in any case.' Especially if you had had the best part of a bottle of Krug and couldn't manage to back your car out of a space the length of a juggernaut.

There was nothing for it but to accede. Not if he wanted to be on that plane ride to opportunity. With a determined effort at boyish good cheer, Matt hailed the cab and clambered in beside his boss. For whatever was on paper, that was the reality of the situation. And didn't they all know it.

In yet another part of town, meanwhile, Dan at least was master of his own destiny. An awesome responsibility and one that had mushroomed along with his nascent empire. Today was D-Day, as in decision-making rather than dosh, although the latter would be more than welcome. Everything they'd done over the past few months, every hour spent working way into the wee small hours, would be worth it if they could now take off from their small-scale launch pad and into the full-blown world of the online big boys. And it was up to Dan to convince the cash handlers that they were worth the punt. A tough task, now that everyone knew the road to e-millions was littered with a thousand wrecked start-ups, but he stood a better chance than most. He'd spent the last eight months quietly buying up one of his rivals after another as they went to the wall. Now he practically had a monopoly, along with a customer service system that was second to none. Survival of the fittest, that's what it was, natural selection determining who made it and who went to the wall. Things may have cooled in the dot.com world since the Internet market went into meltdown, but the hunger for a commercially hot prospect was as strong as ever. Dan knew that he had cornered a niche market, one with enormous potential. Now what he needed was the money to make it really happen, those extra millions to take him on to the next level. It was time to swim with the sharks in a much larger pond and go for a merger.

He straightened his tie for the fourteenth time, the unfamiliar squeeze against his Adam's apple constricting his throat even more than the large lump inside it. So much rode on this meeting that it had got him out of his everyday jeans and sloppy top and into the one suit he had kept from the bad old days. It was definitely a case of when in Rome – and these particular Romans represented all that stood between him and expansion on a spectacular scale. Knowing just how the gladiators must have felt, he stepped out from his untidy corner cubicle into the scruffy main office area, a maze of machinery and cabling marking out a matrix of industry. The tap-tapping of innumerable keystrokes was muffled by a mix of music and the odd burst of laughter but today an unusual tension had reigned. Every one of his tight-knit team knew what was at stake and heads that were usually locked on to computer screens turned as he walked past.

A couple of sarcastic wolf whistles greeted his appearance and ponytailed Jem twirled round from his terminal, baseball cap as ever firmly in place. It served the dual purpose of lending him some dubious street cred while hiding a hairline that was receding faster than Dan's reserves of cash. A stereotypical technical wizard only in appearance, Jem's superior powers represented one of the strongest weapons in Dan's corporate armoury. He was as keen as the rest of them to see it work, to turn theirs into one of the dot.coms that actually made it. Now he had torn himself away from his beloved monitor to make plain his support. Giving his boss a huge thumbs-up even while one hand remained on his mouse, Jem called out a cheerleading, 'Go get 'em, Danno!'

'Yeah, Dan, get those bastards to sign . . .'

'Bring back the bucks, boss . . .'

Even the sparse action around the table football in the chill-out area stopped as they yelled out encouragement or simply grinned their good wishes. As well they might – with stock options a part of everyone's package, each of them stood to gain, some of them big time. Dan repeated the selling points to himself, over and over like a mnemonic. Excellent expansion plans, high visibility and search engine ranking. Click-throughs coming thick and fast. The all-important return customers swelling their ranks by the day. In theory, then, all the angles were covered. Why, then, did he still feel like Daniel entering the lion's den?

Not exactly sure how to go about girding his loins, Dan did so as best he could. Shoulders back, deep breaths, final mental inventory and he was out of the door, the gauntlet of back slaps and high fives sending him on his way. Just for once he was going to blow some precious cash and forgo the Tube. Arriving in a cab would give him a psychological advantage, convince his subconscious of the millions to come. That was the theory, at any rate. It felt like an age before one appeared, although in reality it was probably five minutes at most. Long enough to send the already wired Dan into orbit as he tapped out a tattoo with his fingers on his thigh and thought about the worst that could happen. Then it appeared, sailing over the horizon, the glorious sight of a black cab with its orange light aglow. Practically hurling himself under it, lest anyone else should be foolish enough to try to get there first, Dan hopped in and issued the necessary instructions. He was on his way.

Ten

Fran was flapping. The photographer had not yet shown up, her piece on 'Beautiful Bathrooms' was due in at five, and to cap it all her roots were badly in need of attention. Time management had never been her speciality, but this week it had totally gone to pot.

'Where the fuck is he? I told the little git to be here at twelve thirty on the dot and it's now . . . bloody hell, it's nearly two o'clock.'

'I expect he got held up at another job or something. Why don't we go over what you've already got down, see if there's anything we've missed out?' Handling Fran was rather like dealing with an eight-year-old with an E-number addiction, all hyped out of control and crackling with anxiety. Delilah consoled herself with the thought that it would all be worth it in the end. Column inches in a Sunday national paper were publicity gold dust and they badly needed a boost to their bullion rating. Just as she thought Fran was about to self-combust, an entirely unapologetic photographer shouldered his way in, an alarming assortment of equipment hanging off every available part of his upper body.

'And about time too! Where on earth have you been? I told you, twelve—'

'Sorry, love, got caught up. Shall we get started?' Laid-back was not the word for it – the man was positively impervious to the fizzing ball of fury standing in front of him. Anxious to avoid a confrontation, Delilah stepped in.

'You're here now and that's the main thing. Why don't you dump your things over there? Fancy a tea or coffee? We've had a few ideas about shots already but, of course, you're the expert . . .' This last with a warning look at Fran, who was ready to steamroller the guy into submission. Not a viable plan when a good picture could be worth a great deal more than the meagre 750 words they already had.

'Yeah, great. Tea please, love. Four sugars.' Delilah had an instant flashback to the days when the builders were a permanent presence, but smiled sweetly and asked, 'Twizz, would you mind?'

'Not at all,' came the response in a tone of voice that indicated quite the opposite. As Twizz flounced off to refill the kettle, Delilah got down to the serious business of artistic direction.

'We thought it might be rather nice to have a shot of us drinking our cocktails over here,' she began appeasingly, only to be instantly overridden by a power-crazed Fran with, 'No, no! Right there would be much better. There's not enough light over here and you won't get to see any of the shop in the background.'

The photographer looked glumly around the shop, his eyes flicking briefly over the suggested spots, before announcing, 'Thought I'd go for a shot through that front window. Pretty tasty display you've got there and I reckon the punters would like it.'

Fran's face dropped as the implications hit home. Robbed of a starring role, not even in shot. The very thought brought the blood rushing to her head in a way that clashed unfortunately with her hair. 'Through the window? Oh no, that really wouldn't—'

'I think it's a brilliant idea!' exclaimed Delilah hastily, observing the close-clamped set of the photographer's mouth and the intransigent glint in his narrowed eyes. A true product of the press pack, he obviously liked to get the job done quickly and with as little fuss as possible. Debate did not come into it. Besides, he was probably right. The window told the story far more neatly and graphically than a photo of them pretending to party ever would. It was arresting, unusual, and most of all it was fun. She said as much as Fran continued to pout her one-woman protest.

To her credit, she knew when she was beat. Flinging her hands up in a dismissive gesture, she declared to no one in particular, 'Go ahead. Do what you like. It's only my story after all.'

And it was only *her* shop, although on this occasion Delilah felt it wise to remain silent. The photographer had already nipped outside to frame up his shot, and on his return he gulped down his tea in between fiddling with lights and lenses while they all kept a respectful distance. An hour later they were done. He'd taken shots from all angles, from inside and outside, working with a speed and efficiency that would have done credit to a German production line. As he packed up his gear, Fran gingerly enquired about the finished prints and was briskly informed, 'They'll be done by tonight.' Wishing fervently that she could meet her own deadlines with such impressive ease, she thanked him as nicely as she could and promised to drop by the picture desk later. 'Beautiful Bathrooms' would just have to wait – Fran knew where her bread was buttered and it wasn't within the pages of some middle market decorating rag.

'I'll let you have a look at the final copy,' she graciously offered as she hastily flung herself together and prepared to depart. Once she had made her usual flurried exit, Delilah and Twizz breathed a collective sigh of relief. It had been hard work tiptoeing around the creatives, and even harder work lugging things around and trying to stay out of the way while serving the odd curious customer. Things were slowly picking up as the Christmas shopping season approached, and for a wet Thursday afternoon they had been gratifyingly busy. Sod's law – fill your shop up with a dizzying array of paraphernalia and people were bound to flock in, if only to trip over the cables and camera cases littering the floor.

It took a while to put everything back the way they wanted, and it was close on quarter to six before Delilah glanced at her watch and exclaimed, 'Shit! I was supposed to call Matt.'

Twizz bit back an urge to ask why. About the last thing Delilah should be doing was whatever wonder boy wanted. There was something about him that stank. And it wasn't some poncey aftershave. Delilah, however, was too caught up in her own thoughts to notice Twizz's uncharacteristic reticence.

Exactly a week had passed since that first night together. Uncool as it was even to think of marking the day in any special way, when they had spoken only that morning Delilah had been left with a vague feeling of frustration. It had been he who had called her, just as he had every single day since the main event. Nothing too clingy or cosy, it was usually short but ineffably sweet, at least to her ears. Heaven forbid that she should go all gooey on him but interestingly enough the reverse seemed to be happening. Every morning and evening, without fail, Matt had rung, sometimes just so he could hear her voice before he rushed off to some sale or other. The big art auction season was under way, and both he and Lizzie were run ragged trying to cover them all, make clever purchases and at the same time fulfil the needs of their high-maintenance clientele. The upshot was that Delilah and Matt hadn't seen each other for the entire week and she had been hoping against hope that tonight might be an exception, if only by virtue of its slight but meaningful significance.

'Sweetheart, I'm so sorry, but I have to go. Everyone's about to take their seats and I've a list of orders as long as my arm. It's a nightmare and I've got to get back to the gallery before five and then on to . . .'

She could barely hear him against the background noise of excited Eurobabble, the odd transatlantic twang breaking across the international twitterings of the haute art crowd.

'Don't worry about it. Look, why don't I try you there around fiveish?' It couldn't hurt, her calling him for a change. 'Hard to get' quickly lost the element of play, especially when it appeared he was very much hooked.

Hoping that she might still be in time to catch him, she dialled the gallery and got through to a polite answerphone message. There was always the mobile, although she was somewhat reluctant to disturb him mid-megabucks deal. Torn between acting like his mother and the desperate desire to see him in the flesh, Delilah wavered between the two evils, the receiver still held in her indecisive hand. It was no good asking Twizz – she was at that very moment hauling the rubbish outside and loudly wondering how on earth they had managed to fill three large bin bags in the space of just seven days.

'Life's too short . . .' she muttered to herself. Tapping out his mobile number, she waited for it to connect and her heart leaped as it began to ring. He hadn't switched it off, which must mean that he was at least able to take calls, although it was unlike him not to have phoned by now. It was refreshing, if a tad disconcerting, to come across a guy who had no problem wearing his heart so openly on his Paul Smith sleeve, and it was downright adorable to have one who considered the phone a natural form of communication rather than a power tool.

Delilah waited for him to answer, listening as it rang and rang. A thud of disappointment landed dully in her guts as the ringing tone gave way to his voicemail service and she jammed a finger down to disconnect.

'I've missed him!' she wailed to no one in particular and nearly jumped out of her skin when a voice behind her enquired, 'Missed who?'

'Matt! Oh my God, you bastard, you've got to stop sneaking up on me like that!' Her delighted smile belied her words and he gave her a smacking great kiss before responding with a mock-reproving, 'Oh, that's nice. See what I get for trying to give you a nice surprise.'

'Oh, but you did. You really did. Where the hell did you appear from? I've just been trying to phone you and . . .' Her confusion was compounded when he held up the phone he was clutching in one hand, a flashing orange light indicating her unanswered call. 'I had it on vibrate. Very useful function. You might care to try it sometime.'

Delilah could feel herself blushing even as she giggled out an unbearably coy, 'Is that an offer?'

Mercifully perhaps, Twizzle chose that moment to make a noisy reappearance, much theatrical huffing and puffing indicating the extent of her manual labour. 'It's colder than a corpse's crotch out there,' she remarked en route to grabbing a tissue with which to wipe her semi-frostbitten nose.

'Twizz, you remember Matt?'

Only too well. And her gut liked him even less second time around. Ever the trouper, Twizz delved around for something civil to say.

'We met out by the bins. Nice to see you again,' she managed through several layers of tissue, grateful that she had something in hand to mask her more honest reaction.

It may have been the muffled effect, but to Delilah's ears Twizz's welcome sounded rather more muted than her words. Odd, that. Although, to be honest, so was Twizz at times.

'Good to see you, too. Nice . . . hat you're wearing.' Delilah was so used to Twizz's multicoloured effort that she had ceased to notice its luminescent qualities, even when she insisted on wearing it inside as well as out. Once the temperature dropped below balmy, Twizz wrapped up like a wombat stranded in the Arctic, and steadfastly refused to shed a layer until spring was well into its stride.

'Ta. Anyway, got to get going. New improv group thing tonight. Have a good time. See you in the morning.' Efficiently enshrouding herself in more layers as she spoke, Twizz had more insulation on her than a well lagged loft by the time she waddled out of the door with a nod and a wave from a bright orange glove. You could say one thing for Twizz, she gave great exit.

'Wow.'

'Indeed. Shall we go?'

Outside, they paused a moment in front of the window display, the street lamp providing enough light for them to appreciate its finer points. Matt chuckled and shook his head.

'Incorrigible, that's what you are.'

'Good, though, isn't it?' Squeezed tight by his side, Delilah surveyed her kingdom with satisfaction. Things felt as if they were coming together, despite the final demands and the testy letters from the bank. Just a few more weeks and she felt sure there would be something to show for her efforts. They walked on towards his car in that awkward way people do when their arms are around each other and they haven't yet fallen into a similar rhythm. Delilah usually disliked the three-legged effect but this felt like fun rather than effort. Which brought her back to her idea for the evening's entertainment, or at least the opening act.

'I've got a surprise for you, too,' she announced as he reluctantly let go of her to liberate his car keys from the depths of his jeans pocket. She had to drag her eyes up from the sight of his hand scrabbling round near his crotch. Talk about unleashing a tiger – her libido was sorely in need of taming. And she thought she knew just the man for the job.

'Oh, yeah?' Keys retrieved, he swung them around his index finger teasingly.

'Yeah. You drive and I'll do the directions.'

'God, I love assertive women!' The flash of admiration was genuine, as was the kiss he planted smack bang on her forehead.

They slid into their seats and were off, Delilah issuing rapid-fire instructions to keep up with his road speed. At last they screeched to a halt in front of a building notable for its industrial ugliness and she announced unnecessarily, 'OK, we're here.'

'The Naked Space?'

'Yes, do you know it?' Of course he would, being in the trade. She had been hoping to impress him with her avant-garde art credentials but it appeared he was way ahead of her.

'Only by reputation.' Well, that was something at any rate. They made their way up some spiral stairs until they entered a startlingly light room, the bleached wooden floor and stark white walls making the space seem endless, although in reality it was probably only about forty feet long and half as wide. A couple of pillars punctuated the swathe of space and on them were hung box-framed pieces, the intense colours of their contents drawing the eye immediately as stunning contrast to all that white. Dotted around the walls were similar works, each box containing a miniature world or concept executed in a multiplicity of ways. Pieces of jewellery, household debris, brightly dyed feathers and even the odd dismembered doll's head were juxtaposed with painstakingly painted backgrounds, mosaic-like in their complexity. The accompanying cards revelled in titles such as 'Voodoo Kitsch-en' and 'Household Whores', the latter displaying a fine specimen of a half-smoked, belipsticked fag as its centrepiece.

As they paused on the threshold, taking in the scene,

Delilah explained, 'I read about this in *Time Out*. They referred to it as a "triumph of storytelling within art".'

'They would,' came Matt's response as they headed towards the nearest crop of exhibits. Tacky but truthful, they had their own kind of raw beauty. Not the stuff of drawing room dreams, but Delilah could see where they were coming from. Matt appeared less enamoured. While she dotted magpie-like all over the place as a glimpse of a glittery sweet wrapper or a fluorescent colour caught her eye, he wandered methodically from piece to piece, his expression revealing nothing of his reaction to the work.

'Hey, Matt, look at this one. Isn't it fabulous?' Anxious to show him her personal favourite, Delilah dragged him over to stand in front of a small masterpiece entitled 'Us'. Standing alone in its eloquent simplicity, the clear glass mounting contained two halves of a conch shell made from plaster. Each half was painted in watery colours so delicate that they barely whispered of the sea they were intended to evoke. Tiny pieces of coral, bleached driftwood and pearls adorned the surface, fitting snugly into the curves at the base of each shell. As she stood gazing at them, a gallery assistant floated over and volunteered, 'Gorgeous, aren't they? They're magnetized so that they fit together, but it's a bit hard to display them like that.'

'It's really lovely,' Delilah agreed as, with a nod of acknowledgement, the assistant drifted off again. He was almost as ephemeral as the art, pale face and hair matched by a manner that was decidedly other-worldly, although delightfully unpushy. She turned again to Matt, only to see that he was leaning up against a far wall, his thoughts evidently elsewhere. Not exactly champing at the bit with enthusiasm, but then again, he had been immersed in art all day long. Annoyed with herself for not having thought of that one, Delilah went over to him and said ruefully, 'Bit of a busman's holiday for you, isn't it?'

'Sorry, honey. It's been one hell of a day, that's all. Fancy grabbing a bite to eat?'

They left the gallery, Delilah casting one last look back at the conch shells, now partially obscured by a girl with shaven hair standing in front of them, head on one side and her hand clutching that of a similarly tonsured boyfriend beside her. Matt took her to a place he knew nearby. Never had she come across a man with such an encyclopedic knowledge of great little spots in which to eat. Refreshing but vaguely disconcerting. How had he found them all in the first place? She decided not to dwell too hard on that, concentrating instead on the food and the company. One far outshone the other and her seafood linguine lay largely untouched as they talked and giggled their way through a bottle of wine and a whole evening's worth of nonsense. It was over a shared sticky toffee pudding that Matt suddenly presented her with a slim, gift-wrapped item and said, 'For you. Happy one week anniversary.'

'Is it? Oh my God, that's so sweet of you.' Surprise and pleasure lit up her face all too genuinely. Any sentimental notions having been dismissed much earlier in the evening, she could hardly believe that he had really remembered. This had to be a first – a man who not only thought of such things but also knew where to take her to celebrate them.

'Go on, then, open it.'

Giving the package a good feel, Delilah grinned knowingly at him and said, 'I think I know what this is.' He looked a shade disconcerted but then watched intently as she ripped off the paper, opened the box inside and withdrew a beautiful silver bracelet.

'It . . . it's stunning.' Getting over her initial reaction with admirable dexterity, she held out her arm and draped it across her wrist. It was indeed stunning, being a simple sliver of an almost liquid quality. But it certainly wasn't the beaded choker she had been expecting. As he helped her fasten it, she bowed her head and pretended to be immersed in examining its beauty up close. In actual fact, her mind was racing over the possibilities. So he had bought the choker for somebody else – that didn't preclude a perfectly innocent explanation.

'Suits you. I knew it would.'

She raised her head, smiled so hard that it hurt and responded, 'I love it. Thank you.'

Suitably gratified, Matt insisted on taking care of the bill despite her long and loud protests and led her back to the car, a bottle and a half of wine having rendered the three-legged lurch into something entirely natural. The euphoria lasted as far as the bedroom, where the speed of Matt's demands took her totally by surprise. Whatever had turned him on so hard, there was an urgency behind it that would brook no delay. Full-on, ear-splitting sex without the social niceties. Delilah came to with her skirt round her waist, her knickers round one ankle and her hair all over the place. From the depths of the mattress to her left she could hear what sounded like 'Mmmmtastic . . .' and then Matt pushed himself up on one arm, wiped the sweat from his brow and laughed out loud.

'Christ, you are amaaaaazing,' he announced appreciatively as he eased himself off her, rolled over and lazily kicked off the shoes he hadn't yet removed. Emulating his ankle flick, Delilah managed to land her knickers somewhere in the morass of matter that covered his bedroom floor. As she tugged her skirt into a more seemly position, she fervently hoped that she'd be able to find them again. This time he hadn't so much as stopped to switch on the lights and the overall effect was far more flattering, especially in the current circumstances.

Smoothing her hair as best she could, Delilah had a difficult decision to make. She hadn't really intended for them to end up back at his place, not least because she had spent a good couple of hours the previous evening tidying up the flat in anticipation of this very occasion. It had been that or watch sitcom repeats on the telly, so the choice had not been too hard to make. Now she was stuck. Great sex, wrong venue. She needed to get home sometime before nine o'clock the next morning or suffer the consequences of a sniggering Twizz and a day spent in rumpled clothing. Although at least there would be clean underwear, even if it was of a somewhat saucier disposition than a normal work day merited.

'Um . . .' Delilah hesitated, torn between staying or going. To leave would be sensible, to stay divine.

'Um what? Um . . . how about this? Or this?'

Funny how resolve could melt faster than an ice cube in a frying pan when the man of your dreams is holding you close and his intentions are all too blatantly obvious. Succumbing to the inevitable, Delilah tried reasoning with herself and gave it up more or less instantly as a bad job. Reason didn't come into it when a man like Matt was driving you out of your mind with lust. Even as they began that slow slide back into total abandon, Delilah knew deep down that there was more to it than that. It wasn't just her mind that was giving way here, and the sheer insanity of what lay beyond would have frightened her out of her wits, had they not been already too addled to take a blind bit of notice. Falling in love was not part of her plan. But then again, when exactly did emotions follow the rules?

Despite her best intentions, she was still a good twenty minutes late the following morning. To give her her due, she would have made it but for a bus that stubbornly refused to come. She still thought it politic, however, to stop and pick up a couple of cappuccinos on the way. Twizz always responded well to bribes, and with any luck she might be too busy throwing coffee down her grateful gob to ask too many difficult questions. This was, of course, a hopelessly optimistic approach. No sooner had she shouldered her way in with the coffee cups held aloft like some offering to the gods than Twizz looked up from the paper she had spread across the counter and remarked, 'You look like you've had a right good root.'

'That obvious, is it?' So much for the carefully applied make-up and the sober outfit then.

''Fraid so, love. You really should get him to shave more often.'

Dumping the cups down on the counter, Delilah dashed to the loo to inspect her face at close quarters. Talk about rose-coloured spectacles – in her blurry way she'd fondly imagined that a touch of coverstick would do the trick. She emerged with one hand self-consciously covering the awful truth. 'Christ, it looks like I've taken a Black and Decker to it this time.'

'Look on the bright side. You'll save a fortune on exfoliant.' Twizz was still buried in her paper, oblivious to the depth of Delilah's distress.

'Thanks a bunch. Here, let's have a look at the horoscopes. They might tell me my day is about to improve and you're going to get struck down with laryngitis.' Maturely ignoring the tongue stuck out in her direction, Delilah whipped the paper away and raced off with it towards the sofa, Twizz's indignant 'Oi!' ringing in her ears.

'Oh, great! Listen to this . . . Affairs of the heart are about to take an upward turn—'

'Looks like they already have. Upward, downward, sideways . . .'

'Don't be disgusting.' Twizz's smirk was lost on Delilah, who continued to read on silently. So immersed was she in the vagaries of fortune that when Twizz spoke from over her shoulder she nearly jumped out of her skin.

'I thought you were a Cancerian.'

'I am,' said Delilah, a trifle defensively.

'So why are you reading Gemini, then?'

There was no answer to that one really. Realizing she was beaten, Delilah snapped the paper shut and announced, 'I think it's time for a stocktake.'

'What for? We only did one the other week and it's not as if the stock has been flying out the doors since then. By the way, nice bracelet.' The past mistress of deflection, Twizz knew just when to throw a diversionary spanner in the works, a technique she had been perfecting since her earliest days of homework.

'Thanks. Isn't it gorgeous? Matt gave it to me last night for our . . .' Too late. Twizz's radar was already locked on and Delilah knew that there was no way back. 'For our one week anniversary,' she finished lamely.

'No way! He said that? He actually said that as he gave it to you?'

In the face of such incredulity it was hard to maintain one's dignity but Delilah made a creditable attempt. 'Yes, he did. Is there anything wrong with that?'

Twizz took one look at the closed expression on her face and decided that backing off for once was the wiser move. 'Noooooo . . . not really.'

'I think it's rather sweet, actually.'

Now this was something no self-respecting female Aussie could ignore. 'Sweet? Since when did you want sweet? Sharp, yes, meaty, maybe, but sweet? Give me a break!'

'Just because you only go for guys who are up for a good time, doesn't mean that all men are the same, you know.' Bizarrely for a woman who considered herself a paid-up member of the sisterhood, Delilah was bristling in Matt's defence.

'Oh, yes, they are. Every last one of them. It's just you're too loved-up to see it. Particularly in his case.'

'Loved-up? I am not loved-up! I've barely known him ten minutes and right now what we're doing is having fun. No strings, no commitments. Take it as it comes and see how it goes. And that's all it is.'

'Could have fooled me . . .' As stand-offs went, it was unspectacular. Long hard stares quickly gave way to uncontrollable giggles, and Twizz was the first to hold out a hand and suggest, 'Truce?'

'Truce. You cynical old wombat.'

'Better cynical than shat upon.'

Rather than ruin the moment they wisely left it at that, and the rest of the week passed without incident, the only tension being the build-up to the appearance of the Sunday papers. Delilah could not help pinning her hopes on Fran's article, even as she told herself there were no guarantees. A good response to the feature would be an undeniable boost. Still, there wasn't much she could do now but cross her fingers, wait for the influx of fashion victims and distract herself with the occasional hot flash of Matt. Just thinking about him running his hands all over her was enough to banish business woes, if only for a matter of moments. And what moments they were. She could hardly wait for the weekend and the chance to put some of her steamier thoughts into practice.

They had arranged to catch a film on Saturday night at a cinema not a million miles from Delilah's apartment. It had, in fact, been at her suggestion and she got ready for the date in happy anticipation of coming back to her own freshly made bed near to her own lavishly stocked larder. Rather than leave a message on her voicemail, Delilah had left a note out for Jess. Talk about leading separate lives – they were practically operating in parallel universes. Delilah might have taken it personally had she not known Jess's tendency to behave with the tenacity of a particularly stubborn terrier when the occasion demanded. She just hoped that whatever she had gotten her teeth into this time warranted so much time and attention.

When they staggered back through the door just after one o'clock, having taken the scenic route via a more salubrious spot than the Doom and Gloom, Delilah half expected to find a similarly inebriated flatmate. She was even bracing herself for the inevitable sizing up that would ensue. She needn't have worried. Someone had obviously been home but there was no sign of Jess.

'Must be out on a late one,' Delilah surmised before adding, 'Never mind. You'll meet her in the morning.'

'And what do you suggest we do in the meantime?' teased Matt as he hauled her down on to the sofa and proceeded to divest her of half her clothing with well practised ease. Just as Jess entered the room.

'Ohmigod, you gave me a shock!' Feeling like a sixteen-year-old caught snogging on the sofa, Delilah hastily tugged her top back into place.

'Sorry – didn't hear you come in. You must be Matt. Hi, I'm Jess.' She'd been hiding in her bedroom all along, the sneaky bitch.

Entirely unruffled by the situation, Matt favoured her with his most endearing grin. 'I thought you might be. It was either that or the burglars round here are particularly polite.'

Jess smiled sweetly in response, but Delilah knew her better than that. She looked tired, her hair was ratty and she was dressed in her oldest flock pyjamas and a pair of mismatched bed socks. Clearly all was not well.

'Not out tonight, then?' Still making the odd surreptitious adjustment to her appearance, Delilah watched as Jess crossed behind the kitchen counter and hunted around in the odds and sods drawer. She fished out a packet of pain-killers and proceeded to wash a couple down before answering Delilah's question.

'Nope. Too much work on and then I got this blinding headache. Thought I might try and sleep it off.'

As Jess spoke, Delilah noticed that although she was very pale her eyes were suspiciously red. Could have been too many hours spent poring over paperwork, although it looked more like she'd been crying.

'And I've got this bloody cold as well . . .'

That would explain the nose that matched the eyes.

Relieved that there was nothing more sinister going on than self-sacrifice and a case of the sniffles, Delilah was all concern. 'Oh God, I hope we didn't disturb you when we came in.'

'Don't worry about it. I couldn't sleep in any case. Anyway, I'll shuffle off and leave you to it. Night night. Sleep well.'

That last ironic twist laid any lingering fears to rest. So long as Jess was capable of sarcasm all was fine with the world. It was when she was all sweetness and light you had to watch out.

Matt gave it a bare five minutes before resuming his enthusiastic assault, undoing all her efforts to make herself half decent in the process. He was all for christening the sofa in his own inimitable way but Delilah dragged him to her bedroom door, terrified of another unscheduled interruption. Besides, she didn't like to tell him that the sofa had been well and truly baptized one distant New Year's Eve and that the memory still brought her out in goosebumps of horror. Far better to consummate their passion in privacy than risk sharing the experience with an insomniac flatmate and the ghost of christenings past.

Good sex works better than an opiate any day, and Delilah lay the next morning in a delicious, heavy-limbed fug of love. Eyes still shut, she wiggled a foot towards Matt, cold toes searching for the warmth of his thighs. And kept on wiggling, right to the edge of the bed, before it became apparent that he wasn't there. As realization dawned, her eyes snapped open and she sat bolt upright in bed. A distant murmur of voices could be heard from down the hallway but before she could grab her dressing gown and form a one-woman search party the bedroom door was flung open and Matt appeared, carrying two steaming mugs. The fact that he had found the coffee maker so took her aback that at first she didn't even notice the newspaper under his arm, but when she did her lunge for it sent fat blobs of brown liquid spilling all over the duvet. Completely uncaring of her pristine white cotton, Delilah riffled through the acres of supplements until she got to the style section, and she then proceeded to hunt desperately through its pages until finally she tracked the article down next to a piece on 'Festive Fun with Figs'.

'It's here. Look, right there. Under that bloody great headline.' She waved the page in Matt's face before avidly devouring every word twice over and then declaring, 'And look at the pic. Fabulous, isn't it?'

'It's brilliant. And so are you.' Having placed the mugs out of harm's way, Matt was watching her antics with affectionate indulgence, all the while stroking the leg she had half curled under her.

'I must show it to Jess . . .' Now she was halfway out of bed, practically bouncing with the excitement of it all.

'I already showed it to her in the kitchen.'

'Oh.' Deflated by this, Delilah thrust it at Matt and demanded, 'Well, you haven't had a proper read. Go on, take a look.'

'All in good time. Right now I've got other things on my mind.'

'But, Matt, this is important . . .'

'So is this . . .'

Later, much later in fact, Delilah retrieved her precious article from the floor and admired it just one more time. Sexed-out even by his standards, Matt snoozed beside her. It had been great – thankfully it just got better and better – but Delilah couldn't help feeling he had missed the point. Men. Expect you to let off rockets and streamers when they score the tiniest success but think there's only one way to celebrate when it comes to yours. Maybe that wasn't fair. After all, he had been the bearer of the good news and had even provided refreshment along with it. Bless! Although she really would have to educate him on the fact that it was milk and no sugar rather than the other way round. She trailed an affectionate finger down his back and Matt stirred appreciatively and mumbled something.

'What was that?' she whispered. Not that she was trying to catch him out, but sleep talkers sometimes spill the beans if you do it right. That was the theory, at any rate, although all past attempts had resulted in nothing more revealing than jumbled nonsense and the odd football score. Matt was another of those who was not going to play ball. With a deep sigh he rolled over on to his tummy and snuffled into the pillow. Reflecting that men's infantile qualities were among their more endearing traits, Delilah slid down next to him and enjoyed the warmth of his body next to hers. This was what she had been missing all these months as much as anything else – the sheer pleasure of skin on skin and a heart pumping inches from her own. Sure, they were both at the lust-crazed stage, but even though it was early days she could feel the stirrings of something deeper. Affection growing alongside out-and-out animal passion, and although she wouldn't swear to it, she was pretty sure he felt the same. In his own, entirely masculine, altogether different way.

Eleven

'So, how does it feel to be a hot ticket?'

Fran rocked on her heels, looking on smugly as a bunch of fashionistas fought over the last remaining gold-fringed G-string.

Delilah bit back a wave of irritation and answered, 'It feels very good indeed.' Never mind that Decadence was her baby, Fran had appointed herself fairy godmother and obviously believed her magic pen had made it all happen. And who was Delilah to disagree? It was worth it just to watch them come through the doors, an initial rush to be the first to get there, but even now a steady stream of them dropping by on a daily basis. OK, so they weren't quite in the Harrods sale league yet, but it was still a massive improvement on those first wobbly weeks. The first ever cocktail party for the public and the place was packed. With Christmas coming up to swell the numbers of fevered shoppers even further, things were looking very good indeed.

There was no doubt about it, she owed Fran one, although judging by the satisfaction shining from Fran's face it would appear that payback had already begun.

'Decadence', the article had read,
    a pleasure palace that pleases the palate as much as the eye. As irresistible as the oral experience on

...er are the garments that give new meaning to the concept of instant glamour. I defy any man to resist the allure of the lip-smacking lingerie, and if scanties are not your thing there is plenty to please the most discriminating of boys and girls alike. Jewellery that makes you ache with desire, if only to own it, scented candles that linger long after the event. Talking of events . . .

It had gone on in much the same vein for another 600 words or so with the photo providing the icing on the publicity cake. As for the exclusivity angle, the Bloomsbury set would have been hard pushed to match them. Fran had surpassed herself, forcing the out-crowd to fight for a foothold while the in-crowd dared not miss this latest social must. Whether a solid core would remain once the fuss had died down remained to be seen. Delilah was pretty sure it would – her stuff was good, and unique enough to make a permanent mark. As she repeated this to herself like a mantra she couldn't help but draw a parallel with her personal life, thoughts of Matt popping unbidden into a mind trying to focus on business and bringing an involuntary smile to her face.

Matt. Growing more special by the day, even if she hadn't yet pinned him down to the postcard gesture. Every now and again she took it out of her top drawer to run her fingers over it and take a good, long look at the handwriting. He hadn't exactly showered her with billets-doux, which made positive identification all the more difficult. As far as romantic gestures went, his tended more to the tactile, the bracelet being the most material example although it still raised a bit of a question mark in her mind. She brushed away the notion even as it arose, blanking the spectre of the choker from her thoughts. It was a minor quibble, mere birdseed when compared to the way he made her heart and hormones soar. Even Jess had been surprisingly generous in her verdict, although she had baulked at the suggestion of making up a foursome sometime. Maybe that was a step too cheesy but Delilah was surprised at the ferocity of her response.

'Couldn't possibly, absolutely not,' Jess had spluttered at the very thought.

'But why not? There must be someone you can drag along . . . you know, maybe one of those lawyer types you spend all those hours with "working late".'

'I don't know what you mean. You seem to forget I am one of those "lawyer types" and our time is far too expensive to spend on anything other than the work we're paid to do.' So there. God, she could be pompous when she wanted. Even Jess must have realized she had gone a shade too far because she had instantly softened it with, 'Look, hon, as soon as this case is over I promise we'll go out and play. Fraud is complicated enough but this one is a real bugger. Give it a few more weeks and things'll be back to normal. Anyway, you enjoy keeping him to yourself while you can. Don't forget the six week rule. It won't be long before he starts farting in bed and forgetting to call when he says he will.'

Charming, if unfortunately true. Delilah cast a sidelong glance at her forthright flatmate, now standing alongside her with a distant smile on her face. She was touched that Jess had found the time to come along and show support when her life appeared to be so impossibly busy. Although judging from the mayhem taking place all around them it would seem that Delilah's existence was also picking up apace. By the time the evening came to a close, the pile of bottles by the sofa rivalled the shelves for emptiness and glasses were strewn everywhere. Margaret wandered in just as they were starting to clear up. The final stragglers wafted past her at the door, over-bright eyes and shrieks of laughter betraying their enthusiastic consumption of the Twizz special, the Killer Martini. Luckily, lubrication had extended as far as their purses and each was clutching a carrier bag chock-full of tissue-wrapped goodies. Talk about liquidating your assets – Delilah's cup was running over with joy, success and cold hard cash.

'Hope I'm not too late to join the party.'

With her jaunty red bobble hat pulled over her ears Margaret looked like a naughty gnome. They had barely seen her in the recent mad rush, but Delilah noted with satisfaction that her eyes were clear and her cheeks were more full of colour than they had been of late.

'Margaret! Brilliant to see you. No, of course you're not too late. In fact, as far as we're concerned it's barely begun. Been far too busy pouring drinks for ladies who shop to have one for ourselves. At least, most of us have. Twizz, Jess, leave that for a second. Come on everyone, let's put our feet up and take a breather.' This with a nod to the sofa on to which Fran had already collapsed, worn out by relentless networking and still riding too high on her published efforts to stoop to anything manual or menial.

Twizz didn't need telling twice. Stacking up glasses and wielding a wet cloth were not the most glamorous of tasks and she had had too recent a taste of the social sparkle to come back to earth lightly. 'Excellent idea! Shall I whip up a final round for us all? With a cuppa for you, of course.'

Much enthusiastic nodding from the direction of the sofa had her reaching for her silver shaker when Margaret stopped her in her tracks by whipping out a bottle of champagne from under her anorak and announcing, 'Actually, I brought this. My contribution.'

Fran's eyes widened as she spied her favourite fizz and muttered reverentially, 'Oh, goodie. Krug.'

'Margaret, you shouldn't have.' Delilah was touched. It was typical of Margaret to make such a gesture, particularly when she wouldn't even be reaping the benefit.

'Of course I should. We have a lot to celebrate. Come on, then, dig out some glasses and I'll pop the cork. My father always said the trick was to twist the bottle.' Trust Margaret to be capable of opening a champagne bottle with perfect grace. And all the more impressive considering that she had never been seen to indulge.

'I'll just put the kettle on for you . . .'

'No need. Thought I might have some of the bubbly. If that's all right with you,' Margaret added in the face of Delilah's astounded expression.

'Well, yes, yes of course. I just . . . that is, I thought . . . well, you know . . . that . . .'

'That I might not be able to take a drink?' Margaret supplied, smartly putting Delilah out of her stuttering misery.

'Um, no, of course not. It's only . . . I mean, you never wanted one before and I, we sort of assumed that there might perhaps be a reason . . .' Delilah flicked a beseeching glance at Twizz, busy humming tunelessly as she closely inspected the bubbles rising in her glass. From the other two emanated nothing but thoughtful silence. Some help they were.

'Fair enough. But there is no reason. Not any more.' And having given all the explanation she felt necessary, Margaret raised her glass in a silent toast and drained the contents in one. Her eyes closed for a second in pure pleasure and then they flew open as the bubbles hit the back of her nose and she let out a cross between a hiccup, a sneeze and a giggle.

'Oops. That hit the spot. Twizz, m'dear, could you just top me up here.'

Twizz leaped to her task, curious to see the effect a second glass would have. As it turned out, Margaret was not the first to succumb to its effects. None of them needed much prompting to knock it back, and on top of their earlier indulgence the combination was pretty lethal. It didn't take long for Fran's eyes to fill with sentiment and for her to declare, 'You know what, I really hate Christmas.' Coming apropos of nothing as this did, her remark was greeted with silence. Evidently silence was something Fran hated even more than Christmas, for she carried on in a great stream of Yuletide consciousness. 'It's all so superficial, isn't it? We put up these pretty things and we all rush around and buy these lovely presents and we don't really mean any of it, do we? All that peace on earth and goodwill to men – it's all just crap, really. I hated it when I was a kid and I still do. People are still horrid to one another and they don't love each other enough and I think it's really sad. Really, really, really sad.' A large tear trembled in the corner of her over-made-up eye and then rolled its blackened way down her cheek to end up plopping with great ceremony into her empty glass. Fran swiped at her eyes with a manicured forefinger and succeeded in smearing the rest of her mascara into a charcoaly mess. It was one of those moments when everyone present could empathize, if only because they were enormously grateful that they hadn't been the one to slur out their innermost angst.

Twizz felt honour bound to stick her oar in. 'Too right. You guys don't even have the weather to make up for it. It's a whole lot better on the beach, I can tell you.' Of course. There was nothing guaranteed to send Twizz into seasonal gloom quite like a reminder of the glories of Bondi. What had previously been a jolly gathering now felt more like a wake as Christmas contagion spread throughout the little group. Even Margaret's hat appeared to have lost its colourful vigour, the bright scarlet fading alongside the greyness of the mood.

'You did get to go home last year,' Delilah gently reminded Twizz, only to be rewarded with a deep sigh and a heartfelt, 'I know. And bloody wonderful it was, too.'

'But aren't your housemates putting on some kind of party or something? I thought you told me that South African girl had invited over a whole bunch of people.' Twizz's household was best described as fluid, the members constantly changing as one or the other upped sticks only to be replaced by a remarkably similar compatriot.

'Don't know about that. Last thing I heard they were talking of going up to Edinburgh and staying on for the New Year street party. Scott and Daz are back off home, Sue-Ellen and Janelle are with their boyfriends. I expect you'll be doing the gruesome twosome thing as well,' Twizz added evilly.

Determined not to rise to the bait, Delilah coolly replied, 'Oh, I shouldn't think so. I mean, we've only just met. He's hardly going to be expecting me to spend Christmas with him at this stage.'

'Tricky one, isn't it? That first Christmas with someone new,' Fran pronounced sagely and there was a general murmur of agreement.

'And you've really got to think about the present thing. Too big and you scare him off, too small and he thinks you're a meanie. It's a minefield, I can tell you.'

As Twizz had never been known to give two hoots what any man thought of her, Delilah found this a bit hard to swallow. She had a point, though.

'Oh, bugger that! Let him buy the presents and you get on with what's important.' Drink lent even more ferocity to Margaret's already feisty spirit. Bobble nodding as if to emphasize her point, she stabbed a finger into the air and declared, 'That young man should be crawling over hot coals to get to you and no mistake. And if he doesn't, he's not worth it. Not worth it at all.'

Judging by Margaret's faraway expression, this comment had a more personal resonance than she would ever let on. Another companionable silence fell upon them all and would probably have lasted until the next sagacious remark had Fran not glanced at her watch and yelped, 'Lordy, is that the time?'

The habits of a working lifetime are not changed by fifteen minutes of new celebrity and Fran's deadlines were still stacked against her. Her agitation did not preclude the usual extended leave-taking and it was another half-hour before she departed in a blur of flame-coloured locks and teetering heels. Margaret, too, staggered off into the night, loudly insisting that she'd be perfectly fine, and the three of them were left to the peace of a darkened shop and a bulging bag to be banked the following morning.

'Fancy a last one at the pub?'

It seemed an age since they had fitted in a stint at the Doom and Gloom and Delilah was sorely tempted. Duty, however, called – not to mention desire. 'I'd love to but it's this engagement do tonight. Some old school friend. I told Matt I'd meet him there at about eight.' Even as she said it, Delilah heard the ring of coupledom in her voice.

Never one to miss a nuance, Twizz raised both eyebrows and drawled, 'Very brave of him. I'm surprised he's not worried about you getting ideas.'

'He should be so lucky,' Delilah shot back, but the very same thought had occurred to her the moment he had mentioned it. Most men would rather dance around a handbag than bring their new girlfriend to such a loaded occasion. Then again, Matt wasn't most men, as the constant stream of little presents, phone calls and unremitting attention bore witness. She must be getting soft or something, but the notion of Matt on a more permanent basis turned her innards to a warm, sticky morass of delight.

'I have to be getting along as well.' Something in Jess's voice sounded off-key, a note of unnecessary intransigence that piqued Delilah's curiosity. Whatever her mysterious assignation, she could not have flagged it better. Realizing that she might have given the game away, Jess aimed for a lighter note.

'Let's all go for a drink sometime in the week. When things are a bit quieter.'

'Suits me.' Oblivious to the undertones, Twizz was easy. Especially where a drink was concerned. It was only Delilah who felt the tension as Jess took her leave, eyes carefully averted as she bundled herself up and headed for the door. Had she not already been running late, Delilah would have gone after her and demanded that they talk there and then. As it was, she watched her go off into the night with a sinking feeling in her guts and an inexplicable twinge of fear for her friend.

Delilah took an interminably slow bus ride to the party. Ironic that – for once she had the cash for a cab in her clutches and not a one in sight. A bit like Murphy's law of shopping, when fate decreed that all desirable goods would disappear from the rails the minute the means to spend fell into your hands. For tonight, however, she had managed to treat herself. An insane gallop through late night shopping and the result was a cute little number that managed to combine class with sass. An irresistible combo and she couldn't wait to see how Matt dealt with it.

Matt took one look, let out a long, low whistle and then smothered her with the sort of snog that left nothing to the imagination. Intentions clarified, he led her off to the bar, making introductions all the way until Delilah's head was a whirl of smiling faces and girls called Sophie. The party was taking place in a room above the sort of pub that serves Thai food and Belgian beer to a homogeneous crowd. Matt's friends fitted in perfectly, dragging away on their Marlboro Lights as they exchanged industry gossip, punctuated by the occasional shriek of recognition and much kissing and catching up. Knowing absolutely nobody there freed Delilah up to observe and she drank it all in as they drifted from group to group. About an hour into the party and a face on the edge of the room caught her eye. The stranger shifted out of the shadows and Matt caught sight of him as well.

'Dan! Mate, I thought it was you. Can I get you a drink? You know everyone don't you . . . Ed, Alice . . . and Delilah, you remember Delilah.'

'Of course. Lovely to see you again.'

His touch on her shoulder was even lighter than the brush of his lips against her cheeks. With a sinking feeling, Delilah realized that she had not been wrong about their mutual wariness. Showing determined friendliness, she bared her teeth in a delighted smile and declared, 'Great to see you, too. How are you?'

For a split second, a crazy urge in Dan shouted at him to tell her the truth. That he was at the height of happiness and in the pits of despair. That things were not as they seemed. That it was fantastic to see her in the flesh, even better than seeing her every night in his dreams and every day in his less lucid moments. That life was a total bastard but Matt could be an even bigger one, and that he could cheerfully take the stake out from his own heart and stab it through his mate's instead. He dropped his eyes for a moment and took a Dan-paced pause, a trick which served him well at times like this.

'I'm fine, thanks. Bit overworked but you know how it is . . . Cheers, mate. Cheers.' Saved by a pint, even if it was a poisoned one. As he took his first swig, Matt dropped a casual but definite arm around Delilah's waist and gave her a squeeze. Never had a drop of bitter been so appropriately named. Dan dragged his eyes away, but not before he and Matt had exchanged a look loaded with unmistakable venom. He might as well have erected a 'keep off' sign at Delilah's feet for all the subtlety of his message.

So tight was Dan's throat that the beer was having trouble flowing down his gullet. He swallowed hard and cast around for something diversionary to say while he sorted out his thoughts. 'All set for your ski trip?'

'Oh, yeah . . . all organized.' Matt appeared a shade uncomfortable with that, shuffling his feet around and looking for all the world like a man who has omitted to tell his girlfriend something vitally important.

'Off for both Christmas and New Year again?' Dan persisted, struck by the scenario that was starting to unfold.

'Er . . . yeah, that's right.' More mumbling and shuffling from Matt and Dan was now seriously intrigued. He noted that Delilah's face was registering a hastily disguised mixture of shock and not a little hurt, and for a second he felt like a total shit. But only for a second.

'Same group again, is it? Charlotte and all her girlfriends, Simon, Joe, the rest of the gang?' Dan was beginning to have fun, something that had been in short supply of late.

'Yep. Same bunch. Ah . . . I need another drink. Can I get you anything, darling? Dan? OK, well, back in a sec.' Matt bolted to the bar, leaving a mute Delilah in the company of a marginally remorseful Dan, and then only because he could see that she was visibly upset by this turn of events and doing a heroic impression of not giving a shit.

Dan couldn't help himself. Her wan expression behind the concealing layer of cheer undid his best resolve and he blurted out a sincere and gentle, 'Sorry.'

'Whatever for?' Tone as brittle as her smile, she cocked her head to one side and looked up at him as if for all the world he hadn't delivered a large blow to her nascent romantic hopes. Even while she was doing this, Delilah was talking herself down from the inner explosion of rage that she had hit at rocket speed. After all, she had no right to expect anything from Matt on the thorny first Christmas issue. He was entitled to do what he liked. Entitled, maybe, but from the look on his face he knew he'd done wrong, even if it was only to lie by omission. And there was nothing she hated more.

Looking at her controlled but closed expression, Dan decided it was time to back off. For one thing, he couldn't bear to see her struggle so hard to keep her cool, and for another he knew that if he carried on there would be tears before bedtime. And they wouldn't necessarily be hers.

The party carried on around them but Delilah felt distinctly hollow inside. She had just been sliding into that glorious state when early lust settles and evolves into something more. At Matt's side tonight, she had felt part of something and his evident pride as he introduced her around had softened the edges of the usual 'meet the mates' anxiety. Now this. A great big kick to the guts and they were back on shifting ground. Matt was still over by the bar, no doubt calculating the best moment to return, and this Dan bloke was making her feel very uncomfortable indeed. Her face had always reflected her feelings faster than ripples across a pond, but this time she thought she'd managed to mask the effect. Evidently not, if his galling sympathy was anything to go by. She could do without it – and without Matt's machinations as well. Excusing herself, Delilah slipped through the crowd and hurried out of the room, leaving Dan to stare anxiously after her and wonder how on earth it had all gone so wrong.

'Where's Delilah?' Finally back from the bar, Matt was looking as worried as he ever would.

'Search me. Probably gone to the loo or something. I take it you didn't tell her about the ski trip, then?' Matt's look said it all. Dan was about to bask in self-righteousness when his friend's look of guilt gave way to delight.

'Darling, you're back.' The relief in Matt's voice was unmistakable. So much so that Dan wondered for a second if he had misjudged him, so patently obvious were his feelings for Delilah.

Matt handed her the drink he had ostensibly been fetching and she took it with a cool smile before commenting, 'You took your time. Planning another expedition or something?'

Full marks to Delilah. Dan stood back and waited for the flippant comeback that never came. Instead, Matt's face crumpled into a picture of abject contrition as he shuffled from one foot to another before finally blurting out, 'What can I say? I am a total, 100 per cent shit for forgetting to tell you.'

'Forgetting?' Far from forgiveness, Delilah spoke in that

excessively polite yet pointed manner that couples employ when on the verge of a public argument. If he hadn't been so besotted with her, Dan would have wished himself far, far away. As it was, he stayed, transfixed by Matt's reaction. The guy was practically dissolving, for God's sake.

'Yeah, I know, I know. All I can say is that things have been so hectic and we organized the bloody thing so long ago that it went clean out of my head. Honestly, if Dan hadn't mentioned it right now, I'd probably have missed the plane. And I have had better things to think about of late . . . haven't I?' For a moment there even Dan had been fooled. But only for a moment. Right up until Matt had sidled closer to her and pulled that winsome face. Dan had seen that one many times before and it had yet to fail. Teachers, nurses, female traffic wardens and now Delilah. It was enough to make a man lose faith in the concept of feminine intuition.

'You do forgive me, don't you? Sweetie, I never meant to upset you. I'd never want to upset you . . .'

'Yeah, well, don't forget to send me a postcard.' A pointed enough remark, that sailed straight over Matt's head. Dan, however, felt the blood drain from his face. Surely she didn't think her secret admirer was Matt?

'I'll send you a lot more than that . . .' Matt's tone was suggestive, his hands on her bum, pulling her close.

Now they were nose to nose, Delilah struggling to stay cross. A gentle hand on each shoulder to pull her even closer, a soft line of kisses starting on her forehead and working its way down to her mouth and she was trying not to giggle as he murmured endearments and overplayed his hand outrageously.

'I'll bring you back the best snowman in the world . . .'

Disbelieving snort.

'And a whole bunch of snowflakes as well . . .'

Slight softening of the compressed mouth and a twitch at one corner.

'And I'll write your name on the mountain with my skis . . . with lots of kisses . . .'

There she lost it, unable to resist the mental picture and a mouth that had always had an amazing effect on her senses. The person who could stay cross with Matt for any length of time was either devoid of humour or entirely immune to charm. Luckily, Dan had received his vaccination long ago. He was about to slip away and leave them to it when a brunette rubber ball came bouncing up and squawked, 'Mattie, darling, I thought it was you!'

Overweight but rather pretty, she was jumping up and down with puppyish exuberance. Every man's nightmare come true: the In-Your-Face Ex. Matt reluctantly prised himself away from Delilah and dropped a dutiful peck on each of her ruddy cheeks.

'Lissa!' Hardly surprising that she had recognized him. The mystery was that she was speaking to him at all, considering it was her closest chum he'd been snogging at the time. A selective memory had proved a great healer; here she was, acting as if she had never even crossed him off her Christmas card list or called him every name in her admittedly limited vocabulary. Shame about her timing though – it had always been off.

Lissa was looking at him pointedly. 'Trina's here as well. You simply must come and say hello. Hello, Dan. Nice to see you again.' This last with a coy little glance and a giggle, both of which missed their mark.

Matt sighed inwardly. Lord spare him from ex-girlfriends and overexcited Sloanes, especially when they came in one and the same package. Still, it was as well to get her away from Delilah before any more beans were spilled. With a despairing shrug and a meaningful grimace, Matt allowed himself to be dragged away. Dan sneaked a peek at her face and observed the little frown marring her normally pristine forehead.

'So . . . what are you up to for Christmas?' Hardly the

most appropriate question but it popped out before Dan could run it past his inner tactometer.

Delilah bristled faster than a startled porcupine. 'You mean now that Matt's obviously not going to be around? I do have a life as well, you know.'

'I'm sure you do. I expect you have hundreds of parties to go to followed by a classic Victorian family Christmas with all the trimmings. And no doubt an impossibly glamorous New Year to round the whole thing off in style.' This was something else, the normally taciturn Dan animated by something, even if it was only sarcasm. It was Delilah's turn to apologize.

'I'm sorry. That was a bit prickly of me.'

'Just a touch.'

Something about his expression made her burst into peals of laughter. 'Sorry . . . sorry . . .' she gasped, dabbing at her eyes before daring to shoot him a glance. Far from looking at her as if she were a total head case he actually appeared quite amused.

'You all right?'

'Yep, fine. It's been quite an evening, one way or another.' Still hiccuping with mirth, her attempt at lightheartedness was let down by a stray squeak at the end of that sentence. She flashed him a rueful look that was met with one of such total empathy it quite took her aback.

'So what are you going to do?' Moment over, Dan was steering the conversation back on to its original course. It was either that or head off into some very deep water indeed.

'What? Oh, Christmas. Well, my shop is very busy at the moment. We had a fantastic write-up and what with that and the Christmas shoppers things are going really well.'

'I must come and take a look.'

'You must.' Unbelievable how things change. Half an hour before, she would have sworn this guy qualified for the interfering arsehole award, and now he was acting as if he would like nothing better than to come and rummage amongst her frillies.

'I love to hear about things taking off, especially if I know the people involved. Sounds like it's going great.'

Delilah reached over to touch a table before she spoke. A bit of healthy superstition never went amiss. 'Touch wood. It's worth it, despite the fact that I'm working all the hours God sends.'

'I know how that one feels.'

'I bet you do. Things busy for you too?'

'Manic. We're on the verge of a merger that means everything.' He was off, excitement and energy exuding from every pore. Delilah cast around in her memory for an intelligent question.

'You have something to do with the Internet, right?'

'Right. And it's been a tough few months, I can tell you. But we kept our heads down, concentrated on building the business rather than setting up fancy offices or going for a float. And it's paid off. Got some household names on board, bought up most of my rivals and delivered the product on time to the customer. Now the big boys are sniffing around us. Worth the slog – although some of my staff might not agree. Had to bribe them with pizza to keep going.' He grinned as the memory of Jem hurling pepperoni across the room in frustration popped into his mind.

Looking at him, Delilah wondered what really went on behind those clever brown eyes. 'What sort of business is it?'

Her question hit the right spot. Delilah always found it enthralling to see people come alive when talking about their passion. This quite clearly was Dan's, as evidenced by the way he had lit up as soon as they hit on the subject and was now speaking with the kind of messianic intensity employed by all the best gospel preachers. Endearing rather than fanatical, it was a by-product of his belief that he was offering a great service to the world. It was impossible not to be drawn in by his fervour, his eyes locked on hers as he tried to get his message across. And what eyes they were. She couldn't help but notice their colour, almost amber rather than brown. With tiny flecks of gold that shimmered and danced as he spoke.

'It's more of a portal than a site. A gateway, if you like, to all sorts of products and services, many of which we now own. People used to have to trawl around and hunt down individual sites one by one but we've made it easy for them to find what they want. As it's themed, we know that if they've come to the site looking for one thing, chances are they'll stay to browse around.'

'And what is the theme? Something you're really into, obviously.' She had been expecting a eulogy no less intense in its fervour, so when he hesitated Delilah was instantly intrigued. Surely nothing could be more outré than Decadence?

'Erm . . . actually, it's organic gardening.'

'Organic gardening?'

'And food. My twin great loves,' he said, patting a nonexistent tummy. 'It's a lifestyle site, for all those people who've realized that organic is the only way to go. It's called Grub.com. A play on food, gardening and getting your fingers dirty. Oh, and worms of course. Get it?'

'Great idea.'

'So is yours, by all accounts. Ever thought of having a web site?' He meant it as a throwaway remark but the idea struck him as pure gold the moment it left his mouth. For one thing, it might just mean another precious point of contact.

Unfortunately for him, she shook her head and smiled self-deprecatingly. 'A web site? I had enough trouble getting my head around text messaging. A total technophobe, that's me. Besides, there is still something to be said for the phone and boring old snail mail.'

'Of course there is. I'm a great fan of pen and paper

myself. You can express yourself so much better that way . . .' For a heartbeat there, he thought she might have got it. But then she shook her head and laughed.

'That's just what I was saying to my assistant the other week. She was trying to convince me to at least get a computer in the shop, but I really can't see the point.'

Another chance and Dan seized it with alacrity. 'You have no idea how much easier it makes things. You could do all your accounting on a computer, even set up a stock check system. I'd be happy to show you sometime, teach you the basics. You never know, you might even fall in love with the whole thing and become a total technophile.' And there was always a chance that poring over a hot keyboard together might find her having more buttons pushed than she'd bargained for. An outside chance, but anything was better than watching all his hopes crash faster than an over-extended hard drive.

'Yes, but I'd still have to go and buy one of the damn things and I've absolutely no idea where to start.'

'I'm sure we could sort you out with something. Got a few redundant models lying around that are no longer up to our purposes but would probably suit you just fine.' He'd make sure they did, even if he had to go out and buy it himself.

'Oh no, I couldn't . . .'

'Couldn't what?' Here was Matt again, safely delivered from the clutches of ex-dom and happily handling his present situation as he fondled Delilah. Dan had never seen him quite this overt.

'Have fun?' she teased.

The face Matt pulled was answer enough. 'She was very keen to know all about you. As a matter of fact, she'd read that article and was going on about the shop and . . .'

Talk of the devil. This was one brunette who refused to

be put back in her box. With more shrieks in her repertoire than a cockatiel, she reappeared, chum in tow. 'Matt, you naughty thing, you said you'd introduce us. You must be Delilah. Melissa Payne-Potter. It's so great to meet you. Matt's been telling me about the shop but we'd read it all anyway. It sounds sooooo exciting. This is Trina and I'd love you to come over and meet the rest of the gang. They're simply dying to ask you about these parties you hold . . .'

There was absolutely no stopping her, even if Delilah had wanted to. With the force of character indigenous to her class, Melissa simply wouldn't even contemplate a negative response. Such was the impetus of her gushing that Delilah was swept across to meet her friends almost before her feet touched the ground. Matt and Dan exchanged an increasingly rare glance of understanding.

'Now I know how I ended up going out with that girl for so long,' he exclaimed, eyes rolling at the memory.

'I hardly think three weeks counts as an eternity.'

'It sure felt like it at the time.'

Dan couldn't help but smile at that one. This felt almost like old times. Nostalgia, however, was superseded by a pressing need to know.

'How long's it been now with Delilah?' he asked, as indifferently as he could. To his dismay, Matt's eyes went all misty.

'Five, six weeks. Feels like yesterday. I tell you, mate, I think this might be the one. She's just so . . . so . . . well, you can see what I mean.'

He certainly could. From across the room, Dan could make out Delilah patiently responding to the pressing attentions of her clucking coterie. Whatever they were angling for, it was clearly bigger than a 10 per cent discount. Being male, the significance of the social scrabble passed him by. All he knew was that the way the light caught the edges of her hair and burnished it a bright copper gold was enough to bring a lump to his throat and an itch to another, less obvious part. It suddenly seemed imperative to get things straight, find out what Matt's true intentions were. Not to mention how he'd come about them in the first place. Had he really done Dan over or was it by genuine chance that he had come across Delilah? For the sake of their faltering friendship, if nothing else, he needed to know.

'Listen, mate, why don't we get together? Have that game of squash? It's been ages since we did that.'

'Sounds great. Give us a bell and we'll fix it up.' Matt looked genuinely pleased at the idea and again Dan wondered if he had somehow been mistaken. Suckered by the moment, he made another stab for the truth.

'Look, Matt . . .'

What might otherwise have been seminal was lost in a sudden clashing of fork against glass as a skinny bloke with a big voice leapt on to a table and began yelling for quiet. Speech time. What joy. In the ensuing chortles at unfunny jokes, Dan had a chance to kick himself good and hard for missing his moment. Another time. There would surely be another opportunity to tackle Matt head-on. Of course, Dan already knew what he would say. Protest his innocence loudly to the last, express his hurt and amazement that his best mate should think so badly of him. Blah blah blah blah blah. Dan knew the score. He might hope for an attack of honesty, but there was fat chance of that happening at this late stage in Matt's development.

As the cries of 'Speech! Speeeeeeech!' echoed around the room, Dan glanced at Matt, over at Delilah and then back to Matt again. Nope, he couldn't see it. No shift in species, no alteration in plumage. The leopard was still sporting his designer spots. So there was a remarkable softening in Matt's attitude and a demeanour that in anyone else would have looked suspiciously like love. Dan was not so easily convinced. Nor, more importantly, did he want to be. He might be doing them both a disservice but he prayed that

when the inevitable fall came he would be there to catch
her, or at the very least to soften the blow. From there on
in, he didn't dare think of the consequences. Much less hope
for a happy ending.

Twelve

'I knew we should have taken the bloody train.' Twizz's mutterings were not exactly subtly pitched, and neither was her extravagant shivering and pacing as they stood beside the raised bonnet of Fran's car. A drive that normally took just over an hour had never felt so long, and now it looked as if it was to be extended into infinity by the imminent collapse of Fran's carburettor.

'Oh, give it a rest,' retorted Delilah, driven to distraction by the demands of holding together a group that was growing more fractious by the minute. Never had Jess's absence been so keenly felt – Delilah could have done with a dose of her down-to-earth advice to keep herself sane, if nobody else. Jess, however, was already happily ensconced at her parents' house, doubtless gorging herself on her mother's home cooking and toasting her toes by a roaring fire. Lucky cow. As for her other human rock, Margaret had taken it upon herself to disappear into the drizzle just when Delilah needed her most. It was all very trying. Sometimes Delilah wished she could keep a lid on her big ideas.

The expedition had come together in the usual spur-of-the-moment, haphazard manner. One moment Fran was moaning on again about the ghastliness of it all, the next Delilah was suggesting that they all decamp to her father's house for a Christmas with a difference.

'After all, it's better to spend it in like-minded company

than stuck away with your rellies. Or worse, on your own. Twizz was saying only yesterday how much she was dreading the Springbok invasion. Fran just wants to forget the whole thing. What about you, Margaret?'

She had avoided giving them her own reason for refugee status but Twizz thought she could guess. She might have known that the slimy bastard would have other plans.

'Sounds good to me,' had been her instant response to Delilah's suggestion, overriding the polite wavering of the more timorous Fran, who was secretly thrilled at this further sign of her acceptance into the clan. It had taken longer to persuade Margaret, who demurred on grounds ranging so far and wide across the excuse register that even Twizz had to applaud her ingenuity. Once committed, though, Margaret had remained a fount of enthusiasm, her stalwart nature providing a welcome sense of order to the otherwise chaotic little group.

Her absence, therefore, was only adding to Delilah's anxiety. She peered into the gloom, unable to make out more than a lumpy hedgerow and the road snaking away into the gathering dusk. Suddenly she spotted a small, determined figure trudging towards them, recognizable through the mist only by its jaunty headgear. Margaret stomped up the final incline to where they were stranded, arms cradling what appeared to be a number of steaming packages.

'I knew there was a roadside cafe along here somewhere. Been there for donkey's years, ever since I used to come this way to lecture. And that is going back a while, I can tell you.'

Not for the first time, Delilah sent up a silent prayer of thanks for the miracle of Margaret. Not only had she managed to procure hot drinks but there were also a couple of parcels of chips on which they fell with cries of delight. Even Fran ceased peering hopefully into her engine to delve into the fat, golden pile. When needs must, there was no standing on ceremony and what had been a miserable moment acquired some sense of festivity.

'These are fabulous. Mmmm, yum.' Strop forgotten, Twizz was licking her fingers with all the fervour of a child faced with candyfloss. Life took on a whole new rosiness when frozen fingers were thawing against the side of a styrofoam cup.

'Do you think you should give them another call?' Aware that the goodwill would not last forever, Delilah was anxious to be rescued as soon as humanly possible. No sooner had the words left her mouth than a bright yellow rescue van drew up alongside them, and within twenty minutes they were chugging on their way, Fran having promised faithfully to get her car to a garage just as soon as they arrived. Quite how she was going to find one that was open on Christmas Eve was another matter, but for the moment at least they were back on track.

'Maybe you should phone your father and tell him we'll be a bit late,' suggested Margaret, but Delilah shrugged that one off with a, 'Don't worry. He won't even have noticed.'

Twizz darted her a glance and was met with an expression so shuttered that she immediately turned her attention back to the countryside whizzing past outside the window. Not that she could see much. The fields were dusted with a sprinkling of snow, the trees stark against a sky the colour of a city pigeon. The rain persisted in that annoyingly impotent way that ensures you get absolutely sodden without even the pleasure of a damn good downpour. Altogether the weather presented a most depressing prospect and Twizz counted on the fact that things could only improve.

After several more uncomfortable miles, Twizz urgently needed distraction. It was now too dark outside to see the bleak scenery and the conversation within the car had dwindled to the odd please and thank-you as the boiled sweets were handed around. There was nothing for it but to go for the coach party approach. 'How about a sing-song? Something Christmassy like . . .'

' "Silent Night"?' suggested Delilah, a tad sarcastically.

Fran, concentrating grimly on the road, murmured a feeble, 'We could always try the radio again, see if we can get some kind of reception . . .' but was instantly drowned out by the opening of Twizz's lungs. Soon they were all bellowing along to a ragged chorus, Twizz and Delilah competing to see who could best sustain their 'Gloria's' and Margaret happily joining in at patchy intervals. Even Fran forgot herself so far as to hum along under her breath, really letting go when they got to 'Jingle Bells' and the little car practically jiggled in time to their energetic efforts. The road lighting grew sparser, the junctions smaller and further apart as they entered deepest countryside. Finally they shook, rattled and rolled their way up a minor road that petered out into an unmade track. Fran brought the car to a shuddering halt and the sudden silence was a startling contrast.

Before them was a large stone house, the only illumination a light in the porch. Set between the well lit windows of the dwellings to either side, it made the place seem extremely unwelcoming. Through the undrawn curtains of the nearest cottage could be seen a feast of twinkling decorations adorning a Christmas tree, while the other, larger Georgian effort sported a tasteful wreath. They piled out and trooped behind Delilah as she headed for the forbidding front door. She seized a large brass knocker and rapped as hard as she could, explaining, 'Pa's a bit deaf, I'm afraid,' waiting a few seconds and then giving it another go. This time the response was miraculous. Lights snapped on, a dog could be heard to bark somewhere way down a corridor and footsteps headed audibly towards them. Just as well – it was absolutely freezing and, given their earlier adventures, they were all dying for warmth and sustenance.

'Just a second . . . Harvey, get down. Down!' There was

the sound of keys being turned and a bolt drawn back before the door swung open to reveal a tall, spare figure and a highly excited Jack Russell.

'Come in, m'dear. Lovely to see you.' Delilah's father beamed collectively at them all and stood aside to let them in, his efforts to drop a peck on his daughter's cheek somewhat hampered by Harvey's determination to sniff out thoroughly each and every member of the invading party before leaping up at his mistress with high-pitched yelps of delight.

'Hello, Pa. You look well,' Delilah murmured as she ushered the rest of them in, leading the way through the wellie-bedecked ante-room into a huge hallway cum reception room beyond. Twizz tried to keep the awestruck look off her face but couldn't help but be impressed. Fran, too, was looking about her with no small measure of admiration. Granted, the furnishings were faded and in places well worn, but their quality and innate grace shone through. No wonder Delilah had such immaculate taste, having grown up in surroundings such as these. Only Margaret appeared unmoved, staring ahead into space with a strange air of preoccupation.

They walked on into another, smaller sitting room and the dancing flames of a real log fire immediately drew them in. Given the distance between this and the front door, it was hardly surprising that it had taken some time for Delilah's father to respond.

'We've put your friends in the blue and the yellow bedrooms, darling. Mrs Gilling thought those would be warmest. Perhaps you should settle everyone in and then we can all have a drink.'

Whatever Twizz had been expecting, it certainly wasn't this gentle, unassuming man. From the odd oblique reference, she had divined that he and Delilah had a distant if cordial relationship, but from the evidence before her it seemed that her mental picture of a cold academic was wildly inaccurate. True, he had the faded blue eyes and faintly distracted manner of the cerebrally inclined, but he also had the high cheeks that spoke of a ready smile and an aura of intense compassion. The face and manner, in fact, of someone who had suffered and had come out of it much the wiser.

'Thanks, Pa. Let me just introduce everyone first. Twizzle, my assistant, Fran, who wrote that wonderful article about us—'

'Ah yes, marvellous,' her father murmured as he shook them both warmly by the hand before turning his attention to Margaret.

'And this is—'

'Good Lord,' interjected her father, a light switching on in his eyes. 'It can't be . . . Margaret? Margaret Pilkington?'

Now this was too weird for words. Here was her father looking at Margaret as if she were a blast from the past and Margaret giving him the once-over in equal measure.

'It most certainly is. Give or take the odd spot of decline and decay.' This time, Margaret didn't need a red bobble hat to animate her features. Happy realization having cleared away the clouds of distraction, the smile on her face said it all.

'Well, I never . . .' Geoffrey was shaking his head as he peered at her, his gaze behind the spectacles taking in every tiny detail. Delilah had only ever seen him like this when he came across an especially fascinating specimen of flora or fauna. It was quite something else when applied to a fellow human being.

'Margaret was at university with your mother and I. Even then she was a woman with a magnificent memory and a tendency to call a spade a spade.'

'A blooming shovel, more like.' Margaret was giving her father more twinkle than next door's Christmas lights and, for a second, Delilah felt rather faint. Discovering that they knew each other was bad enough, but the prospect of anything more was so far beyond the pale as to be unthinkable. The fact that there was a history was intriguing in itself but there was clearly more to it than that. For one thing, they obviously hadn't been in touch for many years. Since before she was born, in fact, otherwise Delilah was sure that her name, if nothing else, would have given the game away. The plot was thickening faster than a good béchamel sauce, and the sooner she got to the bottom of things the better.

Not that she had any chance to dig further that evening. Once settled in their various rooms, Twizz and Fran having eyed each other warily across a mercifully spacious shared twin, they all gathered again for a drink and a plateful of Mrs Gillings' famous mince pies. As Delilah bit into hers, she made that first mince pie wish and opened her eyes to find the all-seeing gaze of Twizzle resting on her in an infuriatingly knowing manner. So she was transparent. Better than being so opaque as to be unreadable. And anyway, what was wrong with wishing your boyfriend was right here, right now, kissing you as if his life depended on it?

'Another pie?' she offered, as much to cover herself as to force Twizz into eating something she obviously hated out of pure politeness.

'Thanks, but I've really had enough,' responded an unmoving Twizz, rubbing her abdomen for added dramatic effect. She occasionally tried to convince them that she really did suffer from a gluten allergy, but somehow the confectionery consumption didn't quite square with that, to say nothing of the beer guzzling. The fashionability of her complaint had far more to do with it, alongside a perfectly healthy desire to keep her stomach flat.

'Well, we'd better bundle up and get ready for church.' For a lifelong atheist, her father's attendance at the Christmas carol service remained a puzzle to all concerned. Only the vicar understood, and that understanding was based on many years' acquaintance and a shared fondness for a decent single malt of an evening. When she was younger, Delilah had thought that he took her out of a sense of duty and respect for his late wife's background. Now it was part of tradition, something the two of them shared as the tiny family they represented. And, once they entered the low slung country church, they instantly became part of a much larger family as old friends and nodding acquaintances alike acknowledged them and marvelled over Delilah's development. Christmas without the carol service would not be Christmas at all and she hoped that her straggly gang would enjoy it every bit as much as she did.

In the event, they were quite overcome. The candelabra alight with real candles and ivy-bedecked pews lent the little church a sense of enchantment, appealing to the performer in Twizz and the drama queen in Fran, while Margaret the aesthete merely drank it all in with quiet appreciation. As their voices soared with the rest of the congregation, Delilah was amazed to find that a lump in her throat prevented her from giving full welly to 'Good King Wenceslas'. Whether it was the presence of almost all her closest chums or the absence of a certain person, the whole thing was making her far too emotional. It was a relief to sit down and listen as the vicar began his sermon and the gentle wisecracks were interspersed with a more serious message.

He had just got to the bit about renewed hope and faith for the future when Delilah's mobile emitted an embarrassingly piercing beep from her handbag. She had forgotten to switch it off and her face turned crimson as she hastily bundled the bag under the seat in front, trying to catch a sneaky peek as she did so. A flashing envelope indicated that she had a message, but a reproving look from her father and a sharp kick from Twizz meant that she had to stop scrabbling around by the kneelers and contain herself until a more appropriate moment. Her contribution to the last couple of carols was not as lusty as it could have been had her mind not been wandering over the possibilities. It couldn't be anything to do with the shop: the insurance company only had her home and business numbers and everything had been secured before they locked up at lunchtime. Jess? Unlikely. She knew Delilah's Christmas routine to the last Noel and was even now sitting in similar circumstances not five miles distant. Which only left one other person, given that all the other likely suspects were sitting here with her now. Matt, it just had to be Matt, and the thought of any communication from him made her pulse race and she longed for the service to swiftly reach its conclusion.

Finally they were clustered at the end of the aisle, enjoying the traditional mulled wine and yet more mince pies. Twizz had been accosted by a keen-eyed little girl handing around a plate and was munching her way heroically through yet another allergy-inducing experience, while Delilah's father was regaling the vicar with the Christmas miracle of Margaret's presence. Delilah saw her chance and slipped past Fran, who was enthusiastically partaking of the liquid refreshment. She passed through the heavy wooden door as anonymously as she could and into the chilly church porch. A tough task when half the village has known you since you were tiny and everyone you see wants to say a big hello, but she finally managed to snatch a window between hugs and handshakes to scroll through her text messages and find the precious missive.

'MISS U XXX', it read, and her face broke into a spontaneous grin.

'Nothing to worry the poet laureate, then,' came a familiar voice over her shoulder, followed by an explanatory, 'Sneaked out for a fag,' as Delilah turned on her tormentor.

'Nosy cow!' First the horoscopes, now this. Soon Twizz would be popping up in the bathtub, explaining that she'd been down there practising her scuba skills.

'Not my fault if too much sex has left you deaf.'

Delilah's immediate thought was to stoop to Twizz's level

and stick out her tongue as an appropriate response. The timely appearance of yet another motherly sort anxious to know what she'd been up to in the big, bad city put paid to that notion, and by the time news had been exchanged Twizz had stubbed out her cigarette and gone in search of another stimulus. No doubt she was even now chatting up the choirmaster. Delilah took a few precious minutes of peace and quiet alone in the porch, relying on sensible layering and love's young dream to keep out the bitter cold. A message. He'd sent her a message. It showed that even now he was thinking about her rather than propping up a bar with some glamorous ski bunny. Sure, he could have sent the message from anywhere, dodgy dives included, but it was the thought behind it that counted.

She looked out at the dusting of snow on the ground and saw that it was denser than before. A few flakes whirled in the air and she moved out of the porch so that she could feel them flutter past her face or even try to catch one on her tongue. Who cared if that was a regressional move – she felt as giddy and light-hearted as a child so why not act the part? The sky was still thick with unfallen snow and she was unable to see them, but she was sure that some-where above her the stars shone bright. Far away in an Alpine village Matt was very probably looking at those same stars, perhaps even waiting and hoping for a text message back. The very prosaic nature of the idea gave her an insane urge to giggle. Progress was a wonderful thing, but somehow a digital one-liner could never replace the romanticism of the pen.

She had the postcard tucked away, a bit more battered and bent thanks to being carted around and handled, but still enough of a puzzle to keep her intrigued. Attempts at handwriting comparison had continued to prove hopeless. The only thing she had ever seen him scribble down was a phone number and he never left her alone long enough for a thorough search of his personal effects. In fact, he never left her alone at all, physically speaking. Matt's libido seemed limitless and he was a huge fan of quick-fix sex. According to him, it was the panacea for everything from a bad hair day to PMT, although he was admittedly more into short, sharp shock treatment than TLC. Still, what he lacked in the slow hand department he more than made up for in quantity and vigour. A great change from the once-a-night types she had encountered in her bedroom travels.

'There you are, darling. Vicar was just saying he hadn't had a chance to say hello.' It was her father, come to drag her back inside and do the decent thing before they all took their leave and headed back to the house for a generous nightcap. Geoffrey had never been known to stint with the pouring and they would all be guaranteed a good night's sleep after his hospitality. Which, now that she thought of it, seemed like a very good idea indeed. The run-up to Christmas had been exhilarating, but exhausting and Delilah for one could do with a few days' rest before sales mania began.

Sure enough, the measures were large and resistance low. Goodnights were said with uncommon warmth and the noises of bathroom doors opening and shutting and feet padding along corridors eventually subsided into blissful silence, with only the odd creak to disturb. Delilah lay tucked up in her old room and decided this was the perfect time to tap out her response. The only problem was, she was desperate to hear his voice. And surely it was much more romantic to wish him a happy Christmas in person, as it were, than in the cold, hard way of the digital display. Any hesitation she might have felt was swept away in the residual tide of Glenmorangie, and she hit the speed dial without a second thought. Straight to the voicemail, without even a ringing tone to raise her hopes. Damn it. There was nothing for it but to laboriously type out a message, the pedant in Delilah fighting with her more pragmatic side when it came to the accepted abbreviations. Satisfied with her efforts, she pressed the send button and 'MISS U 2' was winging its way across the continent before her head hit the pillow.

Christmas Day was a dream. Generally there was the odd spare friend or student to add new life to the lunch table, but never as close a bunch as the one she had gathered about her this year. Breakfast segued seamlessly into an orgy of present opening, oohing and cooing. When it came to unwrapping Matt's small but beautifully wrapped gift, she had quite a keen-eyed audience.

'Tiffany – you lucky cow,' was Fran's exclamation on spying the familiar bluey green box, while Twizz was more interested in scrutinizing the card that came with it. Disappointed that it yielded nothing more than a row of kisses under the printed message, she turned her attention to the gift itself. Delilah, daft bat that she was, was still shaking and feeling it, obviously building up to the big moment.

'Oh, for God's sake, open it!' came the impatient shriek, and finally the lid was lifted and the contents revealed.

'Elsa Peretti – and in gold, no less,' Fran approved, obviously au fait with the etiquette of the Tiffany heart hierarchy. Delilah held it in her hand and admired the sweeping curves and simplicity of the line, thankful now that she'd gone the distance and given him a silver art deco card holder as her Christmas offering. As she felt the weight in her palm, a memory knocked at the back of her brain, a passing thought of another, slighter necklace purchased by Matt. Before the fleeting memory could turn into anything more concrete, Delilah was distracted by an eager Twizz.

'Well, go on, then. Try it on.'

She slipped it around her neck and they all admired the effect against the dark green of her sweater. Her father, oblivious to any nuance of meaning or merit, merely nodded approvingly and said, 'Very nice. Now, would anyone care for a sherry before lunch? Or if you'd like to join me in a whisky, you are more than welcome.'

Margaret kept the side up with a hearty, 'Lovely, m'dear. Suits you very well,' even as she graciously accepted a brimming glass of fino. None of them commented on the fact, but her sudden switch in drinking habits was most intriguing, and Delilah determined to tackle her father on the subject just as soon as she could get him out of earshot. As it happened, she didn't have too long to wait. Lunch was a joint effort, Mrs Gillings having provided every possible permutation on a traditional Christmas dinner, and Delilah had slipped off to the kitchen to baste the turkey and fruitlessly check for text messages when her father came ambling in to tend to his one area of expertise, the brandy sauce. It was now or never, so she took a deep breath and dived in at the deep end.

'So . . . what was Margaret like at university, then?' She watched as her father licked the spoon, frowned and then sloshed in a good measure of cognac.

'Like? Oh, great fun. Always a good sport, our Margaret.'

'Oh yes? In what way?' Her father might be vague when it came to the intuitive stuff but he was certainly no dummy. It was hard, however, to keep the questions casual when so much lay unanswered. The drink issue for one, and what on earth had led them to lose contact with one another for nigh on thirty years?

'What? Oh, all the usual things young people get up to – parties, dancing, picnics. And between them your mother and Margaret edited the student newspaper – very political, the pair of them. Frightening they were, with their rallies and marches. Not, of course, that they ever frightened me. I thought the world of them both, although your mother held a special place in my heart.'

Whether it was the booze talking or the blast from the past, Delilah had seldom heard her father wax so lyrical. Even his eyes shone with an unfamiliar gleam as he recalled the glory days. Looking at him, she felt the usual reserve between them softening. Reaching out, she placed a hand on the arm still clutching the brandy bottle and said warmly, 'Sounds great. I almost wish I'd been there.'

'Ah, well, I suppose you were, in a way. As a twinkle in my eye.' Amazing. Not only had she extended an affectionate gesture but he hadn't fidgeted or fudged in the way he normally did when emotion threatened to ruffle the rational surface. Perhaps he realized this because he shot a shy glance at Delilah before continuing, his other arm working furiously at his sauce as he spoke. 'Of course, that's where your name came from. Your mother always said she regarded Delilah as an early feminist.'

Now this was news. Delilah had always assumed that her name had been the result of a mad moment of suspect '70s taste rather than a political statement. The idea, it had to be said, was rather appealing.

'So how come Margaret wasn't around when I was born?' Her imagination had been working overtime on this one. Had there been some kind of bust-up, a trivial incident that spiralled out of control or even, heaven forfend, some sort of emotional thing that went horribly wrong? There were all kinds of ménages à trois, not all of them sexual, and Delilah wondered if it had been a sudden case of 'three's a crowd'. As it happened, she had hit upon the right area but totally the wrong participants.

'Let me see . . . How old are you now?'

How like her father to forget her age. 'Twenty-nine. I'll be thirty this year.'

'Ah, yes. Well, I expect Margaret had gone abroad by then, lecturing and researching all over the place. You must remember that by the time you came along we'd all left university a good ten years before.'

As if she could ever forget. Almost an afterthought, she'd spent her whole life feeling like an interloper in a perfect love story. More so since her mother's death. Apparently oblivious to the darkening of Delilah's face, her father continued.

'Your mother and I would get the odd postcard for a while, but we moved and then lost touch completely. Margaret was very busy building an academic career and we, well, we were also caught up in life and then you, amongst other things.'

Her pa had gone almost puce as he said this and his eyes glistened dangerously. Very, very rarely had she heard her father open up this much and it was always when they got on to the subject of her mother. Sixteen years after her death, the torch shone as brightly as ever. It was one of the things she found most endearing about him, as well as the most irritating. She had never been the recipient of such open affection from him, and that hurt.

'So why did she go? Itchy feet?' Delilah could sense that the crux of the matter lay within the answer to her question. As if to verify her hunch, her father deliberately stopped his stirring and put aside the wooden spoon, wiped his hands absently on a tea towel and then finally found the right framework for his words.

'Not really, no. She was very much in love with someone and that person decided to marry someone else. Poor Margaret could see no option but to get as far away as fast as possible, and who could blame her?'

Who, indeed? The romantic in Delilah thrilled to the thought even as she felt a wave of sympathy for her friend. Margaret had followed that noble tradition of fleeing abroad from a broken heart. OK, she hadn't exactly joined the French Foreign Legion, but it was close enough. She had to know more.

'And did you know this person well?' She tried to imagine Margaret, young and in love, a handsome rat on her pretty arm. It was a tough picture to conjure up.

'Oh, yes. Yes, indeed. We'd often go around together as a foursome. Still, these things happen in life.' Her father

was back to his tasting and stirring, glad of the distraction
in what for him was a mildly uncomfortable situation.

Delilah looked at his averted face, gaze fixed on the task
in hand, and a flash of realization hit her. He was shy,
desperately so. Not cold, not deliberately remote, just plain
old timid when it came to showing his emotions. Hardly a
revelation when it came to his type and generation, but teen
angst and a host of other resentments had blinded her to
the fact. He was also extremely loyal, as evidenced by the
care and discretion with which he described his old friend's
painful past. Delilah didn't want to push him, or to pry, but
there was one more thing she needed to know.

'Pa . . .'

'Mmm?' Still stirring away. Any minute now the sauce
would curdle under his attention.

'Was drink anything to do with it?' There, it was out.

Her father threw her an astonished look and demanded,
'To do with what?'

'You know – the break-up and everything. It's just that,
well, I've noticed that Margaret hardly ever drinks. In fact,
when I first met her she never did. But recently, and
especially now, she's swilling it with the best of them. If
you know what I mean,' she added hastily, aware that her
father might not appreciate her use of the vernacular.

Again he frowned, and this time seemed genuinely
puzzled. 'Not that I know of. As I said, Margaret was always
up for a spot of fun. And of course that included the odd
tipple. We weren't drunks or anything, but we certainly
knew how to have a good time. Why? What exactly is your
question?'

Now she felt like one of his students, caught out positing
a particularly ill thought theorem. Delilah could feel herself
flushing and felt about thirteen again but doggedly pursued
her point.

'No, I know you weren't alkies. I thought it was a little
odd, that's all. I was a bit worried about her. You know, she

could have been on medication or something. I mean, she has been a bit quiet recently and I was concerned.' Interesting how the reflex response kicks in. Try as she might, Delilah could not help her voice rising in the self-justificatory way familiar to parents of teenagers the world over. Her father must have noticed it too, because his tone took on an equally familiar placatory note as he aimed for reason.

'I'm sure you were, darling. You're very thoughtful. But if there was anything wrong she is obviously over it, and I can assure you that Margaret is not the type to turn to the bottle. She's far too strong a character for that.'

Yes, but even the strongest of us can only bend so long before we break, thought Delilah. To her father, however, she merely smiled and said, 'Yes, I'm sure you're right,' and the next minute the kitchen was invaded by an advance party consisting of Twizz and Fran, both ostensibly asking if they could help, although the real reason lay in their rumbling tummies.

The rest of the day passed in a contented orgy of eating, drinking and slumbering on the sofa, the traditional teatime walk attracting only three takers. In need of air, Delilah joined her father and Margaret on a tramp down the valley and up through the woods beyond, watching and listening as they chatted away or fell silent with equal ease. Delilah tried to imagine her mother as the third member of the triumvirate. That was tough enough, but then attempting to add a mysterious fourth member to the group was nigh on impossible. It was difficult to envisage the sort of man Margaret would go for – tall and thin? Short and sharp? The life and soul or the more retiring type? Whatever he had been like, he had to be a total shit to walk out on Margaret. Not to mention a blithering idiot.

As they returned to the house and came back within range, Delilah's mobile emitted another ear-splitting beep. Mumbling some inane excuse, she sneaked off to the downstairs loo and rapidly scrolled to her messages. There it was, shining out at her from the tiny screen. 'BIG X 4 XMAS'. Who needed mistletoe when there were the joys of the virtual kiss? Perched on the old wooden loo seat, she tapped back 'BIG X 4 U 2 THANX 4 PREZ', beaming as she did so. As she pressed the send button she closed her eyes and made a silent wish, hoping that it would somehow travel out into the ether and reach him along with her message. Illogical, she knew, but since when did logic have anything to do with the insanity of emotion?

Slipping out of the loo before someone came knocking, she headed for the kitchen to make her customary Christmas Day phone call to Jess. This comparison of booty had progressed from the days when Barbie's new outfits had been the subject of excited conversation. Now they were far more likely to enthuse over their own new finery, and this year Delilah had been thrilled to discover the perfect pale green pashmina all wrapped up with a sweet note from Jess.

'Forget fashion,' it had read, 'you always look fab,' signed off with a row of precise Jess-type kisses.

They might have been deemed passé, but Delilah had always hankered after a pashmina and this one was embroidered with a darker green thread in the most intricate pattern all around the edge, tiny bugle beads finishing off the effect. Rarely had she seen anything so beautiful and certainly nothing that was quite so 'her'. Even Matt's pressie, slung with great pride around her neck, shone a little dimmer alongside this, not least because she had been so anxious about their friendship. The work thing she could understand, up to a point, but it had never intruded this much before. On the few occasions they managed to bump into one another Jess appeared listless, pale and exhausted. Even their traditional decorating jamboree had diminished to a couple of hours spent alone, half-heartedly tacking up tinsel and cards until Jess burst through the door, late, flustered and full of apologies. True, they had smoothed that one over with the aid of a bottle of wine and an exchange of the 'sod-its', but it still hung in the air and the majority of the baubles remained in their box.

Jess had obviously taken this on board, despite her constant air of distraction. She knew how much Christmas meant to Delilah, who had always loved pageantry in any shape or form and the exchange of presents even more. Normally Delilah took an age to choose her gifts, thinking carefully about the recipient before landing on the one thing she considered perfect. This year, despite being up to her eyeballs with the shop, she had managed to pick out a fabulous leather bag for Jess, the sort of classic item that whispers style through its lines rather than through some obvious logo. And now Jess had returned the compliment, squeezing time out of her unbelievable schedule to hit the shops and buy with Delilah in mind. She was enormously touched and conveyed as much as soon as Jess picked up the phone.

'Jess, it's stunning. Perfect. Thank you so, so much.' She could almost hear Jess smiling at the other end of the line.

'Glad you like it. And thank you for my bag – gorgeous. Great choice. You having a good time, then?'

'Brilliant. How about you?' Good – Jess sounded more relaxed than she had done of late. No doubt the result of being back home with three brothers and her mad but lovely parents to distract her. There was no way you could remain stressed-out for long in that household. A propensity for cheerful chaos and a refusal to leave anyone alone for long meant that any form of deep thought was out of the question. Not even Jess could take her work home with her and expect to get away with it, and by the sound of things she hadn't even tried.

'Oh, y'know, mad as ever. Rory, put those down, you pig. Auntie Ellen gave them to me . . . sorry about that. The little bastard was nicking all my favourite chocs and didn't think I'd notice him sneaking up. I tell you, you've got to

have eyes in the back of your head to survive around here.'
Delilah could just picture the scene, although she would
hardly categorize the six foot three inch Rory as a 'little
bastard'. Sisterly prerogative. Satisfied that all was well with
Jess's world, Delilah rang off with lots of love being sent in
both directions and wandered back towards the small sitting
room to find everyone engaged in a game of contract whist.

It was amazing how seriously everyone took it as the
bids flew fast and furious and furtive glances were cast
at tightly held cards. Fran, in particular, was a revelation,
concentrating fiercely on the cards and acting as if the whole
thing was quite literally a matter of life and death. This
hitherto unseen competitiveness culminated in a comprehensive win for Fran, who let out a great whoop of joy and
then grinned sheepishly at the rest of them.

'Used to play that with my husband. Would never let me
win and hated it if I did.'

Now this was a new one. Fran had never mentioned a
husband before. Confronted by blank expressions, she
realized some explanation was required. 'It was only a brief
thing. We decided we were better off as friends. He's in
India now, doing his spiritual thing.'

Somehow Delilah could not picture Fran with a whist-
playing sandal-wearer. No wonder the marriage had
foundered.

'Of course,' Fran added hastily, 'there's nothing wrong
with anything spiritual. I tried to get into it but it wasn't
for me. Even went to the Ashram and hated it. All that self-
denial and stuff. I'm more of a material girl, if you know
what I mean.'

'Quite.' Geoffrey's comment was succinct but his eyes
were kind. 'Anyone for a nightcap?'

And with that the subject was dropped, although Delilah
continued to ponder its ramifications. It added another piece
to the jigsaw that was Fran, filled in a few gaps. She would
love to find out more in the fullness of time. Several night-

caps apiece having been enjoyed, a happy party eventually
hiccuped its way to bed, the festive spirit once again perme-
ating hearts, minds and stomachs.

Delilah had always thought Boxing Day represented the
greatest anticlimax of them all. Generally her father would
take himself off to his study, leaving Delilah to her own
desultory devices. There were only so many dreadful programmes you could sit through before getting a desperate
urge to hurl the Christmas tree through the telly, and only
so many articles you could read before ennui took its inevitable toll. This one, however, started in true Twizzle style.

While the rest of them had gathered in the kitchen for a
civilized breakfast, Twizz had tiptoed out the back door for
her customary coffee and a fag. It was unfortunate that she
had chosen to wear the brand new pair of in-your-face
animal print trousers she had so thoughtfully given herself,
and doubly so that Harvey was also snuffling around the
lawn, indulging in the canine form of an early morning
routine. One look at the trousers and he was off, racing
towards her as if life and his masculinity depended on it.
Her shrieks and shouts of, 'Get off, you little bugger!' alerted
the rest of them to the fact that something was afoot and
they rushed as one to the window to be treated to the sight
of Twizz frantically jerking her leg as she attempted to shake
the humping Harvey off. Game dog that he was, he clung
on grimly as with glazed eyes and pink tongue hanging out
he dedicated his most energetic efforts to impregnating her
shin. It was only when Geoffrey turned the hose on him
that he reluctantly desisted and slunk off to sulk beneath a
bush. By this time, Margaret and Delilah were weak with
laughter although it was all a bit too graphic for Fran, the
closest she ever came to nature being the pre-packaged meat
counter in Tesco Metro.

'Christ, thought I was a goner there.' The stress of it
all had reduced Twizz to a chain-smoking wreck but her

quivering state did nothing to impress her more country-wise companions.

'And you a good Aussie girl. You must have coped with worse than that out in the boondocks.' Revenge at last for all those straight from the hip comments. Delilah could have kissed the now detumescent Harvey, although there was always the danger that it might get him going again. As it was, Twizz had rapidly changed into a drier, more sober outfit that only another denim could possibly have found sexually attractive.

'Less of the boondocks, mate. I'm from Sydney and the only bloody wildlife we have there hangs out in the bars.' At last, her hands had stopped trembling and she could take a restorative swig of coffee without sloshing it all over the place.

'Not been out of London much, then?' enquired Geoffrey innocently.

'Nah, makes me nervous. Give me a city pub any day. Not that it's not lovely around here,' Twizz added hastily. 'Great place you've got here. We've had a fantastic time, haven't we?' She looked around for support, and much enthusiastic nodding signalled a general consensus of assent.

'Pity that you're set on going back this evening.' Geoffrey was looking at Delilah as he spoke and she shrugged help-lessly.

'I know, Pa, but I've got to be there to open up the shop.' Not to mention charge up her mobile in case Matt decided to call. Pathetic, she knew, but she had forgotten to pack the charger and the phone was flashing its last gasp. Although, judging by the fact that Matt's phone seemed to be perma-nently switched off, he was probably in a similar plight. Whatever the reasons, she felt a mild sense of panic at not being contactable – something she dared not confess to her accompanying crew.

'We could always go back first thing in the morning.

Didn't take that long to get here, did it, Fran, all things considered?' Coming from Twizz, that was a real accolade. She must be having a good time if she was trying to drag it out, freakish canine behaviour notwithstanding.

'Just over an hour, as long as the car holds out.' Fran, too, appeared anxious to stay.

Delilah was touched even as she silently cursed them. She had worried about what they would make of her fusty father rattling around in a house full of memories, but it seemed that her anxiety had been ill-founded. Little did she realize that for them the house held nothing more than warmth and hospitality and her father was an integral part of it. He might be slightly out of touch with reality but that was no bad thing, considering the company he found himself keeping. Delilah was far more like him than she realized, a fact that would have had her protesting in adolescent horror had it been voiced.

In a last-ditch attempt to get back to that charger, Delilah went for a grown-up assessment of the situation. 'It would mean getting up at the crack of dawn . . . and you know what you're like in the mornings . . .'

'You can talk!'

She had to admit that Twizz had a point. Many a morning had passed with the pair of them incapable of speech until enough cappuccinos had passed their lips and loosened their tongues.

'OK, OK. Crack of dawn it is. Now, someone put the kettle on and we can move straight into elevenses.' Which was, of course, what Christmas had truly become – a nonstop orgy of eating and drinking with an occasional nod to the spiritual to appease the Frans of this world.

'Allow me.' Her father was up and out of his chair, an extra spring in his step now that he could rely on there being jovial companionship for at least another day. He was far too self-sufficient ever to be really lonely, but the presence of his daughter and her friends meant a great deal to him, in his own undemonstrative way. He was delighted to buzz around the place playing the perfect host, if never quite the perfect parent.

'There we go... Darling, would you get that?' Far happier fussing around with a pot of tea than answering the phone, Geoffrey piled whatever food offerings he could find in front of his guests as Delilah obediently picked up the receiver.

'It's for you.'

'Oh, right.' Geoffrey was endearingly baffled by the fact that a phone call in his own home might actually be for him. He reluctantly abandoned his ministering to the bloated masses and spoke gingerly into the phone.

'Hello? Hello? My God, Archie, is that you? How marvellous to hear from you! Where are you, old fellow? With your sister... well, you must come over. Delilah is here, along with some pals of hers, and you'll never guess who is amongst them. Margaret! Margaret Pilkington! Yes, that Margaret. Hell of a surprise, I can tell you. That would be wonderful. Well, what about this evening? Oh, oh I see. Ah, well apparently they have to get back to London in the morning. Yes, all of them. Yes, I know. Archie, hang on a second...'

Holding his hand over the receiver, Geoffrey looked over at Margaret, who had been listening intently ever since Archie's name had been mentioned. Delilah's scalp prickled. Could this Archie be the mysterious heartbreaker?

'Margaret, my dear, Archie Outhwaite's on the phone. Back in the country for Christmas. Says he'd love to come over and see us both but there's some sort of family thing tonight. Don't suppose you'd like to stay on another day or so... catch up and all that...'

Delilah flicked a glance at Margaret, hesitating over her Breakfast Blend, and blurted out, 'Go on, Margaret. You could always get the train back. Couldn't she, Pa?'

'Of course. Be happy to drop you off at the station. No

trouble at all.' Anxious not to press her but evidently keen, Geoffrey looked questioningly at Margaret.

'Well, if it's no trouble I'd be delighted. It'd be lovely to see Archie again.' How easy was that? Delilah was thrilled, as was her father, who immediately removed his hand from the mouthpiece and announced, 'All set, Archie. Come over tomorrow evening, any time after seven. Margaret and I are very much looking forward to seeing you.'

His sentiments were reiterated by Margaret, who took a sip of her tea and declared, 'Archie Outhwaite. Well, I never! First your father and now this. Marvellous, absolutely marvellous.' She must have been overwhelmed with excitement because she gripped Delilah's wrist to emphasize her words; the equivalent of a ferocious hug as far as Margaret's tactility quotient was concerned.

Only the fact that Decadence's first ever, eagerly anticipated sale started in the morning prevented Delilah from suggesting that they all stay on another day. She was dying to sneak a peek at the mysterious Archie but pragmatism won the day. It was not for this reason alone that they piled regretfully into Fran's car early the next morning. Delilah could not remember a Christmas at home she had enjoyed quite so much, and both Fran and Twizz seemed equally loath to leave. They hugged her father in turn, which was almost affection overload as far as the reticent Geoffrey was concerned, and chugged off down the lane with many a glance back at the pair of them standing waving outside the front door.

Harvey was nowhere to be seen, no doubt out attacking some other unsuspecting inanimate object. At this, Twizzle was vastly relieved. She had been anticipating the same sort of tortuous farewell scene that took place after the vast majority of her sexual encounters. It was probably only the fact that Harvey was a Jack Russell that prevented him from breaking down and begging her to stay.

Thirteen

They got to the shop a bare five minutes before opening time, thanks as much to a toilet pit stop as anything else. 'Told you to leave off the coffee,' was Twizz's unsolicited advice as Fran made a mad dash for the loo. Then there was a sticky moment when the engine lost all signs of life until a final, desperate turn of the key kick-started it back into action. All in all, Delilah was delighted when they finally turned into Durber Road and she saw that her baby was still standing, if looking somewhat forlorn. A flick of the light switches and one brew-up later and it was as if Christmas had never happened. The precious phone charger was located and plugged in to do its work, but in the meantime Matt's mobile was still sending her straight to voicemail, its standard network message not even offering her the vicarious thrill of listening to his voice. She toyed with the idea of calling his home phone but that would really have been sad, especially under the all-seeing eye of Twizz.

There was no mad rush but the afternoon brought with it a steady influx of family escapees and those with fresh cash to spend. Fran toddled off home just before lunch after big hugs all round, Christmas together having cemented their friendship. It seemed quieter and emptier after she had gone, and at four thirty Delilah and Twizz voted themselves a cheering sherry, the legacy of unwanted loot from under Geoffrey's Christmas tree.

Her father's loss was their gain, and they were just cracking open the Tio Pepe when the shop door opened and in swept a woman with home counties stamped all over her. From the tips of her careful blonde coiffure to the immaculate cashmere sweater and shoes worn for town, she was the elegant epitome of her type. Aware that this was the sort of customer who tended to abuse her husband's gold card, Delilah passed the bottle to Twizz and pleasantly enquired, 'Can I help at all?'

'Actually, you can.' The woman's discreetly made-up face gave little away but there was a definite note of anxiety in her voice. Delilah's antennae twitched into action. 'I believe that we have a mutual friend in common . . .' she began, the tiny hesitation before the word 'friend' adding fuel to the fires of intrigue.

'Oh, yes?' Well schooled in the art of letting the customer show her hand, Delilah tried to sound as neutral as she possibly could.

The woman appeared to be wrestling with her words. She opened her mouth, shut it and then cleared her throat before beginning again. 'Er . . . yes. Yes, her name is Margaret Pilkington. I was a little worried about her.'

'Worried?' A twinge of alarm clutched at Delilah but she reasoned calmly with herself. Margaret had appeared perfectly fine when she had waved them off only that morning and she was in more than capable hands. This woman was obviously either not au fait with the current situation or she knew something Delilah didn't, and she would bet Matt's Tiffany heart that it was the latter. Wearing a face that would have done a professional poker player proud, Delilah smiled sweetly and waited her out, unwilling to give anything away until she knew exactly where this was coming from. It took the woman all of about ten seconds to crack.

What had been an immaculate mask crumpled and her
nose appeared pinched with the effort of not crying. Unable
to contain herself, she opened her coral lipsticked mouth
and blurted, 'Oh, please, if you know where she is then
please, please tell me. I've phoned and I've rung the doorbell
and the car is outside but there's no sign of life. I even went
round to the back door, terrified that she'd had an accident
and was lying there . . .'

'Whoa! Hang on a second . . . look, why don't you sit
down? Twizz, have you got a tissue?' The woman was by
now dabbing futilely at her eyes with a finger, unwilling
even in her current state to risk the pale cashmere sweater
against the effects of mid-brown mascara.

'It's all right, I have one here somewhere.' Now she was
unclasping her good bag, digging around sightlessly for her
travel packet of Kleenex. They waited respectfully while
she extracted one and blew her well chiselled nose. More
composed, she looked apologetically at them both and said,
'I am terribly sorry. But I've been so afraid that something
awful must have happened. I sent a card, I left messages
and haven't heard a thing. Not a dicky bird. When she
didn't call me on Christmas Day, I just knew that something
must be very wrong indeed.' Her voice wobbled again and
Delilah raised a hand as if to ward off her fears.

'Margaret's OK. She's absolutely fine. The reason she
hasn't returned your calls is because she's been away.' Even
that might be more than she needed to know but Delilah
couldn't help it. The woman looked utterly desperate and
she was sure that Margaret would forgive her for imparting
such an innocuous item of information.

'Away? Where? With whom?' There was an interesting
new timbre to her voice. Something sharp, demanding.
Reminiscent of something altogether too raw. This time
Delilah took a longer beat before replying.

'With . . . friends.'

'Friends? Which friends? I mean, anyone in particular?

That I might know?' Realizing that she was giving herself away, the woman attempted to batten down the hatches of her rising hysteria. It was all most bizarre. If she'd been a man, Delilah would have sworn that the jagged edge in her voice signalled jealousy, so uncontrollable was its quality. If she'd been a man . . .

'Actually, she's with my father. Geoffrey Honey.' It was a calculated risk and it paid off big time. The woman's mouth formed a small 'o' of astonishment and she echoed, 'Geoffrey Honey?' in a way that confirmed at the very least no small acquaintanceship.

'Geoffrey Honey?' she said again, twisting her tissue in her hands as her mind worked over this unexpected fragment of information. 'Geoffrey Honey who was at King's with . . .'

'Margaret and my mother. Yes, that Geoffrey Honey. And you are . . . ?'

'Laura Godfrey. Laura Miller as was. So you are Geoffrey's daughter. Well, I never.' Her hands had stopped working at the tissue and her gaze had swum back into focus, fixing its sights on Delilah's face. It apparently met with her satisfaction for Laura's mouth stretched into a watery smile before she pronounced, 'Not so much your father's daughter as your mother's. I was sorry to hear about poor Olivia's death.'

Delilah inclined her head in the way she always did when acknowledging sentiments which had become familiar over time. Familiar, if no easier to bear.

'Thank you.' Still, she was waiting, hoping that Laura would say something to confirm her growing suspicions. She had an inkling that she was right on the edge of indiscretion and there was nothing like silence to topple someone into the pit of disclosure. She only hoped that Twizz would keep her big mouth shut long enough to encourage Laura to open hers. She needn't have worried – Twizz was far too fascinated to toss in her tuppence worth and surprisingly sensitive when it came to situations such as this. Their patience was well rewarded.

Once again averting her eyes, Laura took a deep breath and slid inexorably into confessional mode. 'I was at college with both your mother and your father. And with Margaret, too, of course.'

'Mmmm.' Delilah hardly dared breathe, terrified she might say the wrong thing and scare her off completely. It was like coaxing a hamster out from behind a skirting board, only a darn sight more frustrating.

'I haven't seen your father since, oh, the year we all graduated. Gosh, what a long time ago that was.'

'Nnnn?' An interrogatory grunt, just to keep her going.

'So, how is he?'

'Who?' So intent was Delilah on squeezing the juice out of her that the tangential question took her by surprise. She looked in confusion at Laura, who was waiting politely for a sensible answer.

'Oh . . . ah, my father. He's fine. Very well indeed, thank you.' Oh God, she wanted to scream, Just cut to the chase! Dish the dirt! Tell me what I think I already know. Instead, she folded her hands in a totally alien gesture and tilted her head to one side as receptively as she possibly could.

'Oh, good. Good. And you said you saw Margaret only this morning?'

Ah, this was more like it. Restraining herself, Delilah nodded again and stated noncommittally, 'Yes, I did.'

'Oh.'

Impasse. Laura lowered her eyes and chewed this over for a moment. 'And you say she's well? And happy?' Her voice rose plaintively on the second part of her question and it flashed across Delilah's mind that revenge for Margaret was within her grasp. This, however, was real life rather than soap opera and she had to keep Margaret's best interests at heart, even while her protective instincts came into play. Her mind and body ached from the restraint but she determined to stick to her course.

'She's fine – and happier than she's been in quite a while. Wouldn't you say, Twizz?' Despite her best intentions, Delilah couldn't help slipping in that little dig.

'What? Oh, yeah, on top of the world. We had a ball this Christmas.' Twizz had that faux innocent look on her face that spoke of impending mischief. Delilah wondered quite how much she had cottoned on.

'Oh . . .' Sounding deflated, Laura seemed at a loss. Delilah decided there was nothing for it but to help her out.

'Shall I tell her you called? Give her a message?'

'A message? Um . . . no. No, nothing special. Perhaps you could just tell her that I dropped by. In passing.' The snapping shut of the handbag clasp indicated that Laura was doing her best to rally for the return to whatever situation she had created for herself. Shoulders back, she smoothed her hair and then rose to her feet. Delilah and Twizz rose with her and the three of them stood there for one of those awkward parting pauses.

'Well, it was lovely to meet you, Delilah. Do give my best to your father when you next speak to him.'

'Oh, I most certainly will.'

If Laura had noticed the absence of reciprocal goodwill she refrained from reacting. Gathering herself together, she nodded in Twizz's direction. 'Nice to meet you too.'

'Likewise.' So choked up was she with questions that Twizz could barely manage to get a coherent word out. They all smiled stiffly at one another.

'Well.' Held rigid by a mix of embarrassment and horror, Delilah watched Laura's mouth attempt to form words that simply would not come. Her face worked and she appeared to be yet again on the verge of tears, unwilling to leave and unable to stay. Finally she gulped, cracked a social grimace and was gone, a lingering trace of Arpège the only evidence

that she'd ever been there. They exhaled as one and Delilah
dived for the sherry bottle.

'Bloody hell, mate, who on earth was that?' Twizz had
got there before her, cork already out and amber liquid
being splashed with indecent haste into the waiting glasses.
There was only so much discretion a girl could manage in
one afternoon.

Without so much as a second's hesitation, Delilah took a
generous swig, coughed, spluttered and said, 'That, if I am
not mistaken, was Margaret's lesbian lover.'

'You what!' Twizz gaped at her, for once dumbfounded
by the random weirdness of life.

'It was something my father told me about Margaret,
some story about this lover who did the dirty on her. I don't
know why but when that woman walked in it all fell into
place. The fact that Margaret had never spoken about it, the
way she went all quiet and mysterious on us. It's to do with
Laura, I just know it is. I could feel it in my bones. Then I
could see it written all over her face.' Delilah's eyes were
shining with the certainty of someone who has stumbled
on the truth and has held on to it with both hands.

Twizz was not so easily convinced. 'Oh come on, give
me a break. She's just an old friend who's maybe fallen out
with Margaret in some way and wants to make it up to her.
I mean, how many lesbians do you know who go around
in cashmere jumpers talking like that? Go on, name me one.
Ha, you can't, can you?'

When Twizz was like this, Delilah could cheerfully have
wrung her scrawny neck. Antipodean straightforwardness
was all very well, but not when it relied on the bleeding
obvious as a benchmark for life.

'So what would you expect? Short hair, dungarees and a
copy of *The Second Sex* tucked under one arm?' So that was
a bit snide. Twizz could take it.

'You think I'm so bloody unsophisticated, don't you? We
do have Mardi Gras back home, you know. And lipstick

lesbians have penetrated as far as the "former colonies".'
Not the best choice of words but it would do in the circumstances.

'You only have to look at *Prisoner Cell Block H* to realize
that . . .' Delilah quipped and it was a stand-off to see who
could stay on her high horse the longest. It was a draw,
both of them cracking at exactly the same moment and, like
all their spats, this collapsed amid hoots of laughter. Which
was a good thing, considering they were thrust together in
the small but perfectly formed confines of Decadence for
up to ten hours a day, six days a week. Longer, when the
week was as busy as this one turned out to be.

Three days after Boxing Day and the sales were in full
swing. Word of mouth was a powerful factor, and it had
taken no more than a small sign in the window to advertise
their entry into elbow land. If they thought car boot sales
were a hotbed of bad behaviour, this was an eye-opener.
Perfectly respectable middle-class matrons slugged it out
with the trashier fash pack to get at the goods and, as the
days passed, the pace only accelerated. Back from seasonal
duty visits and burning with the need for retail therapy,
this bunch released their pent-up festive aggression in an
outpouring of snarling and snapping, the like of which had
previously been seen only on safari.

In the midst of all this, the flowers arrived. Too dazed
from dealing with her crazed customers to realize that this
one was different, Delilah absently took a huge bouquet
from a woman standing at the cash desk and began looking
for the price tag. It was only when she came across the card
in its little envelope that it dawned upon her. Thanking the
woman profusely, she tore it open and pulled out the card
within.

'Miss you loads,' it read, signed off with a row of kisses
and a 'Love, Matt.' Written, inevitably, in a florist's loopy
hand. Turning to Twizz with a broad grin on her face,

Delilah interrupted her frantic wrapping and ringing up to demand, 'Do we have a vase?'

'Over there.' A distracted Twizz waved vaguely in the direction of the shelves, indicating their small selection of bejewelled bud vases.

'No, I mean for these.' A ripple of impatience rustled through the queue in front of them but Delilah did not care. A well timed bunch did it every time and she was no exception to the power of flowers. In amongst the lilies and twisted willow were a gratifying number of red roses, proof if ever it were needed that Matt was falling as fast as she was.

'Bloody hell, they're nice.' Finally taking the time for a proper look, Twizz was suitably awestruck at the size and splendour of the bouquet. 'There's that bucket out back. Only thing that's big enough,' she added, before enquiring, 'Need I ask who sent them?'

'You need not,' declared Delilah loftily, before abandoning Twizz to the howling mob as she went off to see to her flowers. It wasn't every day that this happened and she wanted to snatch time to savour it. Serving her customers would have to come second while she marvelled over the deep crimson petals and arranged the willow in just the right way.

The bucket disguised by an artfully draped length of cloth, the afternoon proceeded much as before. Now and again Delilah would glance over at it and feel a frisson of both delight and desire. There was only so much you could say in a text message, and although she had transmitted her gratitude immediately, it wasn't the same. She was longing to speak to him in person but, frustratingly, his mobile remained permanently switched off. There was nothing for it but to concentrate on her clientele, by now behaving worse than ever. It appeared that, as the afternoon wore on, things only got more fractious. More than once the girls had to referee over an item, Delilah only just managing to declare one woman the rightful owner before said sexy camisole was ripped clean in half. Bargain fever also did strange things to discernment, and several customers had to be talked out of buying something two sizes too small simply because it was cheap and their optimism boundless. The competitive spirit encouraged the unlikeliest purchases, and the pair of them shared more than one quiet giggle over the glitzy riding crops and homages to bondage finding their way into suburban homes. At least their hapless husbands would think Christmas had come all over again.

It was as she was placing the last pair of crystal-studded handcuffs in their gift box that the phone call finally came. As soon as she heard the first ring Delilah knew it was Matt. Leaving the rest of the transaction to a tired-out Twizz, she grabbed the receiver and gulped out, 'Hello?'

'Delilah?' He sounded a million miles away, his voice faint against the fuzziness of the line.

'Matt? Can you hear me?' Turning away for an illusion of privacy, Delilah tried not to shout.

'Loud and clear. How's my girl?' The crackling had stopped and she could hear the chuckle in his voice.

'Thank you so much for the flowers . . .' Feeling unaccountably at a loss, Delilah wished with all her heart he was there in front of her rather than at the end of a temperamental telephone line.

'My pleasure. I wish I could have sent myself with them.' He was fading again, his words dissolving into static.

'Me too.' She couldn't keep the longing out of her voice. 'Matt?'

'Hmm?' He was really muffled now and she spoke louder as if to compensate.

'Can't wait to see you. I miss you so much.' Delilah was aware that everyone in the shop could hear but she was past caring. Ostentatiously not listening in, Twizz sensed trouble ahead.

His goodbyes disappeared into a snowstorm of static but

it was enough for Delilah. Aching back forgotten, she sailed home that evening and was even in early the next day. It was no different to the preceding day, save that Delilah's feet hurt that tiny bit more and her cheeks were beginning to follow suit from the effort of diplomatic smiling. A cushion of happiness could only help for so long. It was at the tail end of the scrum that Dan walked into the shop, his keen intelligence instantly taking in the scene as if it were an interesting anthropological experiment. Which, for him, it probably was. Harassed and harried, Delilah was busy persuading a punter that fuschia was not the most flattering choice for a woman of a certain age and complexion. Steering her instead towards the cream ensemble at exactly the same price, she tried a tactful, 'This will be so much more next season,' but her customer was having none of it. Realizing that this was a no-win situation, and that she ought to have guessed as much from the cerise fingernails and matching shoes, Delilah graciously conceded defeat and allowed Twizz to wrap up the offending spoils. Her policy had always been to encourage repeat custom with ruthless honesty, but there were some instances when it was best to keep your mouth shut and your coffers open. No doubt this woman would be back for the gold lamé she had lingered over and frankly there would be nothing Delilah could do to stop her. She only hoped her partner had a sense of humour, if indeed there was a man in Ms Mutton's life.

Mentally slapping herself for this brief bout of bitchiness, Delilah turned back to the throng and instead of yet another designer-clad dame, found herself face to face with Dan.

'Oh my God, it's you,' was her first, unflattering response.

'Nice to see you, too,' he replied, affably enough. He gave her a searching glance before extending his observation to the chaotic piles of goods around him. His eyes flicked over Matt's flowers, resplendent in their bucket, registered them and moved on. Taking in the flimsy underwear, the jewellery and the more outrageous objects, his gaze lit on the piles of Oral Sex, some packaged into pretty boxes and some lying enticingly loose on a great silver platter. His hand reached out and he barely managed a 'May I?' before sinking appreciative teeth into one of the luscious orbs. His eyes closed for a second to denote total ecstasy as the chocolate coated his mouth in its complexity of flavour, then opened again for him to pronounce, 'Fucking unbelievable,' in ringing tones.

One or two Kensington types standing close by edged away, mouths pursed, and Delilah couldn't help but grin.

'Here, have another one, they're organic,' she offered, holding out the platter in a way he found completely irresistible. The woman he lusted after was feeding him chocolate to die for – heaven would have to be beyond incredible to compete with this. Refusal for the sake of politeness was not his style. Without a moment's hesitation he reached for another and wrapped his taste buds around it with an enthusiasm Delilah had never seen before in a man. Chocolate was normally a female thing and yet here was a guy who so obviously got off on it. It would have been an enormous turn-on had not her own appetites been so thoroughly taken care of elsewhere. Literally so, at present. Still, there were finally text messages, each fruitier than the last, and another hurried phone call from what had sounded like the noisiest bar in town, even though Matt swore he was saving his strength for the skiing.

Dan, however, was expending all his energies on savouring the bonbons. After another bout of appreciative eyerolling, he licked his lips one last time and demanded to know, 'What on earth are these?'

'Oral Sex.' It was their name, after all, and she had never been one to shirk the truth. After a pause to take that one in Dan was roaring with laughter, his sense of humour tickled as much as his taste buds.

'Seriously? But that's brilliant! Did you name them or did they . . . ah . . . come like that?'

'Actually, it was my idea,' she retorted.

'Well, I think it's superb. And so is your shop. Simply amazing.'

His genuine delight in everything he saw was heart-warming, if a shade disconcerting. This was the guy, after all, who spent all day and night being a technofreak and what spare time he had found him strung out on the stress of it all. Admittedly he had been far more user-friendly at the engagement party, but Delilah had still felt as if there were a 'handle with care' sign hanging around his neck. Now, however, he appeared amazingly relaxed, picking up candles and giving the lingerie a more than cursory glance. Dan was definitely a man for the hands-on approach. When he got to the CockTail glasses his lips twitched and he shot a very naughty look at Delilah.

'Subtle.'

'Aren't they?' Interesting that. It took most people a moment to realize the implications of the suggestive stem but he'd spotted it straight off. Clearly someone who was in touch with his baser tastes.

Finally having had his fill, Dan leaned back against the counter, surveyed the now near empty shop and proclaimed it, 'Fabulous. You've got something really good going here.'

'Thanks. I hope so. Can I offer you a cup of tea or anything? I expect Twizz and I will be having something a tad stronger. It's been yet another of those days.' Ears alert even when engaged in keying a complicated transaction, Twizz nodded her enthusiastic assent. The end of the after-noon rush had prevented close inspection, but what she saw of this visitor, she liked. A lot.

'Mmmm.' Dan made one of those vague noises that could mean anything and continued to stare into inner space, obviously off on another thought plane altogether.

Delilah sighed. She knew it had been too good to last.

'We have tea, coffee, sherry . . .' She barely restrained herself from clicking her fingers in front of his face. Thankfully, he came back to earth with a start.

From her corner by the till, it occurred to Twizz that there was only one other person she had seen do that quite so well. And that person was even now standing there, hair flying around her face and foot tapping with impatience. Hypocrite.

'Sorry. Um . . . tea, tea would be fine. Thanks.'

'Sure you wouldn't like a slug of sherry in it? Might do you good.' There was something about Dan that did this to her, brought out her mothering nature. Rather than think about that one in too much detail, Delilah dipped out back and flicked on the kettle, at the same time extracting the sherry bottle from its hiding place under the loo rolls. The temptation to keep taking a surreptitious swig was far too great to leave it within reach.

'There we go. Sugar?' Delilah dumped his mug down by the sofa and indicated with a flick of an eyebrow that Twizz's sherry was ready and waiting for her just as soon as she had dispensed with the last customer.

'Sorry?' This guy was almost worse than her father when it came to being lost in cogitation. She held up a teaspoon as a cipher and he got the message.

'Oh, right. Um, not for me, thanks.' Dan picked up his steaming mug and took a thoughtful sip. 'You know, this place is crying out for a web site.'

'You never give up, do you?' Delilah was still not sure about that one. After all, the whole point of Decadence was its touchy-feeliness. Whack that on the Web and its sex appeal would be lost in a welter of 2D images and inadequate descriptions.

'Think about it – you have an appeal and a range that would easily reach a national, if not international, audience. All you need is a means to access them and, more importantly, to let them access you. And for that, the Web is perfect. Even *you* have to admit it.' He was such an evangelist, his face earnest as he preached to the unconverted. Delilah could see his point but took umbrage at his choice of words.

'Even *I*? What exactly do you mean by that?'

Dan loved it when she was riled. For one thing, it made those remarkable eyes shine all the brighter and, for another, it meant that he was getting through to her on one level at least.

'You did say you were not exactly a fan of technology, if I remember rightly.' Such reasonableness would have been infuriating had it not been married to that disconcerting directness. It was the absence of malice that always saved the day for Dan and it was to this that Delilah responded.

'True. But I don't think a web site is what we need. For starters I know bugger all about it and I wouldn't have the time or resources to run one, even if I wanted to.' And in any case, she wanted to add, can't you see that this is absolutely not what I am about? That this is my baby and I know how to nurture it, thank you very much.

Picking up on the subtext, Dan said soothingly, 'Look, it was only an idea. I can see how much this place means to you and I wouldn't have suggested it if I didn't think it could work. As for all the technical bits – piece of piss. Take it from me.'

'Hey, Del, it's worth thinking about. You don't want to get left behind in the Internet rush.' Having finished with the faffing and wrapping, Twizz was ready for a drink. Debate was a welcome extra, and besides, there was something about this guy.

Outnumbered, Delilah threw up a hand and conceded, 'OK, OK. I'll think about it. Now get off my back, the pair of you.'

This was all the encouragement Dan needed. In his business, the ability to run with an idea was half the battle, and now that he had her at least wriggling around the bait it was time to get her hooked.

'You know, I reckon Oral Sex could be an absolute winner,' he said in all seriousness.

'Always is for me,' Twizz muttered into her glass but Dan was not to be so easily deflected. He looked straight at Delilah and she was at a loss for words. If he hadn't been her boyfriend's best mate she could have dismissed the whole thing out of hand but he was totally upfront and obviously keen. There was nothing for it but to play him along a bit and hope he'd quickly see the sense of her arguments.

'That's as maybe, but think of the logistics. I only have this tiny space, the one assistant' – this with a nod to Twizz, who was guzzling sherry and itching for a fag – 'shipping chocolates all over the place would be a nightmare and I simply don't have the infrastructure to do it.'

'You may not, but I do.' At least she was thinking about it, albeit negatively. Now all he had to do was deal with the practicalities and it was in the bag. He could feel it in his bones and they had never let him down, bar once during a game of rugby and that didn't count. 'I told you about Grub.com – that besides being a portal we own quite a few of the actual sites. It means we get a larger slice of the action and it also comes in useful where you are concerned.'

'How so?' Delilah was beginning to see his point but she wasn't yet ready to concede. In any case, it was fun watching him lay all his cards on the table.

'It's obvious. The infrastructure you need is already in place and you have a product we could sell easily. We could set you up with your own web page and all the dirty work would be done through us.'

When Dan got excited, his hands began to flap about in a most unbusinesslike fashion. As they did so now, Delilah began to fear for her fixtures and fittings. It wasn't that he was particularly large – more that his personality expanded to fill the space, making everything around him seem smaller and more fragile. She wondered how she had never noticed this before.

'And what would you get out of this? Presuming that your reasons are not entirely altruistic?' She softened her words with a knowing grin and he laughed as he opened his hands in a placatory gesture.

'Of course they're not. Although I'm not as mercenary as you appear to think. We'd work on a percentage basis, one that would allow both of us to make a decent profit. Can't say fairer than that.'

'I'll think about it.'

'You'll think about it?'

'OK, I'll think about it very hard. Now will that do?' God, but he could be persistent. Even through her laughter, Delilah caught the look of triumph on his face. Gotcha! it said. Well, maybe, but Delilah was no pushover. Especially not when it came to Decadence.

'I'd better be off. Got a meeting to go to – just around the corner, as it happens.' Better slip that one in, just in case she thought he had stalker-type tendencies. As a variation on the 'I was just passing' technique it would have to do, even if there was a distinctly sceptical look on her face.

'Around here?' And dressed like that, she might have added, reassessing his baggy pants and sneakers in one swift glance.

'Some of the best start-ups still happen in people's back bedrooms.' Dan was entirely unflappable. A useful asset when it came to persuading people to part with their millions and even more so when it came to situations such as this.

'You will think about what I said?' Doggedly having one last go at the door, Dan would have given Harvey a run for his money. Although, hopefully, he could keep a tighter lid on his appetites.

'Course I will. But I'm not promising anything.'

Even while he was dying to make her say yes to everything, Dan had to respect her stance. It was that very
strength that had shone through in the photograph. The one
which, despite himself, he kept safe between the pages of
his favourite book, taking it out now and again to keep his
dreams alive. Of course, the real thing was so much more.
So much so that he decided he had better quit while he was
ahead and depart before he did something stupid.

'I'll call you,' were his parting words, ones that sprang
from a thousand male lips and generally carried limited
currency. In this case, though, he meant what he said. Absolutely. But then, Dan always did, often to his detriment. At
least as far as the opposite sex was concerned.

With a hint of amusement still playing around the corners
of her lips, Delilah closed the shop door and shot the bolt.
The end of another day. Another successful day. What a
difference a bit of publicity could make. True, it could only
set the ball rolling but, once in motion, it was unstoppable.
There had already been enquiries from other, glossier maga-
zines and she was becoming an expert at playing spot the
snooping stylist. Soon they would be tapping her for free
loans in return for coverage and then she would know
they'd truly made it. And all of it was due in no small
part to her happy helper, more and more deserving of that
sobriquet these days. Making money obviously suited her
meritocratic instincts, especially when it was from those
who clearly had plenty. Delilah looked at Australia's own
version of Robin Hood, splayed out with her sherry on the
sofa, and giggled.

'What's so bloody funny? And who was he, by the way?'

So she was more grumpy than happy. Delilah could
hardly claim to be Snow White herself. Especially not when
Matt was around.

'Dan? One of Matt's mates. His best mate, in fact. They
were at school together.'

'Oh yeah? Seems like a good bloke. And very sexy, in a

broody kind of way.' That was interesting, coming from
Twizz. Intense was definitely not her style, preferring cor-
poreal to the cranial any night of the week.

'You think so? Yes, I suppose he is. To be honest, I hadn't
really thought about it.'

Like hell she hadn't. Delilah might be kidding herself
that all her electrons were safely streaming one way, but
Twizz knew better than that. And if that wasn't an under-
current flowing in a different direction, she would hang up
her Geiger counter now.

Fourteen

New Year's Eve did not get off to a promising start. For one thing, Delilah's mobile had finally died an inexplicable death and there was simply no time to do anything about it and, for another, she still had no clue what she was doing that evening. The past few days had whizzed by and, come closing time, any partying was distinctly unplanned.

'We could always crash Jake's. I'm sure he won't mind. Probably welcome two gorgeous creatures like us, considering the dags he usually hangs around with.' It was a thought, but not a pleasant one. The last thing Delilah was up for was a backpackers' booze fest. The lure of home and hearth held much more appeal, deeply sad though that might seem. Maturity was obviously imminent. If only Jess had been around, they could have gone for the civilized option and slobbed out on the sofa. Much as Delilah adored parties, neither of them were big fans of the New Year nightmare. A takeaway and the telly had more than once been the celebration of choice, loath though they were to admit it in public. Far better than some romantic interlude that aimed for a fumble at midnight and invariably went horribly wrong or, even worse, those dinner parties where as soon as pudding was digested the Twister mat appeared. Poor old Fran was off to just such an event, coerced into it by her old school chum Felicity. More fool her. Someone inevitably puked all over the place, down the loo if they were lucky, and it was usually that same someone who expected a snog come twelve o'clock. With tongues. No, as far as Delilah was concerned, you could keep New Year and all the perils it promised.

Twizz, however, was adamant that she couldn't be a party pooper. 'There is no way I'm letting you spend this evening on your own. It's New Year's Eve, for chrissake!'

'So? It's just a day like any other. Listen, I'll be fine. Really. The last thing you want is me tagging along and being miserable all night.'

She had a point there. With a deep sigh and a look that said it all, Twizz gave up the fight. Much to Delilah's relief. Now all she had to do was hit the video store before the shelves were entirely denuded and order in something really scrummy. Oh, and allow herself a bottle of fizz. Fizz and chips – her favourite combo. Fizz and Chinese. Fizz and pizza. The permutations were endless, the possibilities too delightful to contemplate. Just her, the remote and a constant supply of munchies. Bliss.

She wasn't even too bothered about the mobile. OK, so there wouldn't be any text messages winging their way across time and space but, as he'd proved himself capable of good old-fashioned dialling, a repeat of the post-Christmas communication problem was entirely unnecessary. Margaret had already rung the previous evening to say she would be staying on with Geoffrey for a couple more days, couldn't begin to describe what a wonderful time she was having and would Delilah be kind enough to look in on her plants. Delilah was glad. It wasn't often that a break with her father could be construed as just what the doctor ordered, but this case was clearly the exception. Two mould-breaking types together, probably even now happily pottering about in comfortable silence with only the odd comment to break the peace. Perhaps she was wrong. Perhaps Archie was a right old raver and leading them all hopelessly astray. She

hoped so – it would do them both good to clamber off the
cerebral plane and party on down.

Margaret had sounded so chilled out that Delilah hesitated to tell her of Laura's visit. Reason, however, won the
day and she broached the subject with some trepidation. As
it turned out, she needn't have worried.

'Thank you for telling me,' had been Margaret's calm
response before going on to speak of other things, and with
that Delilah had had to be content. If Margaret had anything
else to say on the subject she would no doubt utter it in her
own good time. Until then, Delilah would keep quiet and
try not to over-water the winter cacti. Appropriate plant for
Margaret, really – prickly on the outside but capable of
producing the most ravishing flowers when least expected.

By the time Delilah staggered home with her booty, she
was well and truly ready for a comfort fest. Her paper-
wrapped parcel of cod and chips was clutched close to her
chest, warming the cockles of her heart even while it drove
her half mad with hunger pangs. A couple of carrier bags
were looped over her wrist, their contents the ingredients
for the perfect orgy of self-indulgence. Champagne, of
course, and a box of Pringles. A glossy mag, a couple
of candles pillaged from the stock room, the essential
supply of Oral Sex . . . Delilah was armed and ready for
anything. Anything, that is, except the snivelling heap she
found curled up in the dark on the sofa, identifiable only
by a familiar moth-eaten jumper and a tear-soaked mop of
mousey hair.

'Christ, you made me jump . . . Jess? Jess, honey, what's
happened? What's wrong?' The minute she flicked on the
light it was apparent all was not as it should be. The phone
was lying in the middle of the floor, the receiver off and
flung to one side. An open bottle of vodka lolled against the
sofa, the half-empty glass beside it evidence of conspicuous
consumption. Delilah chucked her package on to the nearest
surface and her bags on to the floor before sinking to her

knees beside Jess, whose shoulders were shuddering in great heaves of despair. In one tightly curled fist, she clutched a screwed-up ball of tissues while her other hand beat against the arm of the sofa in time to the moans emitting from somewhere in the depths of the cushions. The girl was a mess.

'No, no, no, oh shit, shit, shit . . . nooooooo,' was about all Delilah could discern by laying her ear next to the cushion in which Jess had buried her head. Figuring that it was best to let her get it all off her chest in one fell swoop, she laid a comforting hand on her friend's back and made hushing sounds, rocking her gently as she did so. Slowly, the uncontrollable shaking diminished and the sobs grew softer and softer until, finally, a tear-streaked face emerged from its sanctuary and Jess wailed, 'Oh God, whatamIgoingtodo?'

To that, Delilah had no straight answer, especially as she had not the faintest clue as to what catastrophe had struck, so she simply carried on shushing and stroked Jess's hair until the gulps for air had calmed to normal breathing and Jess was capable of coherent speech.

'It's over. Took me out for lunch and told me. Said his fiancée had finally found out . . . he had no choice . . . although if it was just up to him . . .'

Here her voice cracked, whether in pain, contempt or anger Delilah could not be sure. Jess made a heroic effort to bring herself back under control and continued, her quiet deliberation only emphasizing the venom in her voice.

'If it was just up to him then we'd have "found a way" but, all things considered, at the end of the day and with any other fucking cliché he could think of, it might be best if we forgot it ever happened. As if I fucking could. All that time being strung along, wondering if he was going to leave her or not. He told me he'd never forgive himself for what he had done. Like hell. I hate his guts. The rotten, stinking bastard.'

Delilah didn't need to hear that crack in her voice to

know that it was matched only by the break in Jess's heart. Love and hate – not so much opposites as twin bedfellows tugging at the same duvet. Roll over to one side and one emotion was exposed, the other way and its partner in crime was the one wiggling its toes in the air. Whoever had been sharing Jess's duvet had obviously upped and left and taken every ounce of bedding with him, not to mention the pillow talk.

'Jess, who on earth are you talking about? Who's the shithead who did all this to you?' For a moment she thought Jess hadn't heard, so still and quiet had she gone. Then, slowly, she turned red-rimmed eyes to Delilah and spat out one word. 'David.'

'David? Oh my God, you mean that bloke in the bar that night?'

Jess gulped and nodded at one and the same time. 'The very same. He called me up at the office and invited me to lunch. It went on from there. He told me all about his fiancée but he said he was going to end it. That it hadn't been right for a long time. And I believed him. Christ, I know it was wrong but I liked him so much . . .'

She trailed off miserably, lips working as self-recrimination set in. Looking at her, Delilah could cheerfully have swung for the self-serving creep, but rather than do twenty years she reached for Jess's glass and made her take a healthy slug before partaking of the calming elixir herself. Her day in court would come, she'd make sure of that. In the meantime, she had a best friend to put back together. Looking down at her devastated face, Delilah felt something implode inside.

'Jesus, Jess, how could you? I mean, do that to yourself?' It burst out before she could stop herself. For a second, Jess looked absolutely stricken and then she turned beseeching eyes to her friend and gulped out, 'I dunno. It just hap— I mean . . . The thing is, I love him. I do. I can't help it but I do. I really thought he felt the same way about me. I

waited and I hoped and I got more and more unhappy.
I even snuck around the way that he wanted, with him
telling her he was working late at the office. How fucking
original is that? And all that time I really was nothing but
his bit on the side. God, how could I have been so stupid?
The oldest fucking line in the book and I fell for it. Shit,
what am I going to do?'

'OK, Jess, it's OK.' Even as Jess pitched forward into
her arms, Delilah was trying to formulate a plan of action.
Recriminations were clearly not the way to go. Letting her
talk in her own time was a given, but the main aim was to
put a stop to the heart-wracking sobs which were again
building to a crescendo. At this rate, she would make herself
sick. There was only one thing for it. The crisis had to be
contained one way or another and old-fashioned methods
were invariably the best. As soon as the crying again hiccuped its way towards a halt, Delilah eased Jess away from
her chest and settled her back against the sofa.

'Back in a sec,' she reassured her before disappearing off
to put plan A into action. She hoped to God it would work
– she hadn't actually got as far as plan B and was casting
around helplessly for any better ideas.

As she came back into the room, Jess looked up listlessly
and Delilah saw that she had to assume her brisk, bossy
persona or all would be lost. Taking a firm grip, she hauled
her gently to her feet and propelled her towards the corridor
before Jess had time to protest. From the bathroom the
sound of running water could be heard and the smell of
Delilah's most soothing bath concoction was wafting out
through the door.

'Come on, you. Hot bath, big glass of fizz. Fluffy bathrobe
and then we'll talk some more if you want. And if you don't
want, that's fine as well.' For a moment she thought Jess
was going to dissolve again. Her eyes filled up and her
lower lip trembled but the only sound that came out was a
teeny hic of gratitude, acknowledged by an understanding

pat and an exhortation to get into the bloody water before
it got cold. By the time Delilah returned, with a brimming
champagne flute, Jess had sunk to her shoulders beneath
the bubbles, her eyes closed in a way that would have been
beatific had the rest of her face not been so ineffably sad.

'There you go, love,' said Delilah, placing the glass at the
side of the bath. Jess's mouth formed a thank-you, her
powers of speech having finally run out. Probably just as
well – there were only so many ways you could say the
word 'bastard'. Looking completely done in, Jess again
closed her eyes and sank back into her semi-catatonic state.
Delilah left her to it, tiptoeing out to get the second part of
plan A underway.

By the time Jess reappeared, wrapped in her bathrobe, it
was to be greeted by a feast that spanned the takeaway
section of the phone book. Delilah had gone mad with the
Yellow Pages, adding to her already impressive supplies.
Chinese and Indian jostled for space alongside a pile of
reheated chips, the cod having been cut into bite-size chunks
for shareability. There would have been pizza as well but a
wait of forty minutes had put paid to that one. Double-
stuffed crust with extra mushrooms was apparently the
thing to order this New Year's Eve. Their naffest compilation
CD blared out from the stereo, the glasses were generously
filled and, to top it all, there was a glistening pile of Oral
Sex just begging to be attacked. Delilah had come as close
as she possibly could to creating home bird heaven.

Barely had they settled on the sofa and stuck their forks
at random into their indoor picnic when the phone rang.
Their eyes met and Delilah barked, 'I'll get it,' diving across
the sofa to make sure she got there first. She could feel the
tension emanating from Jess as she spoke into the receiver,
followed by an audible sigh of relief as she heard Delilah
say, 'Twizz! Everything OK?'

'That's exactly what I was going to ask you,' came the
predictably pithy reply and, for a lengthy pause, Delilah

was at a loss. The jungle drums might beat fast but surely she couldn't have heard about Jess already?

'Thought I'd have one last go at dragging you out on the town,' Twizz continued, and realization dawned. No wonder it had taken her a while to work it out: in another rare display of her softer side, Twizz was being nice.

'Oh, right.' So taken aback was she by this slip of standards that Delilah had to take a moment to absorb the seismic shift. 'It's really sweet of you but the thing is, well, Jess has had a bit of an upset and I think we'll just stay in and make our own fun, if you know what I mean.'

Ensconced on the sofa, Jess was pulling faces, dragging her finger across her throat and generally making it plain that her business was not to be shared. And especially not with her old adversary, of all people. Aware of this, Delilah was doing her best to couch her words, a fatal mistake when it came to Twizz. A born bloodhound, she could sniff out man trouble at thirty paces.

'Been dumped, then, has she?'

'Er . . . something like that.'

'I knew something was up. All that furtive behaviour. Bloody obvious she was fooling around if you ask me. Already taken then, was he?'

Sometimes she was so spot on it was frightening. No doubt the result of cynicism honed on the back of a thoroughly misspent youth. With Jess still flapping her hands in her face, Delilah trod as carefully as she possibly could.

'You could say that.'

'Well, either he is or he bloody isn't. Poor cow – they're all the same, the tossers. She wants to get out there and get back on the bike, not sit around moping over some no-good bastard who wants the lot. So you'll be stuck providing the shoulder. And on New Year's bloody Eve as well. Her timing's a bit off, isn't it?' Ah good, a reversion to type.

This Delilah could cope with – it was the new caring, sharing Twizz she found hard to handle.

'Whatever. In any case, you know I'm not in a particularly sociable mood. I'd have been a total drag and that's the truth. But thanks for double-checking and, look, have a great time.'

'No worries about that. Might speak to you later. Get some grog down yourselves and tell her from me – they're never worth it. Arseholes.'

Definitely back on form. Delilah relayed her message to Jess, who screwed up her face and spat out, 'For God's sake, why did you have to tell her, of all people? She's probably laughing all over her face at me. She's never liked me and you know it.'

'Now come on, Jess, that isn't fair. Actually, she was very concerned. And I didn't tell her anything, apart from the fact you're a bit upset.' Trying to make allowances for irrationality, Delilah carried on in a gentler voice. 'Look, hon, you need your friends around you right now and I can promise you that Twizz does care. She's just not that great at showing it a lot of the time. Now, come on, eat up before it gets cold.'

'Yes, mummy.' They exchanged evil looks and then, to Delilah's relief, Jess managed a wobbly grin. Nothing to challenge the Cheshire Cat, but it was a start on the road back to normality. They were making decent headway on the food front and even more impressive inroads into the booze supply when the telephone rang again, sending Delilah back into her sofa dive. Jess was doing a superb job of affecting cool, but judging by the way she choked on a chip, her heart was definitely somewhere near her mouth, if not actually in it.

'Hello?'

Delilah hated to admit it, but there was always the hope that it was Matt on the end of the line. Fifty-one hours since they last spoke and eleven since she had informed his voicemail she was completely out of cellular contact. She prayed to the god of digital communications that he'd checked in and would make an attempt to reach her on her home phone instead. Heaven was obviously off-line. It was Fran, sounding flustered and speaking in a very furtive manner.

'Delilah? Is that you?'

'Fran? You'll have to speak up. This is a very bad line.' Delilah automatically assumed the polar position and articulated loudly and clearly down the line.

'Shhhh. They might hear you. I told them I'd picked up a message about some family crisis.'

Fran had either gone completely bonkers or she'd been at the bottle again. Adopting a less strident tone, Delilah demanded, 'What on earth are you going on about? And who the hell are "they"?'

'I'll explain later.' Without warning, Fran let out an ear-splitting squeak of alarm. 'Oh, my God! Why didn't you tell me earlier . . . Yes, of course I'll come at once. You just tell her to hang on in there . . .'

'Fran? Are you OK?' This was beyond bonkers, even for her.

'Oh, don't worry about me. It's Aunt Eleanor I'm concerned about. No, no it's no trouble at all. I shall leave immediately.' Determined to give a side of ham a run for its money, Fran was giving it her am-dram all. Members of the Academy could rest easy with their awards but it was clearly having the desired effect, judging by the concerned murmurings that could be heard offstage.

'I'm afraid it's Aunt Eleanor . . . been taken terribly ill. I'm just having a word with her, um, housekeeper. Doesn't sound too good, I'm afraid.' Full marks for the catch in the voice. Delilah hoped she was crossing her fingers to ward off fate. Evidently, Fran had found her friend Felicity's soirée too smug even for her tolerance levels, stretched as they were by exposure to the ungracious world of the glitterati. Or perhaps that should be tinselati.

Catching on fast, Delilah went for the death rattle, safe in the knowledge that Aunt Eleanor existed only in the dubious depths of Fran's fertile imagination. Unfortunately, she rather spoilt the effect by dissolving into a snort and a giggle at the end that she hastily turned into a last-gasp cough. From the other end of the sofa, Jess stared at her in utter amazement.

More concerned whisperings and then Fran came back on the line. 'Hello, I'm on my way. Felicity is going to organize a minicab . . . No, really, you simply cannot give me a lift . . . you have dinner guests to look after and everything but it's terribly sweet of you to offer . . . Hello? Sorry about that. As I said, I'll be there as soon as I can. About an hour. Call me on the mobile if you need me.' And she was gone, escaping as fast as she could from the clutches of Felicity and her friends. Quite where to, Delilah could only imagine, although when the doorbell rang not twenty minutes later it wasn't too much of a stretch to work out who might be peering through the peephole.

'Delilah! Thank goodness – I thought I'd never get out of there. I was getting completely desperate until I remembered what you said about staying in. Eurgh – those people. Sat there in little frocks and smart casuals, talking about which school to send Tarquin to and who was shagging whose personal trainer. Of course, they didn't actually say shagging. That would have been far too much fun. It was all this nudge nudge, wink wink nonsense. Then some person called Nigel started telling me about his kitchen garden, going on and on about how it had changed his life and would I like to come over and see his cucumbers sometime. That was it, the final straw. Sorry about the phone call – you must have thought I was barking mad. But it had to be done. It was either that or hurl the sorbet at him and I don't think Felicity would ever have forgiven me.

Particularly as she'd obviously invited him for me. Heaven forbid. Hi, Jess. How are you doing?' Having thrown off her coat and flopped down on the sofa, Fran noticed belatedly that she was not the only person to occupy its squidgy depths.

The look on Jess's face was something else. At least all the excitement had stopped her thinking about 'other things'. She raised a hand in greeting and said, 'Hi, Fran. Nice to see you again,' even as the look on her face conveyed a rather more mixed message. Delilah could empathize. Their previous encounters had been fleeting affairs and Fran at full tilt was something else, especially when she appeared to have taken an overdose of verbal laxatives. The only sure way to shut her up was to slap a large drink in her hand. As ever, it proved remarkably effective and, despite already having consumed a large portion of (organic) beef Wellington and pavlova with a post-ironic twist, Fran was soon picking away at the makeshift picnic.

Towards eleven, the telly went on, deeply dodgy programmes replacing the constant stream of suspect CDs as entertainment. Fuelled by an interesting mix of every drink they could find in the cupboards, the three of them shouted abuse at the screen as Delilah flicked between channels. They were hurling insults at one hapless presenter, doing his best to make a Highland gathering of fiddle players seem entertaining, when a loud knocking set them looking at one another in drunken astonishment.

'Did you hear that?'

'What?'

'That!'

'D'you know, I think it's the door.' As the others were obviously not going anywhere, Delilah heaved herself off the sofa and wove her way across the carpet to investigate. Throwing caution to the wind thanks to the alcohol-induced loss of inhibition, she flung the door wide, yelling, 'Hello!' as she did so. A startled Twizz took a step backwards, such was the force of the greeting, but she managed to hold on to the armful of cans and bottles that were clutched to her bosom. No doubt it was a mantra taught to every Sydney-sider at birth – never let go of the booze.

'Twizz! What the hell are you doing here?' Delilah held on to the door jamb, swaying gently backwards and forwards. Twizz gave her one scorching look and strode past her into the sitting room.

'Happy New Year to you, too. Thought I'd drop by and see how you were all doing. Very well, by the look of things.'

From the sofa, Jess and Fran beamed and cooed hello. Whether it was Twizz or the fresh supply of alcohol they were so pleased to see was debatable, but at least the thought was there.

'Sit down. Plenty of room. We can all squash up, can't we?' Fran was patting the space next to her and Twizz gingerly levered herself down, opened tinny in hand. Conditions were distinctly cosy by the time Delilah had also taken up her place but it was fine once a certain amount of shifting and shuffling had taken place. And by the time everyone had replenished their glasses, raucousness was re-established and the sofa was party central.

The chorus that accompanied the countdown on telly would have done credit to a bunch of rugby supporters and when midnight chimed, they all leaped in the air with the fervour of true sports fanatics. Much hugging and kissing followed and Delilah was particularly touched to see Twizz envelop Jess in a sisterly embrace that managed to combine empathy with the offering of an olive branch.

'Happy New Year, love. Be much better without the bastard, you'll see.'

Jess's eyes welled dangerously, but she gave her a watery smile and squeezed the arm around her shoulder. 'Yeah, you too,' she whispered before moving on to Delilah and a hug that said it all.

Love-in over, Twizz had just slammed on an appropriately appalling choice of music when above the tinkly sounds of '80s disco came the even tinklier sound of the telephone. Delilah's reaction demonstrated once and for all the speed of her reflexes as she grabbed it before anyone else could and gabbled a greeting.

'Hello? Hello, hello? Oh my God . . . Matt. It's you. Hang on a sec – let me just take this into the other room.' Twizz nudged Fran as a huge smile lit up Delilah's face, and she stuck her tongue out at them before dragging the phone into the corridor and pushing the door to. The thud of the disco beat receded and she settled back against the wall, phone on her lap and abrim with happiness, not to mention a healthy dose of relief.

'Sorry about that. The girls are going mad out there. So how are you? How are things going?' She could hear similar partying noises in the background, Matt's voice manfully trying to rise above the music and laughter.

'I'm fine. Took me ages to get a signal – the whole bloody mountain seems to be on a mobile. I miss you so much, sweetheart.'

'You do?' A huge smile shot across her face and her pulse went into overdrive. 'Well, I miss you too. Tons. Thank you again for my flowers. They're still gorgeous.'

'Not half as gorgeous as you. Delilah?' He suddenly sounded very serious. Her guts heaved and her scalp prickled ominously. She hated it when that happened, when she could feel the portent of something big about to be said.

'Yes?' Steady as she could, Delilah kept it light. After all, what he was about to say might be entirely innocuous. And pigs had wings.

'I just wanted you to know that I'm thinking of you . . . and have a Happy New Year. And I love you. I really do.' She had to strain to catch that last bit, so softly had he spoken. She felt as if she were in a lift plunging forty floors with her life whizzing past her. He'd said it, he'd actually gone and said it. Of course, it could be the drink talking,

but then they did say you should always trust a drunk.
Drunk or sober, it had popped up from his subconscious
and out of his mouth. And she had absolutely no clue how
to respond.

'You do?' Pathetic, but the best she could manage.
Bleating out 'I love you too' had always seemed so lame
and unoriginal a response although getting in there and
saying it first was a definite no-no. It was a tough one.

'Delilah?' He began to break up, his voice disintegrating
into Dalek-speak. 'Ba . . . soon. Lots . . . go . . . ca . . . rrr'

'Matt? Matt? You're breaking up . . . Don't know if you
can hear me. Hello? Matt . . . I love you too.' But he was
gone, dispersed into a thousand digital fragments. Delilah
could only sit and stare at the receiver in her hand, the
creeping warmth in her chest the last tangible reminder of
their earth-moving exchange.

Slumped against the far corner wall by the telephone, Matt
stared blindly at his mobile for a second. A few feet forward
and the signal would be perfect again. Luckily, there were
many dead spots in the village and this happened to be one
of the best. Ironic, really. Damn useful, though, when it
came to keeping a conversation to the right length. Long
enough to keep Delilah happy and short enough not to piss
off Serena, at the moment sitting pretty at the bar. He could
see her from where he stood, head thrown back to toss her
blonde hair effectively as she laughed, the men surrounding
her apparently mesmerized. Sure, she was hot, as well as
being a right little goer. But a holiday fling was as far as it
went and he had ensured she knew the score from the start.
It was only sensible, however, to keep her sweet. That way
the home fires burned happily while the away sheets were
kept warm. As far as Matt was concerned, it was the perfect
arrangement.

Fifteen

The next few days passed in a flash. Delilah had expected time to crawl past until Matt's return but once the holidays were over, the spenders were out with a vengeance, anxious to get their hands on the remaining bargains. In the midst of all the madness, Margaret made her unannounced re-appearance, slipping quietly through the door in the wake of a departing flock of shoppers, each one bearing the grim look of triumph that comes with retail victory. She came bearing gifts: a clump of winter jasmine from Geoffrey's garden and a fresh bottle of sherry with a handwritten label attached that read, 'Another unwanted offering – pour down the sink or imbibe as you prefer'.

Delilah giggled when she read this and passed the bottle to Twizz. 'Good on, your dad,' she said and tucked it away with the rest of their supplies. To Delilah's considerable pleasure, Margaret had roses in her cheeks and a renewed skip in her step. The country air obviously suited her, as did the like-minded company.

'So how long was this Archie bloke around?' asked Delilah, passing around the mugs as they took a well earned breather.

'Saw him a few times. Hasn't changed a bit. And nor, may I say, has your father.'

'Really?' Delilah wasn't sure if this was a good or a bad thing. Wafting through one's life in a state of academia abstracta was all very well, but hard on those around you, as she could heartily attest.

'I mentioned that Laura had dropped in on you,' continued Margaret, as cool as you like.

Delilah could feel Twizz's ankle pressing meaningfully against hers, but she maintained a casual air and responded with a noncommittal, 'Oh, yes, right.'

'Your father remembers her well, of course, as does Archie.' Was it Delilah's imagination or was there an edge to Margaret's voice?

'Uh-huh.'

Both Delilah and Twizz addressed themselves to their coffee cups. Margaret, too, stared into her pool of tea for a moment, then raised her head and asked simply, 'So, how was she?'

'Er . . . Laura? Oh, she seemed all right. Anxious about you, as I said before, but, um, generally OK. Wasn't she, Twizz?'

'Oh, yeah. Bit highly strung, if you ask me. But then those women always are.' Twizz took another gulp of coffee, apparently unaware that beside her Delilah had frozen, faux pas feelers on red alert.

Margaret had also stiffened slightly, pausing before demanding, 'What exactly do you mean by "those women"?' in a voice honed by forty-odd years of lecturing to recalcitrant students.

'Oh, you know, those county types. Bored out of their blonde highlights if you ask me. Can't blame them, though, when you take a look at some of the blokes they've married. It'd send me right round the twist as well. Not that your friend is anything like that, of course,' she added hastily, aware that she might have exceeded even her own extensive boundaries of acceptable behaviour.

'You're absolutely right. That's exactly what she is. Now, do you think there's another cup in the pot?' Not the most graceful change of subject but Margaret could be forgiven for appearing brusque.

'I'll get it!' offered Twizz, glad of the chance to slope off to the store cupboard and out of the firing line. She could have a quick puff while the kettle boiled and return when peace had been restored. As she slunk away, tail dangling near, if not between, her legs, Margaret looked at Delilah and dropped the most enormous wink.

'Sorry about that,' said Delilah, loud enough for Twizz to hear. 'Guess they do it differently in Oz.'

'Oh, I'm sure they don't,' remarked Margaret drily and they both succumbed to a fit of the sniggers.

'Anyway, are you positive you're OK?' asked Delilah, recovering herself.

'Haven't felt better in years and that's the truth. I've realized that ever since Laura reappeared my life has no longer been my own. In some ways I was a prisoner, keeping every Thursday free so I could see her, never daring to go away for longer than a week as I couldn't bear to miss our precious time together. Well, I'm free now. Really free. And I can't tell you how marvellous that is.' Struggling with unfamiliar emotion, Margaret looked at her and gave her one of the bravest smiles Delilah had ever seen. She reached out a hand and covered one of Margaret's with her own.

'You think you're really over her this time?' No further explanation of the whys and wherefores was being demanded. Margaret could see that Delilah knew and understood and, most importantly of all, accepted. It was a valuable gift to be devoid of judgement, and it was that very trait Margaret had also treasured in Delilah's parents.

'Yes, I am. Absolutely. I found out something that was quite unforgivable and that finished it for me. Forever. Laura lies, always has done and always will. I knew that, of course. After all, she used to lie to her husband about her trips up to town. She'd tell him she was off shopping or to the hairdresser and the poor man never questioned the fact.

Although, he was so sozzled most of the time that he prob-ably wouldn't have noticed if she was there or not.'

Margaret took a deep breath and let it out on a long sigh. She was gazing sightlessly ahead of her, looking at someone who wasn't in the room. After a moment, she continued.

'Poor Peter – I always wondered if the drink came between them or if it was there to fill an empty space. She was quite capable of driving him to it. Not that she's averse to a drop of the hard stuff herself. Laura's a lovely person until she's had more than a few – and it was always more than a few. I saw at first hand the damage it can do. Some would say they deserved each other, but I'm not so sure. Maybe I thought I deserved her more. All these years and I would have carried on forever with her. I loved her a great deal, you know.'

'I know.' No more needed to be said. However Laura had betrayed her, it was obviously too much even for Margaret to bear. They'd all been there and it always hurt, no matter whether it was the first time or the tenth. She could only hope for Margaret's sake that this time it was the last.

This was as much of a heart-to-heart as they ever had on the subject. Getting it off her chest once and for all did Margaret a power of good, the roses in her cheeks never fading back to their pre-Christmas pallor. Delilah was glad that at least one of them was blooming. As the time for Matt's return drew nearer, she grew more and more agitated and a couple of spots erupted in sympathy on her chin. Typical – go for weeks with a complexion like a baby's bum and break out the moment your man is due back in town. She put it down to an anticipatory surge in adrenalin, although her increased chocolate consumption might have been the real culprit.

His flight was scheduled for Saturday morning and, by Friday evening, Delilah's frenzy had reached its height. Twizz had long since tired of watching her twitching near

the phone, and had ordered her home with the tart suggestion that she could use the time to slap on a face pack and
slip down some multivitamins in a last-ditch attempt to get
into training for the boy wonder's return.

'Oh my God, you mean the zits are that obvious?' wailed
a distraught Delilah, too beside herself to take offence.

'I wouldn't worry, love. It's not your face he'll be looking
at,' leered Twizz, an insufferably knowing look on her face.

'I have no idea what you're talking about,' huffed Delilah,
all holier than thou, to which Twizz responded with a large
wink and, 'I'm sure you do.'

In the light of her assistant's attitude, home seemed a far
less stressful place to be, and Delilah left her to lock up
while she took the scenic route via a decent cosmetic counter
and her local off-licence. Once home, she poured herself
a frugal glass and slapped on a face pack that made
impressive claims on the miracle front. And so it should at
that price. Keeping one eye on her watch to time it to
perfection, she took dainty sips from her glass and resolved
to have maybe just one more at the most, once Jess got
home. For medicinal purposes, of course. There had been
nightly heart-healing sessions since New Year's Eve, but
surely Jess would forgive her if she abstained for one night.
After all, there was no point buffing up her skin if she was
going to ruin it with great big bags under the eyes and an
incipient hangover. She could feel the mask doing its work,
tightening in a way that boded well for firm features and
an unearthly luminescence. It had just got to the point where
she was afraid to smile when, inevitably, she heard the
phone ring. She had to hold the receiver a good three inches
from her ear so as not to get it stuck in gunk. Equally
inevitably, it was Matt.

'Darling, we're off out for a final booze-up so I thought
I'd catch you while I'm still coherent.' Just hearing his voice,
her stomach tightened as forcibly as her face pack. Articula-

ting without opening her mouth much was hard but she made a brave attempt.

'Oh, well, have a good time.'

'Thanks. Are you OK, sweetheart? You sound a bit . . . muffled. Have you got a cold or something?'

'No, no. I'm fine. Can't wait to see you.' Damn this cosmetic crap. It was either sound uptight or stretch those muscles and feel all her hard work fall off in great flakes of dried green gunk.

'Me too. Listen, why don't I come and pick you up tomorrow evening? Take you somewhere really special?' Sounded fabulous but it wasn't quite what she'd had in mind.

'Um . . . OK.' The disappointment couldn't help but seep through in her voice. She'd had the airport scene planned to perfection and now it looked as if she might be cheated out of it. It was enough to make a three-year-old stamp her foot, never mind a grown businesswoman and style setter to the sensuously deprived.

'Don't sound so thrilled at the thought.' Matt was clearly puzzled at her attitude. Hastily, Delilah tried to make amends.

'It's not that. I'm dying to see you. I just thought it might be rather . . . earlier in the day, that's all.'

She'd put it as tactfully as she could without sounding totally like a toddler. There was a sigh down the phone and then Matt said with what sounded like total sincerity, 'Darling, I'd love to ravish you the second I step off the plane but unfortunately I can't. Lizzie's picking me up from the airport and we have to go straight to an appointment. A new client who's only in town for twenty-four hours and wants to meet us both. It's important I see him.'

It's important you see me, too, she wanted to say, but wisely held her tongue. She couldn't really argue. She'd have done exactly the same in the circumstances, but knowing that didn't help one little bit. It was always harder being the one left behind than the returning hero. They'd simply have to make up for it the following evening. And boy, would they. She'd make damn sure of that.

'Well, I'll just have to control myself until then,' she quipped, and was gratified to hear his best dirty chuckle.

'As long as you let it all hang out later on.'

That, unfortunately, was what she was afraid of – the post-festive tummy effect. Thanks to the demands of the shop the gym was a dim and distant memory, one less treadmill in the great hamster wheel of city life. She liked to think that heaving boxes around at least kept the major muscle groups working, but it probably wasn't enough to combat the excesses of Christmas and New Year. Well, a girl had to keep up her satisfaction levels somehow, and what better way than with bucket loads of oral gratification?

Thankfully the sales rush continued unabated the following day, leaving Delilah little time to get worked up over the evening ahead. She got home in time to whack on the slap and wriggle into a little number she'd been saving for something special. Its snug fit only confirmed her worst fears – she was fat, fat, fat. A pot-bellied, wobble bottom of a woman. An undesirable mass of that subcutaneous substance. She heaved herself out of the outfit and into something else. Equally depressing. Back to the wardrobe and with twenty minutes to spare, she'd thrown half the contents on the floor and settled for the original ensemble. With the cunning addition of an extra undone button or three to draw the eye up and away from the offending area. Around her neck dangled the Tiffany necklace, a tribute to his excellent taste.

'You look great,' was Jess's pronouncement on the final picture, having thankfully not been party to the interim indecision. She'd come through the door as Delilah staggered out of her room on her newest high-heels, humming under her breath in a way that had not been heard since the earliest days of the David affair. An urgent case had fortuitously taken him out of town, although how much that was due to fate and how much to fear on his part was a moot point. Whatever the truth was, Jess was well out of it and the more that sank home, the happier she felt. Hence the humming and the carefree way she tossed her work to one side, ready to embrace the weekend.

It was so good to see Jess happy again that Delilah forgot the butterflies in her stomach and smiled upon seeing her. 'Off anywhere nice?'

'I'm meeting a couple of the girls uptown later for a drink and then we thought we might try that new place at the end of Soho Street. Don't think I need to ask what you're up to.'

He'd arranged to pick her up at eight, but at quarter to he rang to say there was a problem. 'Darling, is there any way you can leap in a cab and meet me at Luigi's? Bastard car refuses to start and if I wait for the breakdown guy I'll be here forever.'

He sounded so hassled she forgave him the fact that it would take her an age to find a taxi on a Saturday night. As luck would have it, she got one almost straight away and within half an hour they were indulging in the sort of snog that causes coronaries in those less young and fit. She had barely had time to take in his ski tan before the view blurred into close-up and his lips were clamped to her own. Never mind chucking water over Harvey – the waiter had to stand there clearing his throat a good three or four times before Matt could bear to prise himself away from her. Thank God the ice bucket was nowhere to hand.

'Your table is ready, sir.'

Full marks to the man – he seemed entirely unperturbed by this open display of lust in his restaurant. Probably saw it at least once a day, if not on quite such a demonstrative scale. Even when they were sat down, Matt's hand rested firmly on her thigh and the other one was more concerned with stroking her face than feeding his own. By the time they got back to her place, the mutual steam had been stoked to boiling point. Which is what made what happened next all the sweeter.

Instead of the unreconstructed enthusiasm she had been anticipating, Matt's lovemaking was distinctly slow and tender. Clothes removed with infinite care, a pause to admire the effect of the necklace against her skin. Plenty of sweet nothings and soft stroking with a restraint that broke only at the final furlong. The mountain air had obviously cleared the way to a part of the brain his libido had hitherto obscured. As they lay in each other's arms afterwards, one of his hands still gently running over her belly, Delilah savoured the feeling of absolute bliss. All her anxieties had been replaced by a sense that they were closer than ever, absence acting as a magnet.

'That felt so good. Being back inside you,' he whispered and she didn't even squirm, she felt so relaxed with him now.

'Mmmm.' No need for words to express how she felt when she could nuzzle close and rely on her fingers to do the talking. Soon they were at it again, this time shorter and sharper than before but still made special by the way they looked at each other intensely all the way through. Delilah fell asleep a very happy woman, satiated and suffused with an unfamiliar sense of security.

'Hello, gorgeous.'

'Nnfff . . . hello.' Fabulous. She was waking up slowly to the feel of someone stroking her hair and the smell of coffee wafting towards her from the bedside table. If he wasn't the perfect man, he came damn close.

'Something I forgot to tell you yesterday . . .'

'Oh yes?' Propped up against her pillows, savouring her first cup of the day, Delilah was ready to forgive him almost any lapse.

'It's Dan's birthday today and I did say I'd meet up with him for a lunchtime drink. Of course, you can come as well. You know I'd much rather spend the day in bed with you but, well, it's only once a year and all that. It's not like he's got loads of friends or anything, so I'd feel bad if I blew him out.'

Matt needn't have bothered with the Andrex puppy eyes. She didn't mind at all, or at least only the teeniest amount. So long as they did it together he could have suggested a stag night in a strip bar and she would have gone along with it. Perhaps.

'Of course you mustn't. Besides, I like Dan. He came into the shop while you were away and was a real sweetie. Says he's going to help me out with a computer and wants me to think about the Internet as well.'

She was surprised by his reaction. The brows that had been arcing upwards so endearingly now knitted together and the corners of his mouth drew down. 'Did he now? Well, well. Good old Dan.' Realizing that he was erring on the side of overreaction, Matt added a hasty and hearty laugh. 'That's him, all right – generous to a fault. Talking of generous, I don't believe you've given me a proper kiss yet this morning . . .'

'Ooh, yes I have . . .'

'Call that proper? How about this . . . and this . . .'

Much improper action ensued and it was a mad scramble to make it up and out of the house on time. It was close on twelve o'clock when Delilah finally locked the front door, giving them a bare half-hour to get down to the pub. They could still have made it had Matt's mobile not gone off at that precise moment.

'Hello? Oh, Millie, hi. What? They what? The bastards – I don't believe it. No, it's not your fault. I'm sure you did. Don't worry about it. Yeah. Well, thanks for letting me know.' He pressed the disconnect button and briefly scowled down at his phone before turning to Delilah.

'That was Millie from the gallery. Fucking traffic people have impounded my car. She saw them loading it up just as she got there to do the Sunday shift. She says she tried to argue with them but they weren't having any of it. Apparently even on a Sunday you can't leave it on certain streets. How the fuck was I supposed to know that?' He was doing his best to control himself but the whitened knuckles and clenched jaw told their own story. Delilah slipped a soothing arm through his.

'So what are you going to do?'

'What can I do? I'll have to get down there and pay the fine fast before they decide to double it or whatever they do. Oh shit, I am sorry about this, sweetheart. Do you think you could get along to the pub and explain, keep Dan company until I can get there? I promise I'll be as quick as I can.'

'Sure. No problem. But why don't you give him a ring on his mobile, let him know what's happening?' Not that it was a big deal, now that the ice with Dan was broken. But it would be the decent thing to let him know and Delilah was nothing if not polite, at least most of the time.

'I would but he hasn't got one. I know – don't ask. How someone like Dan could get by without one in this day and age is beyond me, but he does. He has this weird thing about technology. In fact, as far as I know, he still doesn't have a telly. Travels everywhere by bike if he can help it. The guy's a one-man advertisement for the Dark Ages and he's the one running an Internet company.'

'Bizarre.' Although not entirely at odds with Dan's persona. She could just see him pedalling furiously along, eschewing the closeted sanctuary of a car for the raw thrills of the open-air approach.

'Definitely. Anyway, I'd better get going and so had you. Now give me a kiss . . .' Which added a good five minutes' delay before they could leap into the separate cabs that had fortuitously come along together as if they were buses. As

hers pulled off in a different direction, Delilah gave Matt a
little wave and, despite already being back on the mobile,
he blew her a kiss in return. Whoever was at the other end
of the line was obviously getting the pasting he thought
they deserved, and she would hazard a guess that the car
pound was the lucky recipient of his wrath. No matter – it
would be sorted soon enough and, in the meantime, she
could have a chat with Dan and do her best to brighten up
his birthday. She felt for him; even the most dedicated loner
must want company sometimes. And with Matt spending
more and more of his time with her it meant that Dan was
deprived still further.

It preyed on her mind throughout the short journey, and
by the time the cab drew up outside the White Hart, she
had made up her mind. She would go along with Dan's
web site idea. It made sound business sense and, more
importantly, it might go some way to make up for her
stealing his closest mate. If things were going to progress
with Matt, and she hoped and prayed they would, then she
wanted to be a part of everything in his life. And that
included his friends. Pleased with the thought and full of
purpose, Delilah pushed open the swing door and looked
around for Dan.

He was tucked behind a wooden table, feet up on a stool
opposite, absorbed in the crossword and experiencing a
strong case of déjà vu. Matt was only ten minutes late so
far, but Dan knew from bitter experience that this was
merely the thin end of the wedge. Resigning himself to the
inevitable, he addressed himself to his Bloody Mary and
the labyrinth of cryptic clues. God only knew why he put
himself through the mental torture. On his birthday. And
with a hangover as well. If Matt hadn't been so insistent,
he would happily have spent half the day in bed and the
other half wanting to go back there.

'Hello. Happy birthday.'

Startled, Dan looked up from his paper and saw Delilah

standing before him. He had to pinch himself mentally to make sure she wasn't a mirage. It was definitely her, in glorious fleshly form. Fate appeared to have sent him the best birthday present of all and ten across immediately lost its appeal. Realizing that he was gawping in a most unattractive manner, Dan hastily pulled himself together.

'Hi. I didn't realize you were coming along as well. Matt parking the car?' Not the most effusive of welcomes but she had this effect on his speech centres, not to mention other parts of his anatomy.

'Nope. Actually, he's gone to rescue it from the car pound. Got towed away this morning and, as you can imagine, he's not too happy about it. I've come as the advance guard. Hope you don't mind.' Sweet – Dan looked as if she'd roused him from a deep sleep, all rumpled and distracted. More approachable. And far more attractive.

'Mind? Of course not. It's great to see you. Here, why don't you sit down on this chair. Far more comfortable than one of those poxy stools. Now, what can I get you to drink? Shall I bring a menu over as well?' Dan was urging her towards the seat he had just vacated, moving aside papers and paraphernalia as he spoke. Delilah wanted to giggle at his effusiveness but was afraid she might hurt his feelings.

'Thanks. I'll have a bottle of Stella, if you don't mind. And I'd love to see the menu – I'm absolutely starving.' Although it would perhaps be better if she didn't elucidate the reasons why she could happily eat a horse.

Dan trotted off to the bar and Delilah idly picked up his paper. By the time he returned, she had inked in one down and five across and was wrestling with an anagram that had defeated him for the past half-hour. As he placed the drinks on the table, Delilah glanced up guiltily.

'Sorry. I hate people doing that.'

'What?'

'Having a go at my crossword.'

'Don't worry about it. We can always do it together.' Now

there was a marvellous thought, one instantly consigned to the bin marked 'wishful thinking'. Dan shuffled his stool round next to her chair and nodded approvingly at her efforts.

'Ten down, seven letters ... love spray. Aerosol. Of course – Eros in the middle for love. Aerosol sprays. Perfect. Well done, you.'

Delilah didn't know why, but that made her feel distinctly warm inside. Anxious now for his approval, she turned her attention back to the crossword. This time they worked as a team and did well, filling up three quarters of the blank spaces before Dan called a halt for a loo break. Delilah soldiered on alone, although it was far less fun without his battier suggestions to bounce off. She was wrestling with a particularly insidious clue when she felt a warm, wet kiss on the top of her head and heard Matt say, 'Hello, gorgeous. What are you up to?'

'Ooh, this and that,' she said teasingly before moving her arm so that he could inspect her efforts. 'The crossword, of course. And I'm doing well.'

Matt squeezed in beside her, pulling her on to his knee so that they could both fit on the one seat, and peered at the paper. 'All your own work, huh?'

'Weeeell . . .'

'Lying little toerag,' he said affectionately.

'I don't know what you mean,' she countered indignantly.

'Yes, you do. There's no way you did all this by yourself. There are two sets of handwriting here and if I'm not very much mistaken, one of them is Dan's. I'd recognize it anywhere. Wouldn't I mate?'

'Would you now?' Delilah hadn't noticed Dan's reappearance but Matt certainly had. The two men stared hard at one another and for a moment she felt oddly uncomfortable. An atmosphere had risen up amongst them and she couldn't for the life of her work out where it had come from. All she knew was that it made her feel uneasy. Weird – after all, it had been Matt's idea to meet up for a drink. If there was some problem between them, surely he wouldn't have been so insistent.

'Yeah, well, I've seen it enough. Dan's a bit of a writer,' Matt added for Delilah's enlightenment, 'very good about sending out cards and things, aren't you, mate? Never forget a birthday or Christmas. Pretty good about the old postcards too, unlike me. He's got a lucky pen. The thick nib – gives it away every time.'

Dan smiled thinly. 'Must be losing its touch,' he suggested in a curiously flat voice, his eyes suddenly frosted over.

Attempting to lighten things up, Delilah asked brightly, 'Why do you call it your lucky pen?'

Dan shrugged. 'Oh, just some stupid idea I got at school. I used this pen in all my final exams, did really well and since then I've always thought of it as lucky. Silly, really.'

'Aren't you forgetting the best bit?' Matt was smiling, around the mouth at least.

'What?' Dan looked vaguely irritated, one hand tapping at the table with his precious pen.

'I gave it to him. Eighteenth birthday present, as I recall. I said at the time it was for luck and, look, it worked.'

'So you did.' Dan's tone was flat, his manner curiously cool.

Deciding that they were both acting very strangely, Delilah scrambled up from Matt's lap, evading the possessive hand that tried to stop her, and announced, 'My round. Same again, Dan? Matt?'

'I'll have whatever the birthday boy is on. Happy birthday, by the way. Present on its way, as usual.' As he said this, Matt tossed Dan a card, his tone of voice a fraction warmer than before. Dan, too, smiled with a touch less ice and took the envelope with a friendly enough, 'Cheers, mate. Think I can manage a beer now, if you don't mind, Delilah. Pint of Speckled Hen, please.'

'Same for me, sweetheart. In recovery then, mate?' Matt glanced at Dan's empty glass, a film of tomato juice still clinging to its surface.

'Bit of a heavy night last night,' conceded Dan. 'Went drinking with some of the lads from work and then on to this club one of them knows. Very trancy but Jem is into that. It was a good laugh.'

'Didn't think that was your scene,' Matt commented drily. Not so much of a sad bastard after all, thought Delilah. Interesting.

'Ah, you'd be amazed at what I get up to nowadays,' said Dan self-mockingly. 'Hear you had a bit of a night as well.'

'Sorry?'

'The car. Delilah told me about it. What happened – too pissed to drive it home or was this one of Lizzie's little japes?' Bullseye. A muscle twitched in Matt's cheek and he stared stiffly ahead of him as he blustered, 'No idea what you're on about, matey.'

'Yes, you do,' Dan persisted, adding for Delilah's benefit, 'Every now and then Lizzie gets on her high horse and Matt has to hand back the keys for the night. Never lasts longer than that but it's her way of showing who's boss. Isn't that right, Mattie?'

'Oh, for fuck's sake, can't you give it a rest?' he snarled, his face now blacker than his Calvin Klein sweater.

Deciding that men were indeed temperamental creatures and best left to it, Delilah chose that awkward moment to hit the bar. By the time she returned, the boys were engaged, much to her relief, in a far less loaded discussion on the merits of various squash racquets. She sat herself down on a spare chair and idly picked up the birthday card, a fine example of strictly masculine humour. Flipping it open to read the punchline, she cast her eye over Matt's scrawl. Not exactly a man of letters. He'd adorned the card with a barely decipherable signature in blue biro and that was the sum total of his effort. Typical bloke, as Twizz would have said. Thinking of Twizz brought to mind her comments on Delilah's ineptitude as a girl detective. No doubt she would have purloined the birthday card and got it down to a handwriting lab before you could say analysis. Well, Delilah did things differently. As far as she was concerned, it didn't matter whether Matt had sent the postcard or not. Although she was almost sure he had, big softie that he was.

The topic of squash racquets was exhausted soon enough and lunchtime limped by to the accompaniment of much inane chatter and the exchange of innocuous banalities. Something was obviously eating at both of them but Delilah knew not what and didn't care to enquire. Best to leave the boys to work it out between them, a sentiment that Dan would heartily endorse. He'd have caught the significance of Matt's words even if they hadn't been backed up by a look that underlined everything in neon. So he'd somehow seen the postcard, knew who had written it and why. And gone in there anyway, full steam ahead and charm guns ablaze to win her over. It had worked, of course it had worked. There was the living, breathing proof, sitting there looking at Matt as if he were the best thing since the invention of interest-free credit. Dan could quite cheerfully have choked him.

Such brooding sentiments helped stoke the uneasy atmosphere. Delilah did her best to ignore it. If there was one thing she had learned, it was not to get between two men who were beating their chests at each other. And between them these two made Tarzan look like an intellectual. It was a relief, therefore, when Dan reached for his jacket and announced, 'I'd better be off. Thanks for the card and everything. Delilah, I'll let you know about that computer – I've got someone on the case. Looking forward to that game.' And with a curt nod at Matt he was gone, leaving them to canoodle in peace and allowing Delilah to breathe a surreptitious sigh of relief.

Relief was high on the agenda when the boys met again at the appointed time and place. Relief, that is, of the tension that had all but torn their friendship apart. As Dan pulled on his shorts and T-shirt he cast his mind back to the last time they had met on a squash court. It seemed aeons ago, although it was probably only a few months at most. Then it had been a friendly game, a way to snatch time together between their respectively tight schedules. Now it was a whole different ball game. Tying his laces tight and grabbing his racquet as he strode towards the courts, Dan couldn't help but wonder what lay ahead.

Matt was already there, knocking up against the wall while he waited. Dan paused in the doorway, observing Matt's easy stroke as he hit the ball low and hard. Always a natural athlete, sport came as easily to Matt as most other things. It didn't bother Dan that he had to work that much harder to be as good but it still rankled whenever Matt offered unsolicited advice. It was as if they were stuck in a school day groove, with Matt ever the games captain and Dan merely his stooge. Well, things had changed; they had both moved on. And maybe it was time to see if their friendship had stood the test.

'All right, mate?'

Matt spun round as soon as Dan spoke, acknowledging him with a smile that didn't quite reach his eyes. 'Good. And you?'

'Oh, you know. Trogging along.' Dan's manner was casual but his heart had started to beat faster. There was so much at stake here, so much they could both lose.

'Spin to see who serves?' Without waiting for a response, Matt went ahead, twirled his racquet and won the right to go first. Apparently Dan was not even to be given the opportunity of a knock-up. Typical, thought Dan, and then immediately told himself not to be so negative. His powers of concentration were needed on court. Anything else would have to wait until afterwards.

Matt's first serve was superb, naturally, and Dan soon found himself running all over the court to return his shots. Brilliant tactician that he was when it came to a game, Matt seemed set on establishing his mastery from the off. By the time it came for him to serve, Dan was already puffing. Wiping a bead of sweat from his forehead, he glanced at his opponent, clocked his expression and made two instant resolutions. One was to play him at his own game, get him on the run for a change. The other was to win at all costs.

He calculated his serve beautifully, hitting it so that it floated high above Matt's head. Matt had to turn and run to reach it, awkwardly scooping it up as it hit the back wall and almost fell dead. His efforts were not quite enough and the point went to Dan.

'Shot.' Even when Matt was ostensibly gracious Dan felt patronized. Matt's serve this time was a little less sure, allowing Dan to slam it back fast and so low that it barely skimmed above the bar. Matt returned it in kind, wrong-footing Dan. He heard the metallic thud as the ball hit the bar and could have kicked himself. Another point to Matt. No time, however, for Matt to be complacent. The game was fast developing into a battle of wits as he realized that Dan was more of an opponent than he had thought. Either he had been taking lessons on the sly or there was something else driving his game to new heights. Whatever the reason, he had to be beaten. And if that meant playing dirty then so be it.

Twenty minutes in and they were both dripping with sweat, hair plastered to brows, equally stubborn jaws set and eyes almost fanatical with the desire to claim victory. The court echoed with the noise of the ball ricocheting off the walls and the fetid atmosphere reeked of animal. Forget

civilization, this was king of the jungle stuff. Dan's muscles
were beginning to scream at him but pure savagery drove
him on. It was clear from Matt's play that he intended to
do whatever it took, to drive Dan into the ground if necessary. And by the way the score was looking it appeared that
he might just pull it off. Dan had managed to claw back
into the game but his chest was heaving with the effort and
his legs were beginning to go. Too much time spent at a
computer terminal and not enough tending to his cardio-
vascular needs. Now they were reaching match point, and as
Dan again awaited one of Matt's testing serves, the thought
flashed across his mind that it had ever been thus. Matt
clearing all comers out of his path, even his supposed best
mate. For an adolescent that ruthlessness had been enviable,
to a grown man it appeared almost pathetic. Control freaks
were always afraid and Matt had become one of the worst.

So forceful was this revelation that Dan almost missed
his return. Desperately diving for it, he smashed the ball
with all his heart and soul and it came back hard at an
awkward angle, forcing Matt to improvise as best he could.
It bounced high against the wall and arced back towards
Dan, who realized at the last moment that he had miscalcu-
lated its drop. Running for it frantically, he flicked his wrist
and thwacked it back blind, hoping against hope that he
had somehow saved the point. Sensing the swish of the ball,
Matt tried to jump out of the way and totally misjudged his
move. On hearing his anguished howl, Dan spun round to
find Matt hopping in pain, one hand clasped around his left
calf.

'Didn't get you, did I? Sorry, mate.' Dan suppressed a
smirk as Matt glared briefly at him before growling, 'Don't
worry about it. I'm sure it was an accident.'

'Of course. By the way, that's 9-7 to me. Game over, I
believe.'

'You what?' A deep purple stain rose up from under his
collar and suffused Matt's face. His mouth set in a thin,

white line and his eyes almost bulged with annoyance. On his shin, a distinctive halo-shaped bruise was beginning to appear, its colour matching only too well the hue of Matt's forehead and cheeks. Emitting a grunt that combined both rage and frustration, Matt flung his racquet to the ground, seeming to derive some small satisfaction from hearing it splinter. Watching him, Dan realized once and for all how much Matt hated to lose. At anything and to anyone. It was no basis for any friendship, let alone theirs. With a sinking heart he decided it was all over. What had once been funny and charismatic was now something else altogether. The friendship had passed its sell-by date. It was time to move on.

Within a few minutes Matt had recovered himself to shake hands and offer a half-gracious, 'Well played,' but the damage was done. As their fingertips touched, Dan clasped them tight for a moment and then let go. There was no post-match pint, no promise to call. Matt left the sports club without bothering to shower, anxious to get as far as he could from the scene of defeat.

Left to his own devices under the needle-sharp jets of water, Dan soaped himself over and over as he analysed what had gone wrong. The seed had always been there, that much was obvious. Quite how it had flourished and flowered undetected by Dan for so long was another matter. As with so many friendships it had become a habit, unquestioned and unexamined as the years rolled by. Until something like this happened. Or rather, someone like Delilah. Something mingled with the water streaming over his face, something hotter and saltier that felt suspiciously like a tear. Who or what he was crying for was not altogether clear but wherever it came from, the pain ran deep.

It took him a while thereafter to get round to it but Dan was as good as his word to Delilah. By coincidence or subconscious design, he chose Valentine's Day to drop in to the shop with the promised computer. Of course, he could have sent along one of his team but that would have missed the point of the exercise. Hence the delay, as finalizing finance and forging ahead with his deals took up every spare waking moment. So busy had he been that the significance of the date barely registered until he was inside the shop and dumping the box down in a hastily cleared corner.

'This is very kind of you,' Delilah was saying as she fussed around him with the ubiquitous tea and biscuits. Dan brushed off her gratitude with appropriate modesty. It wouldn't do to live up to the cliché and let her think he was only after one thing, even if that thing was her heart rather than the more obvious parts.

'No problem. I said I'd find you one and I'm only sorry it's taken so long.' Taking a breather from heaving machinery, Dan leaned up against the counter and looked around him. 'Red must be in fashion at the moment,' he commented as he reached out for another chocolate chip cookie.

'What? Oh, it's our Valentine's Day display. You wouldn't believe the number of men we've had in looking for something in either red or black. When they see this they think they've died and gone to a bordello. Nothing like being original, is there?' Delilah looked at him to share the jibe but for once Dan did not appear to be listening to her.

'Valentine's Day? I don't believe it!' He had the stricken look of a man who swore blind he wouldn't forget. And then promptly did.

'Whoops. Slipped up, have we?' she teased and he groaned in response.

'It's not what you think. It's just that every year I send something to my mother, a card and a present to let her know I'm thinking of her. My dad always made a big fuss of Valentine's Day, you see, and I'm trying to keep up the tradition.'

'Oh, I see.' Matt had mentioned something about Dan's father dying a few years back and the effect it had had on him. Sounded like it had been a tough time for all concerned and she was touched by this display of sweetness.

'We could put something together for you.' she offered and Twizz nodded enthusiastically in agreement.

'Sure we could. For your mum, you say? Well, how about one of the lavender-scented pillows – they're pretty.' She was darting around the shop, eyes searching for the perfect present.

'Or one of the French cotton camisoles? They're edged in real lace and they're very sedate,' suggested Delilah.

'And here's the perfect card. One of yours, Del, if I'm not mistaken.' Twizzle was holding up a handmade card on which the silvered silhouettes of the crescent moon and a single rose were juxtaposed against a background of hand-printed silk. Simple but striking, it was one of her favourites.

'Great. Fabulous. All of it. You're very kind, both of you. I'll take the lot. Now, how much do I owe you?' Laughing partly to disguise how deeply he was touched, Dan whipped out his wallet to be halted in his tracks by a stern look from Delilah.

'Don't you dare! After getting us the computer and every-thing. Consider them a present, from us to your mum. Although we'll let you put your name on the card,' she added cheekily.

'If you're sure . . .'

'I absolutely insist. And while you're installing that we can get them wrapped up in something that will withstand the post. Twizz, have we got any of those bubble wrap envelopes left? The large ones?'

'Yup. Should be some right here.' Twizz delved deep into the recesses of the store cupboard and emerged triumphant, A3 envelope held aloft.

Delilah handed it to him. 'Here, write the address and everything on it now. Much easier than doing it when it's all packed up.'

'Good plan,' said Dan, whipping out his trusty pen to

sign the card before marking out his mother's name and address in a thick, clear hand. Methodical as ever, he then turned the envelope over and wrote the return details on the reverse before passing it back.

'I can't thank you enough . . .' Dan began again, his stumbling gratitude acknowledged by a cheerful, 'No worries, mate. Anyone who gets us online is all right by me,' as Twizz gathered up the goods and got down to wrapping them up. Dan left them to their tissue paper and sticky labels and began to unpack the equipment.

For the next ten minutes or so all was peace and industriousness. The gift-wrapped items were being carefully inserted into the envelope when Dan emerged from underneath the monitor, scrambled to his feet and said, 'I reckon that's it. Shall we have a go?'

Temporarily customer-free, they clustered around the machine and watched as Dan booted it up and the icons appeared. He was halfway through an explanation of their dial-up networking when a commotion outside the door caught Delilah's eye and she went to see what was going on, Twizz being far too delighted with her link-up to cyberspace to so much as twitch a muscle. A scrawny youth was desperately attempting to tame a wild bunch of balloons, a combination of their quantity and the wind threatening to lift him off to helium heaven. Trying to sort himself out, he was clinging on to the thin wire of fairy lights that ran between the tree outside and the shop. Any minute now the balloons would get themselves entangled, he'd be electrocuted or probably both. Delilah was aghast. Flinging open the door, she stuck her head out and yelled, 'What the hell do you think you're doing?'

The spotty teenager looked at her with undisguised contempt and stated the bleeding obvious. 'Delivering them. This is Durber Road, isn't it?'

'Yes.'

He was craning to read the envelope attached to the

weight at the bottom of the string. 'And this is Decker . . . Decra . . .'

'Decadence. Yes, it is.'

'Well, there you go, then. These are for you.' And with that he thrust the whole lot into Delilah's hands and strode off, mission accomplished.

'Hey, hang on a second . . . hey, you . . .' The wind was against her and the boy deaf to her frantic shouts. Giving up on him as a bad job, she manoeuvred the bunch into the shop with much ducking and diving and shut the door after her with a heartfelt, 'Phew!'

Twizz and Dan tore themselves away from the monitor and stared at Delilah, hair whipped into a frenzy and engulfed in brightly coloured balloons.

'Here, let me give you a hand,' said Dan, to the rescue as ever. She gave them to him gratefully and let him set them down carefully before she reached out and tore open the attached card.

'I thought it was too much of a coincidence. The idiots have gone and sent them to me instead of delivering them to Matt! Oh, shit – they must have got the addresses mixed up. Now it's ruined, my big surprise.'

Dan took one look at her distraught little face and conceded defeat. If it meant that much to her, and it so obviously did, then he'd be an idiot to harbour any more hopes. Settling for friendship stuck in his craw, but it was in the spirit of this that he suggested, 'Why not take them over there yourself? Then it would be a double surprise.' Full marks for maturity, Danny boy, and zero for happiness.

'Great idea!' exclaimed Twizz, afraid that Delilah's lower lip was beginning to wobble. This love guff was all very well, but it had a disastrous effect on one's sense of proportion. And proportions were very important in Twizzle's book.

'I suppose I could,' allowed Delilah reluctantly, her initial plan in ruins. As a salvage operation it had possibilities.

'Of course you could,' urged Dan, wondering even as he said it why on earth he was being so encouraging. Guilt may have had something to do with it. That and an over-whelming desire to see her smile again.

'I'd give you a lift over but I'm on the b— Oh, bugger!' Dan had made the fatal mistake of looking at his watch. 'Can I make a quick call?'

'Help yourself.' She still thought it odd that a man like him did not have a mobile but she supposed he had his reasons.

'Sal, hi, Dan here . . . they're there already? Shit! Yeah, I know, I know. I forgot about the time. Stall them, will you? Tell them I'm on my way from another meeting. Get them a coffee or something. Yeah. You're an angel . . . I'm sorry about this. Sure. OK. Yup, quick as I can.' Dan's face was set and Delilah forgot about her own disaster for a moment.

'Everything OK?' she asked anxiously.

'Fine. But I have to get going, I'm afraid. Got a meeting with some bigwigs and if I can bag this one we'll really be flying. They're very high profile and that's what we need.' Dan was hunting around for his leather jacket as he spoke and Twizz fished it out from under the counter for him.

'Oh no, and you've been held up here.' Delilah looked stricken and it was all he could do not to grab her and tell her he'd far rather spend an hour with her than a whole day with a bunch of Web whizz-kids any day. Even if they were vital to his success.

'Don't be silly. I've enjoyed myself. Better fly though, seeing as I'm relying on pedal power. Call me if you have any problems.' And he was off out the door like a hare on speed.

He'd barely been gone a couple of minutes when Delilah noticed the parcel still sitting on the counter. She ran to the door and down to the end of the street but it was too late to catch him and she came panting back, under pressure herself to get somewhere fast.

'Missed him! Shit! I know – I could always get them to put it in with the gallery post. I'm sure Matt wouldn't mind and it'd still get there on time.'

'So you are going over there, then?' There was something about Twizz's tone of voice Delilah didn't like.

'Yes, I am. Why? Do you think that's such a bad idea?' She hadn't meant to sound so defensive but somehow it came out that way.

'You do what you want, love. I'm going for a smoke.' Twizz was already reaching for her baccy tin, roll-ups being in favour this week.

'Do you think you could make it a quickie? I need you to watch the shop while I'm gone.' Delilah was hopping from one foot to the other, clearly anxious to act the Cupid.

'OK, keep your hair on. By the time you've slapped on the polyfilla I'll have had my puff.'

'Oh my God, make-up! You're right. And I was going to get changed before I saw him.' Delilah looked down at her perfectly respectable but distinctly unraunchy outfit and decided it would have to do. Surely by now it was her inner self he was interested in anyway? Perhaps not – he was a man, after all.

Rather than suffer her fretting, Twizz urged her into the loo with a reassuring, 'You look fine. Lashings of lip gloss, quick squirt of perfume and he'll never know the difference.'

While Delilah was attending to her sartorial needs, Twizz took reflective drags on her rollie. For a sardonic man-hater she was surprisingly sensitive and she was worried on Delilah's behalf. It all seemed to be going so well, but Twizz trusted her gut instincts and as far as Matt was concerned, he made her colon curl. Always had done. There was just something about him that didn't fit. Nothing tangible, just a sense based on years spent studying the species. She hoped she was mistaken – nothing would please her more than to be proven so. And for Twizz that was saying an awful lot.

Further rumination was prevented by Delilah bursting out of the loo, curls askew and demanding, 'Will I do?'

'Wonderful, as always. Now take the bloody balloons over to lover boy before they burst.' She stubbed out her fag and prepared to hold the fort. 'I guess you won't be back before closing time?'

'Probably not. You don't mind, do you?' Delilah felt a pang of guilt but it was superseded by a desperate desire to be on her way. There was nothing she liked more than a surprise, even if she was the one springing it.

'No worries. I'm not meeting up with the gang until later anyway.' True to her anti-romantic ideals, Twizz and her friends had organized a Death To Valentine Party, a pre-requisite for entry being a curled lip and the absence of a partner. She had thoughtfully invited Jess along, only to be taken aback when she declined on the grounds that she had a date. With someone who, for the moment, would remain anonymous. Jess was being extra cautious and who could blame her. At least she was getting out there again. The news had set Delilah and Twizz all a-twitch and would provide great fodder for a post-mortem once Delilah had returned from cloud nine.

'OK, well, I'm outta here. Wish me luck.'

Twizzle looked at Delilah, swaddled in her coat and scarf with balloons aloft and thought she looked adorable. If totally daft.

'Good luck. No doubt I'll hear all about it.'

'No doubt you will. Be bad.'

Twizz held the door for her as she struggled out, Dan's package under one arm and her helium-filled friends stubbornly refusing to make things easy. She could chart Delilah's progress from the shop doorway using the balloons that bobbed above her, then they turned a corner and were lost from sight. Twizz sighed to herself and went back inside, drawn inexorably towards the large slab of chocolate that would be keeping her company.

To her joy, Delilah's cab luck held and she was soon bowling along towards the centre of town. She had to keep the windows shut for fear of an escape attempt, but apart from that, all went well and the cab drew up outside the gallery just before five. Perfect. Matt had not been expecting to see her until seven thirtyish. She couldn't wait to see the look on his face when she rocked up, riotous display in tow. It was almost worth the delivery company screwing up to be able to see it at first hand. She ducked through the gallery door and smiled at the receptionist, a daffy nineteen-year-old who went by the name of Millie. Matt was nowhere to be seen.

'Hi, how are you?' It always paid to be nice to the person on the front desk, although it had to be said that, beneath the clueless exterior, Millie was basically good-hearted.

'Very well, thank you. I like your balloons.' Millie beamed her toothy smile and added, 'Matt and Lizzie are in a meeting. Said they mustn't be disturbed. Do you want to wait for him, or perhaps you'd like to have a look round the shops and pop back later?'

Right, you daft bint, I always go shopping with a bunch of balloons. Overcompensating for the uncharitable thoughts in her head, Delilah smiled pleasantly at her and said, 'I think I'll wait, if that's OK. Might just nip to the loo.'

'Of course. You know where it is, don't you? Through the back and next to Lizzie's office.'

'Yes, thanks. Could you look after these for a second or . . . no, it's OK, I'll take them with me.' Trying to butter her up a bit more, Delilah added, 'By the way, nice necklace.'

It was lovely, and unusual for Millie. Intricate, delicate and strangely familiar. As Delilah peered more closely at it, the penny dropped. It was the choker. Her choker. Or at least the one Matt had bought from her that very first time he had come in the shop.

Oblivious to the narrowing of Delilah's eyes, Millie simpered sweetly. 'Oh, thank you. It was a Christmas present from Lizzie. Lovely, isn't it?'

Curiouser and curiouser. Delilah let that one lie and headed off for the loo, brightly coloured trail jiggling gently behind her. What a privilege, to be allowed over the marble hearth. No one but the most honoured of guests were permitted to avail themselves of the facilities and then only if they had spent a considerable sum. Slipping down the narrow corridor that led to the administration area was like going backstage at the theatre, the open gallery area giving way to a warren of corridors and rooms. Most of the doors were firmly closed, including Matt's, and she tried to proceed as unobtrusively as she could, aware that Lizzie would not take too kindly to an important meeting being disturbed. The bathroom was between her office and the storage area, a room that harboured some priceless pieces.

The heavy wooden door swung open silently and she squeezed inside, there being just enough room in the vestibule area for herself and her ever present companions. She placed them carefully on top of the basin, put Dan's package to one side and was about to push open the inner door to the toilet when a sound stopped her in her tracks. There it was again, loud, clear and unmistakable. A guttural groan followed by a woman's voice urging, 'Faster, faster. Right there. That's it. Oh yes, lick me baby.' And in response she heard a distinctly masculine grunt and a noise which sounded like a hand working through wet spaghetti.

Rooted to the spot with horror, Delilah listened as the voice carried on. 'Oh yes, yes, yes. Don't stop. Don't you dare stop, you bastard. Ooooooh, aaaaah. Oh God, oh my God. That feels so good. Come on, faster. Harder.' She knew that voice. It was Lizzie's. And unless she was very much mistaken . . . Like a drowning man diving to his doom, Delilah sank to her knees and peered under the toilet door. Facing her were the soles of someone's shoes. Masculine shoes. Matt's shoes. And on his left calf, plainly visible

where his trouser leg had ridden up, were the faint remains
of a bruise. Yellow now, fading fast but still unmistakably
halo-shaped. She had commiserated with him over it, had
kissed it better as he told her how he had let Dan win. Now
she was seeing it under very different circumstances.

Revulsion, rage and despair shot through her in equal
measure as she knelt there, unsure what to do next. One
thing she could not do was stay crouched on the floor
forever. Various scenarios rushed through her mind like a
film on fast forward. She could break down and howl, bang
on the door and cause the most awful scene or creep away
and confront him later. Then again, she could do something
else entirely. Cold fury cleared the way and she plumped
for the most cuttingly adult option.

Getting to her feet as soundlessly as she could, Delilah
slunk back to the sink, put in the plug and turned both taps
on full. Judging by the noises Lizzie was making, she was
yet to reach a crescendo and Matt certainly had his ears too
full of thigh to hear anything. With any luck the water
would be swilling around their feet and into the corridor
before they realized what was going on. Propping the bathroom door open with the weighted balloons, Delilah picked
up Dan's package and strolled back to reception, shock
ensuring that she moved like a sleepwalker even when she
felt like running as fast and as far as she could. She even
managed a bright smile and a cheery, 'Can't wait,' to Millie
as she passed her on her way out of the door.

Once she was in the street it really hit home. Kicking a
handy bin as hard as she could, Delilah swore repeatedly
through gritted teeth, fists clenched and eyes filling up fast.
A passer-by gave her an odd look and a wide berth and she
realized that she couldn't stay there forever, particularly as
it wouldn't be long before her sabotage tactics were discovered. The problem was, where to go? By the time she
got across town in the rush hour the shop would be shut
and Twizz would have gone. Jess was off on her date, Fran

at some singles ball and Margaret was visiting her sister. The last thing Delilah wanted was to be on her own but it looked like she was all out of options.

Hastily ducking down a side street and then on to the main road, she tried and failed for half an hour to hail a cab. Her luck had deserted her. Not only was it rush hour but it had started to rain. Frankly, she had more hope of stumbling across the Holy Grail. Who said miracles never happen? In the blink of a thought a cab appeared, light on and heading in her direction. The chances of that were too infinitesimal for her addled brain to compute. Simply grateful that the gods had not entirely forgotten her, she clambered in and gave directions to her place. The traffic, of course, was horrendous, giving her plenty of time to think over what had happened. Too much time. Terrified that she might break down in the back of the cab, she cast wildly around for something to distract her. Sitting on her lap was Dan's parcel – too late now to catch the post. She only hoped he would understand, given the circumstances.

Idly, she tossed it over and over, her eyes scanning his handwriting even as she was not really reading it. Something caught her eye – the shape of an S, the curl of the D. She turned it over yet again, read the back and then the front. Thought about it. Thought about it some more. Thought about it really hard and then leaned forward and tapped on the glass.

'Sorry, I've made a mistake. I'd like to go somewhere else.'

'You what, love?' Although she was talking to the back of his head, she could feel the cabbie's irritation. He had a right one here.

'I said I'd like to go somewhere else, if you don't mind.' Pain had sharpened her voice and her sense of self-preservation. She was paying for this cab ride, for God's sake. Slowly and clearly she read out the address on the reverse of the parcel. Slap bang in the opposite direction and on the northern fringes of the City. Sounded awfully like an office address. Hardly surprising – he probably slept under his desk. Delilah glanced at her watch. Ten past six. Less than an hour had passed since she had been crouched by the toilet door but it felt like a lifetime. Another lifetime – one that had contained a lover called Matt.

Twenty tortuous minutes later they drew up outside a dingy building in a back street. And not a moment too soon. One more moment spent churning things over and Delilah would have been a blubbering heap. The driver looked only marginally more cheerful when she handed him his money and included a reasonable tip. Years of conditioning. Well, a few more days like today and she would be well on the way to becoming a total bitch. Then let them try and get their 10 per cent. Marching up to a bewildering array of door buzzers, Delilah located the one that read Grub.com and pressed it forcefully. She was about to attack it again when it crackled into life and a faraway voice said, 'Yeah?'

'I'm . . . I'm here to see Dan. It's Delilah.'

'Who?'

'DELILAH.'

A pause and then the sound of a thousand angry bees as the lock clicked off and she was permitted to enter. She found herself at the bottom of a stairwell, to the right of which was an ancient lift. Tacked to one wall was a printed list of company names, and what an eclectic bunch they were. Everything from Health 4 Fun to the Brass Neck Theatre Company with several dot.com enterprises thrown in for good measure. Grub.com was apparently on the third floor and she started on the long hike up the stairs – the way her luck was going it was too much of a risk to step into the lift. She'd probably spend the night yelling for help although at least there would be the prospect of a rescue by the fire brigade. OK, so she was irrational. She was entitled to be.

Much puffing and panting later, Delilah regretted ever

having allowed her gym membership to lapse. Anger and sheer bloody-mindedness kept her going up the steep, dimly lit staircase. She heaved herself up the last few steps and arrived at a door marked 'Grub.com'. Pushing it, she found it was locked although there was yet another entry bell to one side. She pressed it and waited. And waited. Eventually, the door swung open and a ponytailed guy stood there looking at her. Evidently a great fan of street gear, he was clad from head to foot in acid brights. Delilah blinked painfully and then announced, 'Hello, I'm Delilah. Is Dan around?'

'Down the end on the right.' The door swung wider to permit her to enter and she could see one large room jam-packed with desks and computers. The desks were littered with trinkets and toys, the walls covered in posters and charts. In one corner stood a table football game, and around it three or four people egged on the players, beer cans in hand. Plenty of the monitors were occupied as casually dressed girls and guys stared grimly at the screens and tapped away at their keyboards. As an essay in e-enterprise, it was textbook. Trying not to feel self-conscious, Delilah headed for the corner indicated and looked around for Dan. Short-sighted as ever, she was almost upon him when finally she focused on his familiar shirt. He was on the phone, talking quietly but with absolute authority as he issued instructions. Delilah edged closer and he saw her out of the corner of his eye.

'Fine. Send them over for signature in the morning. Yep, sounds great. Thanks, Jerry. Goodnight.' Business done, he replaced the receiver and walked towards her with a wel-coming, 'Delilah! This is a surprise.'

'I'll bet,' she muttered thickly, momentarily unable to articulate any more.

'Sorry?' Dan was next to her now, ushering her towards his desk piled high with papers and looking vaguely confused.

'I said I'll bet it is. A surprise.' Her voice had returned with a vengeance. Alarmed at its ferocity, Dan shot her a look and then said, 'Something's wrong, isn't it?'

'It most certainly is, very wrong indeed.' She was almost shouting now, all that withheld emotion spilling out in her words. Dan tried to take her elbow but she shook him off.

'Delilah, I can see you're upset. Look, why don't we go into the corridor where it's more private and you can tell me all about it.'

So he was embarrassed by her behaviour. Good. Now he knew how it felt. 'I don't want to go into the bloody corridor. I want to stay right here so you can explain to me all about you and your sick little plan. How long did it take you and Matt to cook that one up? Hmm? Bet you loved it, the pair of you, sniggering over it, seeing if it worked.' Her breath was coming in uneven gasps and Delilah knew she was on the verge of losing it. Dan kept staring at her as if she were stark, raving mad.

'You what? Delilah, I have no idea what you're on about. Come on, why don't we just go into the . . .'

'Fucking corridor? No! I'm not going anywhere with you. Not until you tell me why you did it, you and your best mate. Whose idea was it? Yours? Matt's? Do you always work as a double act?' She was rigid, holding the tears in check. Dan looked at her helplessly and then at the package tucked under her arm.

'Mum's presents . . .'

'You left them behind. I was going to get the gallery to post them for you only things got rather . . . busy.' Dignity still intact, but only just.

'Busy? How do you mean? Delilah, what on earth has happened?'

'Why don't you ask Matt and Lizzie? I suppose you knew all about that one, probably set me up there as well. Telling me to go along and deliver those fucking balloons myself. God, I've been such an idiot.' Her chest was heaving and one treacherous tear seeped out and trickled its way down her cheek. Angrily, she brushed it away, daring the others to appear. She knew that once she started to cry there would be no stopping them until she was completely spent, and she hadn't quite finished yet.

'Set you up? I don't know what the fuck you're talking about.' Now he was losing it, although he kept his voice as low and level as he could.

Delilah looked at him standing there innocently and sneered. 'Well, when you do work it out write the answer on a postcard. You wanker!' That was it. She was finished. Her voice gave way completely and with a despairing shake of her head she thrust past him and ran towards the door, leaving Dan to the curious stares. Mercifully, the majority remained glued to their monitors. Just as well for company morale – it wasn't often their boss was at a loss for words but for once he was well and truly flummoxed. It was hardly the happily ever after he'd envisaged.

Sixteen

Three weeks later and the dust had nearly settled. Matt had called, of course. Over and over again. And each time he had received the brush-off from either Twizz or Jess until finally Delilah had felt strong enough to take the phone herself and listen to what he had to say. He'd begged, he'd pleaded, said he'd do anything for a second chance. Then he'd cried as he told her how much he loved her and couldn't bear to be without her. The sad thing was that he undoubtedly meant it. But there was no going back for Delilah and she said as much, putting the phone down on him and consigning the flowers and cards that came to the bin.

Now here they were, sat huddled in the Doom and Gloom as if the events of the past few months had never happened. Of course they had, and the fact that the usual gang was swelled by the presence of Fran and Margaret stood testament to that. They were all there except Jess, held up as usual but on her way. Delilah looked round at her support team and cracked a smile.

'Hallelujah!' exclaimed Twizz and raised her glass for a toast. 'To life after tossers,' she declared and there was a general wave of agreement from those assembled. Delilah joined in enthusiastically, far enough down the road of recovery to have gained some perspective.

'I should have known, of course. Anyone who was that

keen that fast was bound to be a commitment phobe. And if I'd thought about it, Matt was not all he seemed.' She spoke flippantly but none of them were fooled.

'You weren't to know, love. He did a pretty good job of acting the charm merchant – even I was almost convinced.' Amazing how Twizz could mix the soothing with the self-righteous. And get away with it.

'I don't think he was acting,' interjected Fran, 'I think he really believed he was in love with you. The only person he was fooling was himself, when he thought he could get away with it.'

'Maybe. Still, if that's his idea of love then it's not good enough for me.' Delilah's face was sombre as she stared into the past, reliving the tears and trauma all over again.

'Hear, hear. Let's drink to that and I'll set them up again.' There was no way Twizz was going to let Delilah slide back into maudlin; the past few weeks had been miserable enough for all of them. Now there was light at the end of the tunnel of love and she was going to make sure it stayed on, no matter how many pints of vodka it took to sustain.

Twizz stood up and rummaged around in her trouser pocket. 'Might have to ask you to shout me a few quid until I get to the cashpoint. Oh no, hang on, found something.' She pulled out some crumpled notes and a scrap of newsprint. Frowning, she unfolded it and then enlightenment dawned. 'Almost forgot – saw this in the paper. I meant to give it to you earlier but it clean slipped my mind. It's about that Dan bloke. Dan Gallagher. Didn't recognize the name until I saw the picture.'

She passed it over to Delilah who read it through rapidly, Fran hanging over her shoulder to get a good look. It was taken from the business section and there was an unflattering photo of Dan above an article all about his merger with one of the 'big boys'. Fran let out a low whistle.

'They paid him how much?'

'Yeah, but that's all on paper. As it says, he's still running his part of the company. All it means is that he'll have more to play with. Knowing Dan, he'll plough every last cent into making it work even better.' Delilah's eyes kept flicking back to the photograph as she spoke, unaware that she had sounded as if she knew him intimately.

Twizz shot a glance at the other two and then tentatively suggested, 'Why don't you give him a call? Say congratulations or something?'

'God, no, I couldn't. Not after what I said to him.' Delilah's eyes were regretful but her tone was intransigent. She had made enough mistakes without compounding them further. Besides, it was more than likely he'd put the phone down on her. And that she couldn't really bear. She'd thought often in the intervening weeks about that dreadful scene, and the overriding impression she retained was the look in his eyes just before she left in high dudgeon. A look of irrefutable hurt. There was no going back on that one and she wasn't even going to try.

Wisely, her companions said nothing further. They'd tried often enough and each time they'd been blanked. For someone who was good at forgiving others, Delilah was unmoving when it came to herself. Even the argument that she had been temporarily out of her mind did not hold water. She was determined to move on and put the past behind her. Even if that meant losing a chance in the process. It was a bitter pill to swallow, finding the postcard man and losing a lover within a day, simultaneously discovering that they were not one and the same. It had totally done her head in, and if losing Dan was the price she had to pay, then so be it. She had plenty of other friends to keep her company. Good friends at that. As they had proven time and again, especially in the last few weeks. Tonight was by way of a thank-you for their support and what better venue to choose than their favourite scruffy pub. She only wished that Jess would hurry up and arrive so that their little party could be complete. As it was, she got there just in time to buy the next round, looking very swish indeed for a night out at the Doom and Gloom. 'Nice skirt,' grinned Delilah, melancholy having melted away with the aid of several stiff drinks.

'Thanks. Actually, I'm going on to meet a . . . er . . . colleague later. He's having dinner with some clients but I said I'd catch him for a quick one.' Jess looked around as she spoke, daring anyone to comment. Twizz, of course, rose to the challenge.

'A colleague, eh? It'll be more than a quick one for you, then.' They dissolved into cackles, even Margaret permitting herself a quiet giggle. Jess tried and failed to look indignant.

'Oh, go and wash your mind out, you dirty little Antipodean,' she threw back, but her eyes were smiling as she said it. Delilah was glad for her. After the David debacle, Jess deserved a good time and it sounded like this mysterious colleague was going to be giving her one. If not several.

'Almost forgot – there was some post for you.' Jess chucked a pile of envelopes at Delilah and she flicked through them in a disinterested fashion.

'Bill, bill, junk mail, bill . . . ooh, what's this?' She was staring at a postcard, on the front of which was a muscle-bound hunk holding up a packet of breath mints. Plastically good-looking, he was clearly no brain surgeon. Above his inanely grinning face someone had written 'I Am A Dick Head'. In thick, black ink. Aware that all eyes were upon her, Delilah turned it over and read the short message.

'Forgive me', it said. 'I never meant to hurt you and I'm sorry if you took it that way. Friends?'

He'd signed it 'Dan, the not-so-mysterious man'. Delilah read it through twice before she looked up and realized that they were collectively holding their breath for her. Wordlessly, Jess reached across, took it, read it and then passed it to Twizz. Too taken aback even to think of snatching it away from them, Delilah sat and ruminated. He'd written to her, asked for another chance. Wanted to be friends. The question was, how did she feel about that?

'Bloody hell,' said Twizz, handing the postcard on to Margaret, who glanced over it carefully before giving it to a desperate Fran. Ever the voice of reason, Margaret looked at Delilah, all hunched up with thought, and asked gently, 'So, what are you going to do?'

'I know what I'd do. Be over there like a shot, especially now he's worth all that dosh.' Twizz's eyes were alight with possibilities, her mind already out on a spending spree.

Delilah, however, shook her head. 'And that's precisely why I wouldn't, not now. Just in case he thought that's why I was there.'

'Don't be silly,' said Jess. 'He knows you better than that. It's *him* that wrote to *you*, after all.'

'Yeah, and as you said, that money is only on paper. And he knows you know that, so where's the problem?' United by the desire to see her happy again, Twizz and Jess were working as a team. It struck Delilah that it was incredible how much difference a few months and a lot of water under the bridge could make.

'I don't suppose there is one . . .' she conceded reluctantly and they fell on her words like starving jackals.

'No, there isn't! So why don't you get off your arse and get on over there now before you both change your minds.' Twizz was vehement, her hair seeming spikier than ever as if to emphasize her point. There was a well lubricated chorus of approval from the assembled inebriates and even the relatively sober Jess was nodding in agreement.

Delilah attempted one last feeble argument. 'But it's nearly nine o'clock. He won't be there now and I don't have his home address.'

'Trust me, with a deal like that he'll be there till midnight tying up the paperwork.' Jess spoke with the conviction of a commercial lawyer. Delilah was fast running out of excuses.

'You can remember the address, can't you?' demanded Twizz, not to be diverted from the trail of Delilah's ultimate happiness. She'd always liked Dan but his new status added even more lustre in her street-smart eyes.

'Remember it? It's engraved on my heart,' declared Delilah dramatically, although it was in fact true, if only because she could never forget the scene of one of her most ill judged moments.

'Well, then, get yourself together and jump in a cab. Go on, Del, life's too short for this kind of shit.' Twizz was almost pleading with her now, desperate for her not to fuck this one up.

'Sod it, I will.'

A cocktail of derring-do and the demon drink won the day. Delilah allowed herself to be bundled out of the pub and into the nearest taxi before she could begin to fuss over her hair or the state of her make-up. She really must have been pissed. She gave out the address confidently enough but as the journey progressed, doubts began to creep in. What if he'd written that postcard on a whim, what if this was revenge and really he never wanted to see her again? Luckily, Twizz had foreseen this eventuality and she had been sent along with a well filled glass to keep her company. By the time she staggered out of the cab it was practically empty and her Dutch courage level was high.

All was dark outside the remembered doorway but someone let her in when she buzzed, not even bothering to ask what her business was. She climbed the interminable stairs, plenty of vodka adding steel springs to her thighs. By the time she got to the office door, the butterflies were starting to flutter but it was too late to go back, even if she'd wanted to. For one thing, she'd have to explain herself to everyone and, for another, someone was leaving just as she arrived and the opportunity to slip in unannounced was too good to miss. The door shut behind her, she stood for a moment in the semi-darkness and let her eyes adjust, the only available light the glow from scores of computer screens. The place was deserted and her heart sank, all her bravado seeping away as her spirits fell. Then she noticed it, the lone desk lamp on at the far end of the office. Dan's end of the office. Being careful not to bump into the furniture, Delilah set off towards it like a drunken moth drawn to a flame.

Her efforts to steer a straight course must have succeeded because she crept up close behind him without having been detected. He was bent over some documents, completely absorbed in the small print. Delilah placed a hand on his shoulder, swivelled him around in his chair and boldly announced, 'I am not the woman you think I am.'

For a second he looked completely stunned, then he smiled broadly and responded, 'And what kind of woman would that be?'

'This kind.' And with that, she swung her bottom on to his desk, papers scattering to left and right as she pulled him up and out of his chair by the lapels. She'd never seen him in a suit before and the result was very sexy. Very sexy indeed.

'Hey, careful there,' he was laughing now, standing between her dangling legs as his hands reached round to grab her buttocks. In best blue movie mode, Delilah arched her back, pouted and demanded, 'What's the matter, scared I'll ruin everything?'

Dan stopped laughing, stared hard at her and then said in the softest of voices, 'No. I'm scared I have.'

Delilah felt a lump rise in her throat. She was here, holding on to her postcard man by his shirt tails and not knowing what the hell to say. Luckily for them both, Dan was nothing if not a doer. With a sound that was half groan, half giggle he lunged for her at the very same moment she also made up her mind to become a woman of action. Circuits blew and mouse mats flew as they went beyond the virtual and into the realms of the right here, right now. Forget cybersex – this was the real thing. And with their fingers on each other's buttons, both of them knew it.